Final Onslaught

Space Colony One
Part Two
Book 3

J.J. GREEN

ISBN: 978-1-913476-05-2

Cover Design: Erik J. Andersen
Editing: L.M. Lengel

Sign up to my reader group for a free ecopy of
Night of Flames, the prequel to Space Colony One,
and for more free books, discounts on new
releases, Review Crew invitations and other
interesting stuff:

https://jjgreenauthor.com/free-books/

CONTENTS

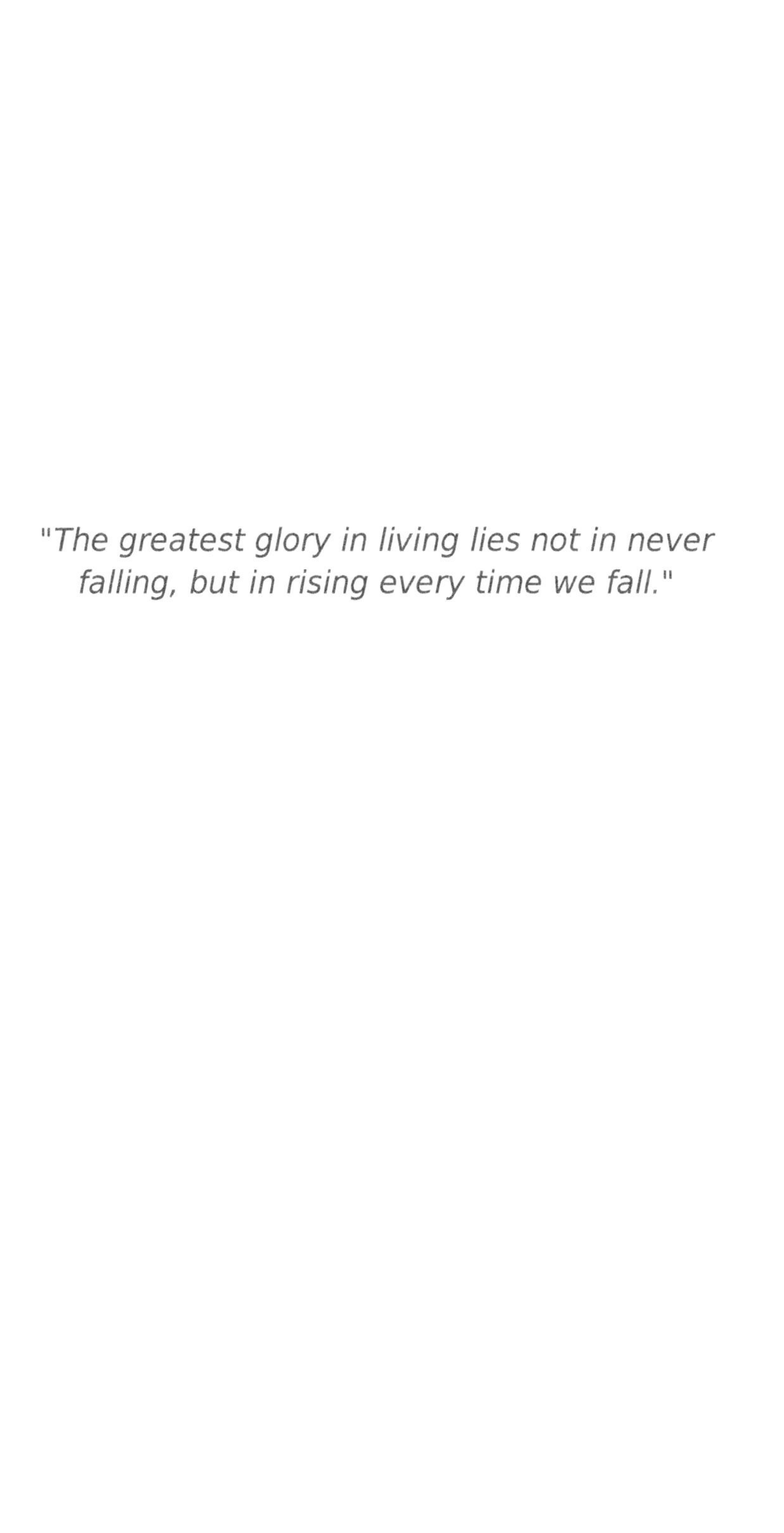

"The greatest glory in living lies not in never falling, but in rising every time we fall."

CHAPTER ONE

Cherry sat at the ocean's edge and wept. The waves were sluggish as they hit the shore, heavy with the bodies of dead and rotting Fila. The stench was overwhelming, indescribable. As far as the eye could see, Fila corpses floated on the water's surface, swollen by the gases of decay. The unique patterning of each body's skin was defiled by corruption, and the tentacle limbs hung listless, moved only by the lethargic ocean current.

It was her fault. Millions, possibly billions, of Fila had died and were still dying due to her rash, unilateral decision to defy the Scythians. If she had only stalled for more time or even agreed to their demand to enslave the human colony so the Scythians could return to their home planet, the Fila would not have died.

The colony could have reneged on the deal. It could have turned on the Scythians who arrived. Or, because the arrivals would have been dependent on the humans for their survival, the colonists could have held them hostage and threatened to murder them if the colony was not left in peace.

So many possibilities had been open to her, but she'd made a snap, rash decision, responding in fury after the

Scythians had blasted apart half of Oceanside without provocation.

She had told Meredith that Ethan would have been ashamed of her, but it was herself who should be ashamed. Ethan would not have been so headstrong or reckless. He would have kept his emotions in check and thought the problem through.

He would not have risked all in a moment of rage and defiance.

Cherry had taken that risk without a second thought, not even considering the impact her decision could have on those who were only tangentially involved in the fight for Concordia. Now she had the blood of an entire population of intelligent beings on her hands. Was there ever such a mass murderer in the history of the human race? She didn't think so. It was an unprecedented genocide.

And there was more death to come. The biocide the Scythians had fired onto the land and into the water continued to spread. The Fila in the oceans were helpless against it. The deadly chemical spread far and wide on the currents and the Fila could not leave the water and live. On land, the spread was slower but no less lethal. Oceanside had been abandoned six days previously, immediately after the attack, when it was discovered that one of the Scythians' biocide canisters had landed there and killed hundreds of people.

A toxic area had been identified near Annwn too, and the evacuation of the small city had turned into a rout. Smaller settlements near and in the mountains had not yet been touched by the spreading devastation, but it was only a matter of time before they were affected. At some unknown point in the future, the biocide would have done its work and no living thing would remain on Concordia. The planet would be a mausoleum, a ghastly memorial to the pride and spite of the Scythians.

Cherry's guilt was an iron spike driving relentlessly

into her chest. Yet the pain was well deserved and for that reason she welcomed it. When the enormity of what she'd done had begun to sink in, she'd wanted to end it all, but then she'd realized that would be way too easy an escape. Now, she only flirted with death, tantalizing herself with the prospect of release but at the same time knowing that suffering was the only penance she could pay.

Over the quiet wash of the waves on the shore, Cherry became aware of another sound. Footsteps trudged through the pebbles, growing louder. Someone was coming toward her.

Cherry did not look around or bother to wipe the tears from her sodden face. The footsteps drew close and then stopped.

"Cherry." The voice was muffled. The person was wearing speaking from inside a haz suit. Anyone who wanted to eke out their last few days, weeks, or months on Concordia before their inevitable death wore haz suit before stepping outside. Cherry wasn't wearing one.

A hand touched her shoulder. The person had used her first name too. It was someone who knew her personally. Cherry felt pressure on her shoulder and heard the movement of the pebbles as the person squatted down.

"Cherry, it's dangerous to be this close to the ocean. The biocide could be carried to you in the spray from the waves. What are you doing here?"

When she didn't answer, the person continued, "What am I saying? Of course I know why you're here. Come on. Come with me. Let's get you inside."

Despite the muffling of the haz suit's helmet , Cherry now recognized the voice. It belonged to Kes. It was naturally he who had come to find her. Wilder—who was no longer Cherry's friend anyway—was aboard the *Opportunity*, the single colonist who remained safe from the threat of the biocide. Aubriot was the only other person who used her first name, and she had not seen him or heard from him since the attack. He could even be dead. She'd left messages on his comm but he hadn't answered.

"Cherry," said Kes, gently tugging at her arm.

She turned to face him. His blue eyes were all that was visible of his face through the visor of his helmet. Kes had such kind eyes.

"I know what you're thinking," he said, "and I know how you feel, but—"

Cherry pulled her arm from his grip. "No, you don't. You really don't."

Kes sat down close beside her, the material of his haz suit pressing against her pants. "I was there too, remember? I was there in the bunker with you. And when you gave the order to retaliate, I said nothing. I did nothing to stop you. I thought Isobel and Miki and my unborn child were dead. I wanted revenge. I wanted every Scythian to be blasted out of the sky. None of us tried to stop you."

"Except Meredith," said Cherry.

"Meredith would have capitulated, it's true, but she did nothing after the decision was taken from her and the battle started. We're all culpable. Not just you."

"I know what you're trying to do, Kes, but the responsibility is mine. I'm the one who gave the order. I'm the one who..." Her words sticking in her throat, Cherry swept her arm wide, gesturing toward the thousands of rotting Fila floating on the waves.

"You didn't kill them, Cherry," said Kes. "The Scythians did all this. Not you. No one guessed what the Scythians were capable of. No one thought their retaliation would be to wipe the planet of all life. No one imagined they would be so evil."

Cherry heard Kes' words but they made no impact on her feelings. She knew his intent was kind but nothing anyone said could absolve her of her guilt in the matter.

It was a plain, hard fact.

"Come back to the shelter with me," said Kes. "Quickly, before it's too late. If a single molecule of the biocide hits you it will run through you like a hot knife through butter. You won't stand a chance."

Cherry didn't know what butter was and she didn't care if the biocide hit her, yet she did feel bad that her friend had come to find her despite the dangers of being outside.

"Cherry, please," Kes urged. "I should be in the lab working on developing a neutralizing agent for the biocide, not out here with you. Please come with me."

Cherry relented. Kes was right. He should not be wasting his time on her. He was one of the few people who stood a chance of saving the remaining life on Concordia. After all she'd done, it would be wrong of her to add to the peril of the colony through her own selfish actions.

"Okay," she said, "I'll come." She began to stand up. Her legs were numb and stiff from sitting so long on the cold pebbles. Kes helped her up.

Cherry turned her back on the seascape of decaying Fila and faced inland. Dusk was falling. Where had the time gone? She had wandered down to the shoreline that morning. Gray and pink clouds overspread the sky and the scrubby beach grass was turning monochrome in the fading light.

It was a regular scene, one of thousands Cherry had witnessed in the years she'd lived on Concordia. No one could have guessed on seeing it that the simple plant life and hidden coastal creatures of the landscape were on the brink of complete and final extinction.

With Kes supporting her by holding her arm, Cherry tramped clumsily through the sliding pebbles. An autocar was parked on the road that ran parallel to the beach. They headed toward the vehicle. Warmth and feeling were returning slowly to Cherry's legs but the terrible weight of guilt remained. She knew the feeling would never dissipate. Not as long as she had breath in her body. But the way things were looking, that would not be for too long.

CHAPTER TWO

The refuge was crowded. It was also shoddy. Hastily converted from storage warehouses into homes and workrooms, it was one of the few places known to be far from the effects of the biocide—for the time being—but it was plain to Kes, as he showered before returning to work, that the building skills of the Gens who had disembarked the *Nova Fortuna* had not been passed on to many of their descendants.

There had been no need. By the time the current generation had been born, the colony had been established and extensive manufacturing processes underway. The proportion of the population trained in practical skills like construction, plumbing, and electrical work had greatly diminished. Twice the Gens had been forced to build underground shelters to protect themselves from Scythian attacks, and each time they had completed the tasks efficiently, effectively, and at a breathtaking pace.

By contrast, the job of creating a safe haven for the people displaced from Oceanside and Annwn progressed slowly and with many errors.

The lab Kes had returned to after taking Cherry to

his home, where Isobel could look after her, was barely functional. The electricity supply was erratic—though, to be fair, that was at least partly due to the fact that the colony now relied on solar power from the plant in Suddene, the Fila's geothermal supply had, predictably, quickly died: the shower heads often spluttered and coughed due to air in the water pipes, and the plasterboard that separated the laboratory from the rest of the warehouse was flimsy and looked about to fall down at any moment.

Considering the lab was the place where the task of saving the colony from disaster was being undertaken, it was pretty poor effort on the part of whoever had built it.

Kes turned off the shower. His skin was covered in goosebumps from the cold water. Showering seemed a pointless precaution considering the biocide appeared to kill on contact. Cherry had been his canary all the way back to the shelter. If the biocide had reached them she would have died immediately. Nevertheless, it didn't hurt to be extra cautious, and, considering he'd instigated the protocol, he could hardly complain. Wearing haz suits with their powered air purifying respirators while outside and following rigorous hygiene protocols in the laboratory were essential if he and his colleagues were to survive working with the deadly biocide.

He quickly dried off with a towel and put on clean clothes and lab coat before entering the lab.

"You're back," Tricia, Kes' colleague, said. "Did you find the general?"

"Yes," replied Kes. "She was at the beach. I brought her back. I'm sorry I had to leave the lab, but I had to go and find her. I couldn't think of anything else after I heard she'd gone missing."

"No problem," said Tricia. "I know how you felt. We all have people we're worried about. She was at the beach, though? Was she on a suicide mission?"

"What do *you* think?"

Tricia turned away, troubled, and returned to her work.

Kes was troubled by Cherry's behavior too, but he'd done all he could for now. Isobel would look after his friend. He had to concentrate on discovering what the Scythian's biocide was made from and then he and his team could work on developing something to neutralize it. They were in a race against time. Not only was the colony facing the inexorable spread of the biocide across Concordia's land forms, it was also vulnerable every time it rained. There was a chance the biocide might enter the water cycle by evaporating into the atmosphere along with the ocean water, forming clouds, and then later precipitating and falling to the ground.

They were lucky it was the dry season and on Lyonesse rainfall was sporadic. Suddene's climate was dry all year round and as far as anyone knew only two of the enemy's canisters had landed on the smaller continent. Those who lived there were likely to be the last who would fall to the Scythians' deadly chemical. Whether or not that would be a good thing, Kes did not know.

He returned to his chromatography test, mentally shutting out the hum of quiet conversation and the movements of the scientists in the cramped space. Setting up the test had taken him back to his college days as an undergraduate in biochemistry. Only then he hadn't been dealing with substances that could wipe out the last outpost of human civilization.

A small team of intrepid, courageous lab technicians in haz suits had harvested several samples of the tissue of a dead Fila, sealed them in water tight and airtight boxes, and brought them to the laboratory. The techs had taken a huge risk in their endeavor. No one knew if the biocide would eat through the tough, inert material of the boxes, but, thankfully, it hadn't. Now it was up to the colony's biologists and chemists to find out what had killed the creature.

It was perfectly possible that the structure of the Scythian chemical altered in some way as it destroyed living tissue. That would make the scientists' challenge exponentially harder. It was also possible that the Scythians had developed the biocide so that it broke down to harmless constituents as soon as it ran out of tissue to feed its processes.

In fact, all kinds of impossible-to-surmount obstacles might stand in Kes' and the other scientists' way, but what else could they do except try? It beat sitting around waiting to die.

The difficulty in identifying the biocide lay in determining what was a constituent of Fila flesh and what was the lethal chemical. Fortunately, Kes and the other xenobiologists had already undertaken studies of Fila morphology. Donating specimens for study had not presented a problem to a species that had the capability of quickly regenerating all parts of their bodies except any of their three brains. Consequently, the scientists had some idea of what they should expect to find in the tissue samples taken from the dead Fila, but the study of the species was nowhere near complete. Many of the substances that made up Fila anatomy and metabolism had been unknown to human science. The scientists could not identify without a doubt what chemicals in the tissue mush of the murder victim were its own and which were the poison.

Kes' gas chromatography equipment stood inside a large transparent box. On one side of the box were two holes at arm height that opened into long, thick gloves. Kes pushed his arms into the gloves to resume his test on a tissue sample. He hadn't been working for longer than five minutes, however, when he received a comm. It was Meredith.

"Hi," he replied, not pausing in what he was doing.

"Did you find her?" asked Meredith.

He'd forgotten to tell the Leader that Cherry was back and safe at the shelter.

"Yes, I did. Sorry, I—"

"How is she?"

"Not good."

"I thought you might say that."

"She blames herself," said Kes. This comment met with silence. Perhaps Meredith blamed Cherry too. Kes hadn't spoken to the Leader much since the attack. There simply hadn't been time to sit down and calmly analyze what had happened. The priority had been, and remained, to save as many lives as possible.

"I hope she can get over it," Meredith said eventually. "There's no point in apportioning blame now."

That was certainly something they could agree on. "Heard anything from the Assembly?" Kes asked.

"Yes," Meredith replied. "That was the other reason I wanted to speak to you. The Fila's distress call arrived and the Assembly has replied using the same method. Now that all the Fila comm stations on Concordia have been abandoned, Quinn relayed the reply from the *Opportunity*. I'm not sure how the Assembly can send information so fast through space, but I'm glad it can. Unfortunately, the Assembly member's ship closest to us will take eighteen Concordian days to reach us. The Fila seeding ship is on the other side of the galaxy."

"Even if the seeding ship was in orbit it wouldn't be much help," said Kes. He vividly recalled the Fila vessel from when he'd briefly visited it in order to embark on his mission to the Galactic Assembly. The ship was large, but not anywhere near large enough to accommodate even a small segment of Concordia's human population. More importantly, it was full of water and Fila.

"I'll take your word for it," Meredith said. "But perhaps this other ship may be able to save some colonists."

"Do you know which species the ship belongs to?" Kes asked.

"It's named in the message but the translation system couldn't handle the word."

Kes wondered whose it was. The species had to be one of the more obscure ones. He'd assigned the Assembly member species English names but he hadn't gotten around to informing the Fila of all of them. Now it was too late. He didn't know how long the translation system would last, either. The situation in their water world was utterly chaotic as far as anyone could tell. Some of the creatures survived, mainly in freshwater lakes and in rivers, but death was moving closer to them, and much faster for the aquatic aliens than for the humans. The worst thing was, there was little to nothing the colonists could do to help them.

"You realize that even if all the Assembly members' ships turned up tomorrow, their efforts might be useless?" asked Kes. He didn't want to crush the Leader's hopes, but it was a fact that had to be faced.

"I do," Meredith replied. "As long as the biocide is ravaging the planet, it could be too risky for them to send any shuttles down to us."

"Exactly. The biocide doesn't only destroy whatever living tissue it touches, it uses the chemicals of the victims' bodies to replicate itself. A molecule of that stuff on the exterior of a shuttle could end up wiping out an entire ship's crew. I wouldn't blame any would-be rescuer who decided not to take the chance."

"Me neither, I guess. Still, I thought it was worth letting you know."

"I appreciate it," said Kes. "Now, if you'll excuse me..."

"Yes, you have a lot of work to do. I hope you find

something soon."

"Me too. Before you go, have you heard anything from Wilder?"

"I try to keep her up to date on the situation when I can."

"How's she doing?" asked Kes.

"Okay, I think. Considering her age. She has Quinn and the other Fila crew on the *Opportunity* to talk to."

"She's tough. As long as her food lasts, she'll be okay."

"I hope it lasts as long as it takes for the Assembly member's ship to arrive. That way, at least one of us will survive."

"The last living colonist from Concordia?" Kes asked. "I don't know if I would like to be that person."

"Let's hope it doesn't come to that. With luck your team will develop something to neutralize the biocide in time and everything will be okay."

"We'll do our best," said Kes. "The alternative outcome is a wonderful motivator."

Meredith closed the comm.

So much had been left unsaid. Realistically, there was little chance the colony's scientists would isolate the biocide and develop a neutralizing chemical in time. Even in ideal conditions, the task would take months. According to the time-lapsed satellite images Kes had seen of the devastation the poison was wreaking across Concordia's landmasses, the colony had only a few weeks.

What was more, at that moment, tens of thousands of colonists remained alive. The luckiest were living on dry Suddene, their lives disrupted but essentially safe over the short term. Others resided in makeshift shelters similar to the former warehouses where Kes lived and worked. The worst off were camping out in the countryside in areas as-yet untouched by the biocide. The Assembly could send a dozen ships and still not have room for everyone, assuming the rescuers took the risk of sending shuttles down to the poisoned planet. The Parvus' ship, which had hung around since the Scythian attack, could not accommodate humans at all.

If it came to facing the decision of who would be saved and who would die, how would they choose?

CHAPTER THREE

Wilder opened the pouch she'd made from a knotted sweater and peeked inside. Piddle and Puddle were sound asleep, curled up together, their arms wrapped around each other's body. They floated gently inside the pouch, which, for once, was clean. The little creatures seemed to have finally become accustomed to micro-g. They hadn't thrown up for three or four days. Even better, they also appeared to understand the basics of toilet training at last. They had a favorite corner where they did their business. Though, without the benefit of planetary gravity, Wilder was forced to keep a close eye on her pets and clean up their messes quickly if she didn't want to encounter unsavory surprises later on.

Was what she was about to propose to Quinn fair on her little friends? Maybe not. The two of them could live for months on the *Opportunity* on her supply of food. Perhaps even years. Wilder was sure that Quinn could devise a way to feed them, or she could simply leave the food cupboard open and Piddle and Puddle could help themselves.

But then what? Would any Galactic Assembly

member arriving to rescue refugees bother with two small, unintelligent life forms? It was unlikely, and the Fila could not offer them a home in an aquatic environment.

Wilder could not avoid the fact that the only possible hope for her small friends was if they stuck with her.

Her mind made up, she pushed off with her feet from the cabin wall and floated out into the operations room where Quinn and his fellow crew members worked behind a transparent wall.

Wilder held up her palms and braced against the gentle impact as she reached the wall. She reached for a handhold and held on.

"Quinn," she said firmly. She would have to be firm and assertive in order to get him to agree to her request.

"Yes, Wilder?" the Fila replied.

"I've decided I'm going to go down to the surface."

"You want to return to Concordia?"

Wilder frowned. Quinn was not usually this stupid. But then again, the flat, emotionless monotone the translation equipment supplied made it hard to tell the intent behind his reply. Perhaps he was only surprised. That would be understandable in the circumstances.

"Yes," Wilder said. "I've made up my mind. I'm no use to anyone while I'm up here. I'm not very good with biology or chemistry—physics and engineering are more my things—but what little help I can offer is useless while I'm in orbit kilometers above the planet. I need to be down there, and the sooner the better. I'll go to a shuttle now and take Piddle and Puddle with me. So if you wouldn't mind, please transport me to the surface. I think if I go wherever Kes is, that would be best."

"No."

Wilder was so taken aback at the Fila's blunt, unequivocal refusal, she was lost for words for a moment. Then she got angry. Her hands curling into fists, she said, "I wasn't asking your permission. I'm *telling* you I'm going down there. I insist you transport me in a shuttle to the planet surface."

"No. That will not happen."

"You have zero jurisdiction over me, Quinn," said Wilder. "And this isn't a debate. You have to do what I say."

Quinn gave no immediate reply. The pause dragged out. Wilder grew angrier. There was nothing she hated more than being told what she could and couldn't do.

"Wilder," Quinn said suddenly. "My people are dying."

Wilder's ire flooded out of her. Her grip on the handhold relaxed and she floated free, slumping in midair. "I know. I'm sorry."

"Humans will begin to die in great numbers soon, too," continued Quinn. "If you go down there you will be one of them."

All the shock, pain, and fear Wilder had endured over the previous few days welled up inside her and spilled out. For several moments she couldn't speak. It became clear to her that her determination to return to Concordia had been a way for her to distract herself from the terrible situation the Scythians had created. She wiped her eyes and nose with her sleeve and said, "I'll die up here. It'll just take longer."

The prospect of starving to death aboard the *Opportunity* while listening to reports of the mounting death toll on her home planet had haunted Wilder ever since she'd heard the news of the biocide. It hadn't taken her long to figure out what it meant for her personally.

"Perhaps you will not," said Quinn. "I have thought of another possibility."

"What other possibility?"

"The *Opportunity's* fuel cells are full. We could leave this system and go somewhere else. I have pondered over this other prospect for some time. I had hoped that the situation on Concordia might improve, but it seems that all is lost. My people cannot escape the poison that is spreading throughout the planet's water reserves. I believe their total destruction is inevitable."

Wilder put a hand on the see-through wall. As always, Quinn's emotion was impossible to tell from the non-inflected translation, but she didn't believe it possible that her Fila friend was not experiencing deep sorrow and grief.

On the other side of the wall, Quinn raised a tentacle and placed it in the same place as Wilder's hand. The two friends hung there, one suspended in air, the other suspended in water, in silence.

"Where would we go?" Wilder asked at last, not at all sure she wanted to go anywhere.

"That question is difficult to answer," replied Quinn. "We would need to find a planet that is similar to Concordia's gravity and that contains landmasses and water. It would also need to offer plant life that is edible for humans."

"And for Fila," said Wilder. "You all need to eat too." Now that she thought about it, Wilder realized she didn't know what the Fila ate, or even how they ate. She'd never seen Quinn or any other Fila take any substance into their bodies.

"We rarely encounter any problems with finding edible organisms on new planets."

"Huh, I wish the same were true for humans," Wilder said. A modest range of Concordian plants and small creatures were eaten on the colony but it had taken scientists decades to discover them and prove their safety. Then Wilder realized what Quinn was saying. "Wait. You mean it would be easier for you to find somewhere to go than me, right? I don't want you guys sacrificing yourselves so I can live. Honestly, though it feels weird to be saying it, I'm not sure I even want to live. What would be the point? I mean, I like you, Quinn, and all the Fila I meet, but I don't know if I want to live a life where I would never see my own kind ever again."

"Humans colonized Concordia from another planet," said Quinn. "We could take you there if you know the coordinates."

"I don't, though they must be somewhere in the data files. But Earth has to be many light years from here. I think the Guardians took twenty years or longer to come to Concordia, and their ship was way faster than the *Nova*. I'll run out of food long before we arrive."

"Perhaps the survivors of the Scythian attack could supply you with provisions for the journey."

"I don't want to take food from them, Quinn. They have it bad enough down there as it is. And there's also the risk of the biocide traveling up here on the shuttle. When I said I wanted to go down to the surface I was planning on a one-way trip."

Wilder and Quinn pondered the problem some more.

"I thought of another reason I can't go to Earth," said Wilder after a while. "The Guardians told us the human population had been decimated by a plague. Assuming they were telling us the truth, I would be infected by the disease if I went there. It would be the same result as if I stayed here." She sighed. "To be honest, it makes me feel sick to even be thinking about how *I'm* going to survive when every single other human being on Concordia will probably die. What a weird fluke it was that I happened to be up here when it all kicked off, right?

"You know, when I was a kid, I read some stories about ancient ships that sailed on oceans before air or space travel were even invented. Sometimes there would be a storm and the ship would sink or break up on rocks, and only a few people would survive. The lucky ones. Only they weren't so lucky because they would end up clinging to wreckage from the ship or isolated on tiny islands in the middle of nowhere. They had no food and no water, no shelter or way of staying warm, and they would die too, like the people who drowned when the ship went down. The only difference was they died slower and more painfully."

Wilder blinked to clear her vision. "I got the a-grav working. Did you know? Yesterday. I finally got the damned machine to work. But no one will know now. It won't make any difference to anyone." She studied the complex patterning of Quinn's skin and then turned her gaze to the three other Fila in the operations room. They did not have English names but Wilder had grown to recognize their patterning too.

"I know what you should do," she said. "You should find a planet where there's water so you can all survive. Your seeding ship will come for you eventually, or perhaps an Assembly member will pick you up. I'd appreciate it if you could find somewhere Piddle and Puddle can live too. I know that's a big ask but I'm asking it. Don't try to save me, though. All things considered, I'd rather not be saved. When the time's right, I'll go out the airlock."

Not wanting to hear Quinn's response to her decision, Wilder quickly pushed herself away from the operations room wall and returned to the living quarters. Quinn could still talk to her in there if he wanted, via the ship's comm, but Wilder hoped he would understand from her behavior that she didn't want to discuss her choice and that he would respect that.

He did.

CHAPTER FOUR

Cherry watched as heavily pregnant Isobel soothed her little girl to sleep. Mother and daughter were lying together on the double mattress that took up most of the floor space in the little family's allotted section of the warehouse. Isobel lay behind Miki, gently stroking the girl's red-black hair as her eyes slowly closed. The child's discarded interface with accompanying keyboard lay on the bed beside her. One of Isobel's lower legs was in a cast.

Cherry didn't like to watch while Isobel performed her motherly duties, but there was nothing she could do about it. Only thin curtains separated the sections for families in the warehouse, providing a modicum of privacy. Unless Cherry faced a curtain or looked upward there was nowhere else to look. The single folk were even worse off, sharing one large space filled with narrow cots.

That was where Cherry should be. That was where she'd slept after helping to organize the search for trapped colonists and then later the evacuation of Oceanside. That was where she would have gone if Kes hadn't made her promise to stay in his and Isobel's makeshift room.

Cherry was sure Isobel didn't want her there. Who would want to share a tiny living space with a suicidal, fatally incompetent ex-general? And Isobel already had enough on her plate with trying to keep a toddler entertained without any toys or room for her to run around. Isobel also looked as though she was about to pop. What a time to be expecting a baby.

A shout from an excited child broke through the general hubbub and echoed around the warehouse. Miki's eyes flew open.

"Shhhh," said Isobel. "Shhhh. It's okay."

Miki's eyes closed again. Isobel continued to stroke the little girl's hair until she was breathing heavily and sound asleep. Isobel caught Cherry's gaze and smiled. Slowly and carefully, she pushed herself to an upright position and then eased herself along the mattress until she perched on its end.

Cherry was sitting in a low camping chair, her knees drawn up, feeling awkward. She didn't know what Kes had told Isobel in their hasty conversation, conducted in low voices, when he'd taken her to his wife. But whether he'd filled Isobel in on the details or not, it was pretty obvious to anyone the state she was in.

"Are you hungry?" Isobel asked.

Cherry shook her head.

"Thirsty?"

"No," said Cherry. "I should be the one helping you, not the other way around. And shouldn't we be whispering?" She nodded at the sleeping girl.

"Don't worry," Isobel said. "Once she's asleep she can sleep through a hurricane. Which is going to be handy now we're living in here."

The noise in the warehouse was indeed very loud. Cherry imagined it wasn't much quieter at night, especially not in the families' section, where there were many children of around Miki's age.

"Can I get something for you?" asked Cherry.

"No, it's fine. A few of the moms and dads organized a meal roster. Someone will bring something over in a little while."

"Okay."

The awkwardness stretched out, seemingly with no prospect of coming to an end. Cherry wondered how long Kes would expect her to stay there. And where would she sleep? There was a space between the edge of the mattress and the curtain wall where she would fit, but lying next to Kes and his wife and child at night would be a whole new level of uncomfortable that had nothing to do with the hard floor.

"I guess this must feel familiar to you," said Isobel.

"Huh? What do you mean?" Cherry wasn't generally in the habit of consigning entire populations of intelligent beings to death.

"I mean the living conditions must have been something like this in the early days of the colony, before you built the first settlement."

"Oh. No. Not really. Well, a group of Gens and Woken did sleep in a big barn on the first night when the sluglimpets attacked. But I don't think anyone did after that. Everyone slept on the *Nova* until the first dorms were ready."

"Right. The First Night Attack. I remember studying it at school. Were you there?"

"No. Only a couple hundred Gens were picked to spend the first night on the planet. I wasn't one of them. I didn't get to go down to the surface until the Naming Ceremony."

"That must have been an amazing experience after spending all your life aboard the *Nova Fortuna*."

"Yeah, it was." Cherry paused. "Feels like a long time ago now."

"It was a long time ago," said Isobel, but then she corrected herself. "Except not so long ago from your perspective."

"No, not so long." Cherry tried to figure it out. She'd returned from the mission to the Galactic Assembly six Concordian years and three Earth years ago. Prior to her leaving, the colony had only just brought in its first major harvest. Was it only such a short time since she'd disembarked the *Nova*? So much had happened, it felt like a lifetime. For most of the colony it *had* been a lifetime.

How many Concordians now living had been born on the colony ship? It had to be a small proportion of the population. Most had grown up planetside and had never even been aboard a starship. Life on the surface was all they knew. And now, soon, it would be all they would ever have known.

"It's hard," said Isobel, "but I'm sure things will get back to normal soon."

Cherry raised her eyebrows. "I beg your pardon?"

"Our house in Annwn is still there, I think. The biocide won't damage it. As soon as Kes figures out the formula for a neutralizing agent, they'll clean all the biocide away and we can move back there. I'm hoping he can do it before the baby comes. I don't fancy the idea of giving birth in here."

Cherry blinked. "Are you sure Kes will be able to do it? Is that what he told you?"

"He hasn't said anything except that he's working on it, but I know he will. He's so smart."

"He is smart," said Cherry. "I hope you're right." She wasn't sure if Isobel was ill-informed about the true situation or if she was only hormonal and slightly deluded. Either way, setting her right about the danger she, her child, her unborn baby, and everyone else on Concordia was in would be no benefit to anyone.

Cherry had a sudden urge to speak to Aubriot. She felt in need of some callous, sour realism. And it wasn't only Isobel's naive optimism that was bothering her, the entire homely set up put her on edge and in her current state it was more than she could bear. She didn't know why exactly, but being around families always made her uncomfortable. Perhaps it was only that she hadn't grown up in a family herself. Many Gens had taken to living in families with ease but some hadn't, and she fell into the latter group. She had no desire for children and the idea of even holding a baby seriously alarmed her.

"I need to go out for a little bit," she said to Isobel.

"Oh, no. You mustn't! You have to stay here. Kes said —"

"I'm not going outside, just for a little stroll around the warehouse. I have to stretch my legs." Cherry stood up.

"But—"

"I'll be fine," said Cherry, touching Isobel's shoulder as she stepped around her. "I'll be back soon."

There wasn't a lot someone in Isobel's position could do to stop her, and she wouldn't want to leave Miki alone. Cherry pulled the curtain aside and walked out into the narrow corridor between the two rows of family rooms. She comm'd the warehouse coordinator and asked to be connected to the countrywide network. Then she comm'd Aubriot.

"Yeah?"

His dour tone made Cherry question her desire to talk to him. "You're alive, then."

"Seems so."

Cherry was about to ask Aubriot why he hadn't replied to her messages but she changed her mind. What was the point? If he'd wanted to speak to her, he would have.

"Are you okay?" she asked. "Were you injured during the attack? Where are you?"

"I wasn't injured. I'm still at Cerberus. Helping with the cleanup. You?"

"An evacuation site outside Oceanside. You should

come here. I gave orders for everyone to withdraw to the east coast. This is the largest habitable area at the moment."

"Can't."

"What? Why?"

"We're cut off. The biocide that landed outside Annwn has spread across the countryside. Can't go over it, can't go under it, can't go around it, and we sure as hell ain't going through it."

"*Shit.*"

"Funny, that's exactly what I thought."

"Aubriot..." All Cherry's terrible guilt and despair welled up in her again.

"What?"

When Cherry didn't answer, Aubriot said, "Don't feel sorry for me. We're all in the same boat, right?"

"What are you going to do?" asked Cherry.

"Carry on clearing up what's left of Cerberus. Those bastards might change their minds and come back to finish us off the fast way. We need to be ready for them if they do."

"That makes sense," said Cherry.

"Keeps us busy."

Cherry had a vision of the biocide creeping nearer and nearer to Cerberus, cutting a swathe of destruction. What would happen when it reached the men and women stationed there? Would the poison cross the inanimate infrastructure of the silo somehow, carried on microorganisms floating in the air? Or would the people at Cerberus be protected by their position underground in chambers of metal and stone, and eventually starve to death?

"Cherry," Aubriot said.

"What?"

"How are you doing?"

Cherry was so taken aback by the question, a gesture of care from Aubriot, she repeated herself. "What?"

"You know, it's not your fault," said Aubriot.

"That's what people keep telling me."

"If you hadn't given the order to fire back, I would have. And the officers would have obeyed me."

"I don't think so, but maybe. It doesn't matter. Might-have-beens won't change what I did."

"You're getting mixed up," Aubriot said. "What's happening is just a slow version of what would have happened anyway, because we refused to enslave ourselves to murderers. No one wanted that life."

"Some might have wanted it." Cherry remembered Meredith's decision to do exactly that, before Cherry took the decision out of her hands. "Even if you're right, the Fila wouldn't have died. They're entirely innocent in this."

"No. They picked their side when they chose to help us go to the Assembly. They're not stupid. They knew exactly what they were doing and the risk they were taking. They were poking the wasp's nest and they knew it. You can't take responsibility for their actions or the repercussion they've suffered."

Cherry was silent. A couple of young kids came racing down the space between the curtained cubicles.

"Hey, I heard one of the Guardians survived the destruction of the *Mistral* and had come back," Aubriot said. "Is it true?"

Faina! Or at least that was what the thing had implied it was. Cherry had forgotten all about the supposed Guardian.

"Yes, it's true," Cherry replied. "Kind of. Something that looked like an escape pod was found crash landed in the wildlands over the mountains. A few weeks later something else turned up in Annwn. It *looks like* a burned Guardian. What it really is, I don't know for sure. I had it locked up in Oceanside jail but it escaped."

"Good idea locking it up," Aubriot said. "That's exactly what I would have done. Do you know where it is now?"

"No, I don't. To be honest, I'd forgotten about it, what with everything else going on."

"Ah well. As long as it stays the hell away from me I don't care where it goes."

"Funnily enough," Cherry said. "A Guardian is about the only thing that could cross the dead zone between Cerberus and Oceanside right now, but I doubt it's going to come for you."

"I wonder what it's doing," said Aubriot. "Their mantra was to save the colony at all costs, right? Maybe that's why it escaped. It saw the attack and its programming kicked in and forced it to break out of the confinement you'd put it in. Disobeying orders for the greater good."

"Yeah, maybe. And we know how well that turned out last time, don't we?"

"You're telling me?"

"You know, you've given me an idea," Cherry said. "Something for me to do. I have to go now. Take care, Aubriot. I know we've had our ups and downs, but you mean a lot to me." The words were out before Cherry even knew what she was about to say, but as she spoke she realized what she was saying was true. She *did* care about the arrogant, oftentimes unbearable asshole.

Aubriot coughed. An awkward beat of silence followed, then, "Yeah. You too." He closed the comm.

A new sense of purpose coursed through Cherry's veins. She would find the escapee and put an end to it once and for all, if she could. The thing looked especially difficult to destroy.

The colony's future would not be further jeopardized by the interference of the strange visitor.

CHAPTER FIVE

"I think we can rule out any kind of proteasome stimulant," said Tricia.

"I agree," Kes said. "The speed and extent of the devastation to the cells is just too fast. I'm betting on a protein denaturing compound. Perhaps something bonded to a virus. That would account for the rapid replication and transmission rates."

Thom, who was a chemical engineer by profession but had joined the team trying to find a way to counteract the biocide, spoke. "Could it simply *be* a virus? I mean, it isn't my field, but that's my guess."

"It's a good guess," said Kes. "All the dead cells seem to have undergone lysis, so it adds up." He was annoyed at himself. Why hadn't he come up with the idea? It was a distinct possibility, given what they knew about the biocide's effects. He'd been working on the assumption that the substance was a toxic chemical rather than something alive.

He was tired. They all were. As Kes sat at the table in the meeting room, the thirty or so faces around him were pale and the eyes were shadowed. Everyone was unkempt, too, and it was getting hard to ignore the smell of dirty clothes and body odor. Ever since creating the lab at the warehouse the team had taken hardly any time off. People would snatch a couple of hours' sleep lying on the meeting room floor and then immediately return to work.

Perhaps they were taking the wrong approach. Fatigue dulled the mind and that was dangerous. Someone could miss something vital, or even slip up and allow the biocide to leak out. Then no one in the warehouse would stand a chance.

"A virus that infects every living thing it encounters?" Tricia asked. "Is that even possible? How would it survive after it first evolved? It would be self-limiting, running out of victims to infect because it kills everything it touches."

"It doesn't have to have evolved," Kes said. "The Scythians could have engineered it."

"Pretty risky," said Dean, a fellow xenobiologist.

"When you're set on destroying an entire planet's worth of life," Thom said, "perhaps any risk is worth taking."

"Hmm," Tricia said. "I guess the Scythians might have discovered a planet where the virus evolved and destroyed everything."

"We're leaping ahead," said Kes. "The virus idea is only a guess. We mustn't close our minds to other possibilities or we might miss something important. But I would still suggest we try to isolate virions from the Fila tissue samples."

"We can try," said Dean. "Kes, what do you say we review *all* the test results we have so far?"

Kes nodded. There were a few soft groans. Kes felt the same. But no one voiced a strong protest. Everyone knew the painstaking attention to detail was necessary.

As the results of all the tests undertaken over the past few days were displayed on the room's interface screen and discussed, Kes forced his tired mind to concentrate. He also had to force himself to ignore the pressure to find the solution to the crisis before it was too late. That was the hardest thing to do. The fear of what would happen if the team failed was so great, Kes sometimes imagined he could feel it, like a high-pitched whistle, too high to be heard by human ears but there nevertheless. Or he would smell it: a rancid, rank odor underlying the smell of unwashed bodies.

He could not—would not—allow the biocide to reach Isobel and Miki. They would *not* fall to the Scythians' evil. He would not countenance it. But he needed an answer. Where did it lie?

A comm arrived for him from one of the warehouse coordinators. They all knew Kes was not to be disturbed unless it was for something vitally important, so he accepted it.

The coordinator didn't waste any time on preamble. "A Fila called Quinn wants to speak to you. He said it's urgent."

"Quinn? Okay, that's fine. Put him through." Kes stood up and excused himself. He stepped out into the lab and waited, listening to the silence for a second or two before Quinn's voice came through. The distance to the *Opportunity* and the sub-par state of the comm system was causing a lag.

"Kes, thank you for speaking with me. I know you are very busy. I tried to speak to you directly but I was unable."

"We're down to a low bandwidth so we're only allowing comms between refuge centers. But if you want to talk to me anytime it's fine. How are you? What's happening up there? How's Wilder?"

Kes had only been able to contact Wilder once, when he had briefly filled her in on the situation on the surface. He waited anxiously during the silence of the lag for the Fila's reply.

"Wilder believes she will die, probably due to

starvation, I believe," Quinn replied. "She is planning on killing herself first."

Kes winced at Quinn's brutally honest response. He knew the Fila couldn't be expected to understand human social sensitivities, but that didn't prevent his emotional reaction. "Uh, okay," was all he could think to say.

"On the other hand," said Quinn, "I don't expect to die."

"Good," Kes said.

"If necessary, I will go with my fellow crew to another planet. But the time to do that has not yet come. Kes, I am now the only channel of communication between your colony and the remaining members of my species on Concordia. I received a message that all sites containing the translation equipment are now dead zones, contaminated by biocide."

"How many Fila are left?" Kes asked. "Is there any way we can help them?"

"That's the second reason I wanted to talk to you. I do not know how many of my kind have died. The situation is too turbulent for a reckoning. But a great many individuals have retreated to the large river that runs along the base of the mountain range in Lyonesse. I believe you call it the Vimur. No biocide landed in it and the flow of the current toward the ocean is keeping the biocide out for the moment. But a canister did hit land not far from the river. The patch of destruction is spreading closer to the water. If the biocide reaches the Vimur, all the Fila sheltering there will die. Even if they leave via underground waterways the poison will follow them."

"I understand," said Kes. "We're doing all we can to create something to neutralize the biocide. As soon as we have it, we'll send some over the mountains. When we abandoned Annwn we flew the helis out. They can't carry much weight, but I'm sure they can transport enough of the neutralizing agent to spray a band along the river banks and safeguard the river."

"Are you close to finding a remedy to the biocide?"

"We're…" Kes could not find it in him to muddy the truth with Quinn. "We aren't close at the moment, but I'm confident we'll have a breakthrough soon."

"I assume you have been conducting tests. Please send me all the data you have. The *Opportunity's* processing power is considerable. It may discover patterns or relevant information you have missed."

"That's a great idea. I'll do it as soon as I can. If you don't have anything else to tell me, can I speak to Wilder?"

"Yes, of course."

Two more seconds of lag followed.

"Kes?"

Wilder sounded so young. She had always reminded Kes of his sister, who had been fourteen when they'd said goodbye for the last time on Earth, knowing they would never set eyes on each other again. Now, he heard the same fear and sorrow in Wilder's tone as he had then in his sister's. It was as much as he could do to hold himself together.

"Wilder," he said, struggling to keep his voice normal. "How are you doing?"

"Oh, you know…I've been better. How are things down there?"

"They could be worse, but not a lot."

Wilder gave a quiet sigh. "After we went to all that trouble to join the Galactic Assembly, I was expecting a tad better benefits."

"They are coming. And that's important for you to know. If they aren't here in time to save us, they could still save you. Are you rationing your food? You have to make it last as long as you can."

"So I can be the last remaining Concordian? I don't think I like the sound of that. I mean, I like solitude, but not *that* much."

"Maybe someone from the Assembly could take you to Earth."

"I already had this conversation with Quinn. You're forgetting about the disease the Guardians told us about, the one that wiped out civilization, remember? I would catch it, and, besides, you didn't hear what I said. I don't want to be the only *Concordian*. I'm not from Earth. Concordia's my home. If my home and all of you are gone, what else do I have?"

"You have..." Kes wasn't sure how to answer. Wilder's point was valid. Home, family, and a circle of friends who loved you, these were all important to human happiness, if not essential. He knew that to him, personally, these things were everything. "You have yourself. You're young and adaptable, and you're so smart, Wilder. Who knows what you might do with your life? You have so much potential. So much to offer other species, other civilizations. And I know Quinn would miss you very much if anything were to happen to you."

"I..." A pause stretched out longer than the lag. "I don't know. Maybe he would."

"Of course he would, Wilder. He wanted to go up there with you to the *Opportunity*, didn't he? That's what you told me."

"Yeah, he did."

"It was because he cares about you."

"I guess so."

Kes closed his eyes, imagining the young girl aboard the starship that had conveyed her, himself, Aubriot, and Cherry so far across the galaxy. He could remember the time vividly, the months he and Wilder had spent questioning and observing the Fila, trying to understand them. He could see Wilder in his mind's eye, floating in the micro-gravity, painfully thin, her hair a mess.

"I guess Piddle and Puddle would miss me too," she

said.

"You...what? Are they the other Fila on the ship?"

"No, they're my pets. I brought them with me when I came up here."

"Seriously? What kind of pets?"

"I don't think they've been classified yet."

"You found a new species and you didn't tell me?"

"I didn't want scientists studying them," said Wilder. "They were happy living with me."

"Well, I can understand that. I'm glad you have them with you to keep you company, and you're right, they would miss you too. So you mustn't do anything stupid, okay? Hang on as long as you can."

The lag dragged out. Finally, Wilder's soft reply came. "Okay, I'll try."

Kes' muscles relaxed in relief. "Thank you. That means a lot."

"Kes, I'm worried about some friends of mine. Could you check they're okay?"

"I can try. The database of survivors and their locations is still being compiled but I'll do my best."

"Thanks." Wilder stated some names and Kes noted them. Then she said, "I have to go now. Piddle and Puddle are waking up."

"If you want to talk to me, anytime, just comm the center. I'll tell them to put you straight through to me. Anytime. I mean it."

"I will. Bye."

Kes' comm went dead, but the center coordinator opened it again. "I have a message for you. I thought you might want to hear it before you return to work."

"Okay. Play it."

As soon as Kes heard whose it was he gave a mental groan. If Cherry had left him a message, he guessed it meant she'd left the center.

Kes, I realized there's something I have to do at Oceanside, but I don't want you to worry. I'm wearing a haz suit. Isobel is nice and Miki is sweet, but family life isn't for me. I'll let you know what's happening later.

That was it.

What was there for Cherry to do at Oceanside? The place was a no-go zone, the biocide gradually spreading over it. But, from the sound of it, Cherry was feeling better and that was the important thing.

Two lives saved in one day. Now he only had another few tens of thousands to go. Something from his conversation with Quinn, which had been niggling at the back of his mind while talking to the Fila and to Wilder, suddenly popped to the front. The helis.

Everyone had been focused on retreating to the areas of Lyonesse that lay as far from the encroaching biocide as possible and then trying to find an antidote to the poison, but Suddene was barely touched. Kes' advice to Wilder to keep going as long as she could applied to everyone on Concordia too. They might not be able to save everyone in time for the arrival of the Assembly's rescue ships, but if they could save even a small portion of the population, that would be something.

They should begin transporting people to the other continent in the helis. The aircraft would only hold one or two passengers and the trip took hours, but it would be worth the effort. After transmitting the test results data to Quinn, he would comm Meredith and suggest the idea. It made sense to transport the most vulnerable people first, such as Isobel and Miki.

If his wife and child were out of immediate danger it would be a great weight off his mind.

CHAPTER SIX

It seemed bizarre to Cherry that the autocars continued to run as normal through the wrecked, dying landscape. All you had to do was tell the vehicle the destination coordinates and it would take you there if it could, driving over the destroyed and broken remains of roadways.

Unless you knew for sure the route was safe, however, the endeavor was dangerous. If a crack yawned wide across a highway the cars' proximity sensors might not detect it. They were made to detect obstacles, not absences. The vehicles could drive right up to a hole and tumble into it. In the days following the battle with the Scythians, the autocars—conveying those brave enough to venture out of the refuges—had encountered road surfaces that were too uneven to cross. Then, cars would either stop and turn around, stating the necessity of traveling via an alternative route, or halt entirely and state that the destination was unreachable.

Cherry guessed the car she was in would do one or the other sooner or later. She couldn't expect to get far into what remained of Oceanside. After that, she would get out and walk. She didn't know where the escaped 'Guardian' might have gone but she would begin her search at the jail. There was only one and she'd brought along an interface in case she couldn't find it by sight in the altered cityscape.

The inside haz suit smelled of sick. Cherry figured the odor was a sterilizing chemical used to treat the air the device drew in. No one knew for sure whether the suits actually protected against the biocide. It wasn't the kind of thing you could easily test.

She was more than happy to take her chances, however. She might not have been able to save the colony from the Scythians, but she might be able to save it from another menace.

Oceanside was unrecognizable. Cherry was reminded of the devastation of the colony's first settlement after the Scythians had bombarded it to the ground and then a tsunami caused by the crash of the *Nova* had finished off the destruction.

She was traveling through the site of the first Scythian strike, where the enemy had concentrated the fire from all its ships in one spot. The blast had leveled half the city's buildings and the epicenter was a molten mess spreading hundreds of meters wide. No one sheltering in or near the main strike had survived. Nothing resembling a human body had been found.

In some areas, smoke still poured from fires started by the blast, but other than the twisting, rising vapors, there was no sign of movement in the rubble.

Cherry's heart and guts ached as she surveyed the desolate scene. What was the death toll? No one knew. The scramble to escape the encroaching biocide had been mad, chaotic. No one knew exactly who or how many had made it to a refuge. The priority was to survive.

A single tree stood silhouetted against the bright sky in the distance. As the car drew nearer to it, Cherry saw it was entirely, utterly dead. The leaves still hung on the branches, but they were brown and desiccated. The tree looked as though a frost giant from a children's story had breathed upon it, instantly killing it.

No frost giants lived on Concordia. They were earthly creatures, if they had ever existed. The tree had been killed by the biocide.

Cherry hadn't realized the poison had spread to this part of Oceanside already. The chemical was moving fast. Even in the man made cityscape it progressed through the soil, carried from one living thing to the next.

She was now within a dead zone. It was a chilling thought. Beyond the confines of her haz suit, death awaited her. What would it feel like to die from the biocide? Cherry had only seen it happen once. In the Leader's bunker, not long after the Scythians had launched the biocide canisters at Concordia, the Fila who had been liaising with Meredith from the adjoining water-filled compartment, Elliot, had suddenly died. He hadn't made a sound, or rather, the translation equipment had not conveyed a word from him.

Had the Fila's death been instant? Or had he communicated with his kind, in their way, in his last few seconds, choosing not to submit his message to the translator? Had he suffered?

Cherry shivered, and then put the questions from her mind. Whatever would happen, would happen. She had to focus on her goal. The task would be difficult enough without the added complication of anticipating her death by Scythian poison.

She would go to the jail and look for any signs that might give her a clue for her next step in locating the Guardian. If she didn't find anything she would have to try to guess where the thing might go.

She remained unconvinced the machine was what it seemed to be. Its appearance only weeks prior to the

Scythians' return had only excited her suspicions. It was too much to believe that the *Mistral's* escape pod had floated around in space for more than a hundred Concordian years only to finally be dragged to the surface within a couple of months of another visit from the colony's number one enemy.

But if it wasn't a Guardian, what was it? The thing had to be connected to the Scythians somehow. It was the only possible answer. And if it was connected to the Scythians, what would it do now? Concordia was heading for global extinction. The strange visitor's original purpose, whatever it might have been, was now irrelevant. Had the Scythians' communicated a new order to it while they were in battle?

Was that why it had broken free from confinement?

Cherry's pulse sped up. She was certain she was on to something. The events surrounding the mysterious arrival were finally beginning to make sense.

The autocar stopped abruptly, forcing Cherry forward into her seat belt. A section of a house was spread over the road. Among the rubble lay a bathtub, upturned. Curtains, still attached to their curtain rods, flapped in the wind. A sanitizer rested on its side, its door hanging open.

"Road blocked," the autocar announced. "Calculating alternative route. Alternative route calculated. Time to destination, three hours fifty-eight minutes."

Four hours? "Stop," said Cherry. "I'll get out here."

In response, the autocar's door locks clicked open and the engine died.

Cherry reached for the button to open the door, but her finger rested on its surface without pressing it. She took a long look at the surrounding scenery. Off to the right stood what had once been a small children's park. The play equipment was untouched by the Scythian attack, but the same could not be said for the vegetation.

The soft, rubbery ground cover that was ubiquitous in Concordia had turned black. Tubular flowers lay scattered around low shrubs, pale brown and papery. The shrubs themselves had the same blasted look of the tree Cherry had seen earlier.

She was still in the dead zone.

Cherry breathed in deeply. The vomit-tinged smell of her suit's interior did nothing to ease the querulous complaint of her stomach. She pressed firmly on the door release. The door moved outward and then slid back. Nothing now stood between Cherry and the air of the dead zone.

She waited, her eyes on the cadaverous playground. Would it be the last thing she saw? Quickly, she looked up into the cloudless sky, preferring that as her final view of the world.

Nothing happened. If the biocide was going to get her, it wasn't happening just yet.

She climbed out of the car, bringing the interface with her. She'd set up the screen so that it would display a map of Oceanside and her position in it. She was surprised to find that she was only about eight hundred meters, in a straight line, from the jail. And, judging by the ruined cityscape, she would be able to walk in a roughly straight line most of the way. In the direction she had to travel, not a building was left standing as far as she could see.

Tucking the interface under her arm, Cherry set off.

CHAPTER SEVEN

Kes woke suddenly. His head was resting on his folded arms and he was hunched over, supported by leaning on a table. For a moment, he couldn't remember where he was. He could hear voices and a faint chemical smell was seeping into his nostrils. Despite his nap, he felt immensely tired and wanted nothing more than to fall asleep again. But his memory of recent events was returning. Disquiet and the burden of the task that faced him forced him to a greater wakefulness. He sat up.

He was in the lab. He'd fallen asleep while reading results on an interface set into the table surface. The other scientists were getting on with their work or talking, speculating on their findings. His co-workers had either not noticed he'd fallen asleep or they'd left him alone, taking pity on him.

Kes stretched his arms and back and then rubbed his eyes.

"Coffee?" asked Tricia, who had come up behind him.

"That would be wonderful," Kes replied. "I guess I dropped off."

"We're all exhausted," Tricia said, "but what are you going to do, huh?"

"That's right. We have to keep working until we hit on the answer."

"*If* we hit on the answer." Tricia stepped closer and checked no one was listening to their conversation before saying, more softly, "I don't hold out a lot of hope. Do you? We're trying to do the impossible. I mean, if we had months to work and fully equipped labs, we might stand a chance. But I reckon we have less than a month, tops, and trying to accomplish anything with the equipment we managed to transport from Oceanside and Annwn at short notice is utterly futile. Half of the stuff hasn't even been properly calibrated. How can we trust our results?"

Before Kes could answer, Tricia walked away from him, heading over to the coffee machine. She brought back a mug of hot, black coffee and handed it to him. Ordinarily, just the smell of strong coffee would perk him up, but this time the aroma did nothing to penetrate the fatigue enveloping his mind.

"Better get back to work," said Tricia.

"Hey, wait a minute," Kes said as she turned. He put down his mug as Tricia faced him again. "You're wrong."

"About what?"

"Everything."

"Gee, thanks."

"We can find a solution to this," said Kes. "I know it. This isn't some airy fairy hypothesis we're testing. No one's working toward their PhD, dotting every i and crossing every t. We're fighting for our lives here, and we're bringing all the brain power in the colony to the table. We've got some damned smart people in this team. The best. And we don't have to get everything one hundred percent correct. We only have to find one thing that will halt the progress of the biocide. We can finesse the details later."

Tricia looked unconvinced.

"But I'll tell you the one thing that will make us fail for sure," said Kes.

"What's that?"

"If we give up. If we stop trying, thinking the situation is hopeless. Then we've lost. You're right about the equipment, and the fact that everyone's tired beyond the point of exhaustion, but those things are out of our control. The one thing we can control is our attitude. We have to be careful not to fall into negativity because that's going to kill us."

Tricia heaved a sigh. "Okay, I hear you. I'll try to be more positive. But it's hard. It's hard to stay sanguine when death is approaching you from all sides."

"I know," said Kes. "By the way, I sent all the test results data up to Quinn. The *Opportunity's* computer is crunching through them. Input from the Fila could shed a new light on things."

"I hope so." Tricia turned again to leave, but then she said, "Why don't you go and get some sleep? A proper sleep, I mean. For more than fifteen minutes."

"I'd love to. I was planning on enjoying that luxury after we figure out how to neutralize the biocide, though."

"So was I, but we're all so tired now there's a danger we'll miss something important. Like our attitude, our alertness is under our control, and even the greatest minds are fallible under extreme duress and fatigue. Go to bed and sleep. I'll keep the show running while you're gone and set up a schedule so we can all get enough rest."

"That's a tempting offer, but—"

"Do it, Kes. You've gotten the least sleep of all of us, and you must be especially tired after your trip to retrieve our errant general."

Kes went to protest again, but Tricia raised a finger

to him and then pointed at the door.

He smiled. "Okay, I surrender." He rose to his feet. "I'll be back in a few hours."

"You come back when you're fully rested, and not before."

Kes left the lab. He couldn't deny that Tricia's reasoning was sound, and even if he wasn't in the lab he could continue pondering the problem of the biocide. Sometimes the simple freedom to think deeply about something brought unexpected answers.

The lighting outside the lab was low. Kes realized it was evening and the colonists were settling down for the night. He walked between the rows of cots in the single person's section. In some places there were no cots available and people were sitting or lying on mattresses or cushions pushed together. The warehouse was chilly despite the many human bodies gathered together. The heat was rising to the high, pitched ceiling.

He reached the curtained section for families with young children. There were no numbers or signs on the curtains by which to navigate, and most of them were closed so he couldn't see inside. Kes wasn't sure he remembered exactly where Isobel and Miki were. When he reached what he thought was the right place, he halted outside, reluctant to disturb the occupants if he was wrong.

"Isobel?" he asked. "Are you there?"

He heard a familiar thump, and he relaxed. He had found the right cubicle after all. What he'd heard was the sound of Isobel's cast hitting the floor as she stood up. A beat later the curtain opened.

"You're back!" she said. "It's so good to see you."

They hugged, and Kes went into the cubicle. He pulled the curtain closed. The lighting was even dimmer in the tiny room, but he could make out Miki on the mattress, her little legs and arms splayed as always.

"Are you hungry?" Isobel asked. "I saved some food for you."

"I'm actually too tired to be hungry. I really need to sleep. Tricia forced me to go and get some rest."

"Good," Isobel said. "I'm glad. Oh, I'm sorry, Cherry left. There wasn't anything I could do to stop her."

"It's okay. I know. And it's fine. There *is* no stopping Cherry once she's set her mind on something."

"I hope she's okay."

"I think she'll be all right. What she does is out of my hands now anyway. I did my best to help her but at the end of the day she'll do whatever she wants."

"Come to bed," said Isobel. "I don't think I've ever seen you look so tired, and I've seen you tired plenty of times."

Kes needed no further persuading. He sat on the low camp chair to pull off his shoes, and then he stood up to take off his pants and shirt. Meanwhile, Isobel tidied their daughter's arms and legs to create space for Kes on the mattress.

Miki was lying next to the curtain. Isobel curled around her, and Kes lay down on the outer edge of the mattress and put his arm over Isobel's belly. He felt their baby wriggle.

Not so long ago, he would have taken lying in bed with his pregnant wife and little daughter entirely for granted. Now, it was the most blissful situation in the world. The only thing that could make it better would be to remove the shadow that hung over them.

He fell sound asleep.

CHAPTER EIGHT

Half of the jail remained standing. A diagonal line cut across the building. On one side stood cracked walls and splintered windows, on the other was empty space. The sun was setting behind Cherry, throwing the exposed interior of the building into sharp divisions of long shadows and rosy light.

She looked around her. No movement of any living thing disturbed the desolate tableau of the ravaged city. If the Guardian was out there somewhere, it was hiding.

Cherry turned on the light on the haz suit's helmet. She swept the darkening cityscape with its beam, checking again for movement. All was still.

The jail stood in a built up area of Oceanside where no greenery decorated the streets, but despite the lack of evidence Cherry guessed the area was within the dead zone. Her suit had protected her so far, however. She could only hope it would continue to do so.

Stepping over scattered, broken bricks and twisted support beams, Cherry walked toward the jail. The entrance door no longer existed. She surmounted the edge that was all that remained of one half of the building and went inside. At one spot the admission officer's desk had miraculously survived intact with its chair tucked in, as if the officer had left it after finishing his day's work only moments previously. Except a layer of plaster dust coated the surface and everything else in sight. No rain had fallen since the Scythian attack, which had probably helped to keep the survivors alive up to that point.

The administration section of the jail had been blown to pieces. Cherry passed through the admitting area to the standing part of the jail. Six cells, a shower room, and a jailer's station made up what remained of the first floor. All the cell doors stood open.

She guessed that, like most of the buildings in Concordia, the jail had been built with a basement area —a shelter where the staff and criminals could go if the Scythians attacked. This standard building regulation was old, dating back to the years when Ethan had been Leader.

Cherry had never been to the jail's basement but it wasn't hard to find. A hatch in the floor between the cells lay open, revealing steps that led down to darkness. Tipping her head forward so that her helmet's light illuminated the steps, she descended.

Twenty steps later, she reached the bottom of the stairs. Everything was pitch black down here, except for the section unveiled by her light. The cells in the shelter were more basic than those above. Simple iron bars ran from floor to ceiling and from the front of the cells to the back, separating each cell from its neighbor.

Cherry imagined the jailers hurrying the inmates down the steps after the warning of the imminent attack had gone out. They would have shut and locked the hatch and secured the prisoners in the underground cells, probably squeezing several people into each. Then the waiting would have begun.

Had the prisoners and jailers maintained their social separation, or had the two sides come together emotionally and mentally as the seconds ticked down, seeing themselves as all Concordians in the end?

Cherry gasped and froze. She had glimpsed human feet and legs in the sweep of her helmet light's beam. Slowly, she turned her head to focus on the spot. A man's boots and legs lay askew on the floor. She raised her head to take in the rest of the fallen figure. The dead man was wearing his jailer's uniform. He sat slumped against the wall, half fallen to one side. His right shoulder was the highest point of his body. Cherry wondered what had killed him. It was possible his death was due to the attack, but it was unlikely in this place below ground. His clothes and skin were not burned as she would have expected if that were the case.

She had not personally received the report that the captive that claimed it was a Guardian had escaped. The message had been relayed to her, and she didn't recall any mention of a death. Perhaps it had occurred afterward. Here, too, the cell doors stood open.

Cherry stepped closer to the dead man and peered over the prone form to catch sight of its head. She quickly took a step back, grimacing. The man's neck had been broken. His face was turned nearly one hundred and eighty degrees from the front, as if something or someone had seized his head and twisted it violently around.

Had the Guardian done that? Others might not believe it, but Cherry could. She knew too well how the androids could behave when they believed they were acting for the greater good. She also knew that though they had looked convincingly human they were much stronger, tougher, and more resilient. Could the Guardian have killed this man? Yes. Absolutely.

But why? Perhaps the guard had tried to prevent it from leaving. The explanation didn't make a lot of sense, however. Everyone else in the basement had left, probably after the attack when all of Oceanside and the rest of Concordia was in chaos. The jailers had probably been scared and wanted to leave but also didn't want to leave the prisoners trapped there.

So if the Guardian had been free to go, why would it have killed the guard? Cherry studied the confined space once more. An anomaly in the regularity of the bars in the cell at the end of the room attracted her attention. She moved closer, and the interrupted pattern was immediately apparent. Two of the bars were bent sideways, creating a gap. It was a narrow gap, but wide enough for a thin person to pass through.

A scene sprang to Cherry's mind. The light was on in the basement. The prisoners were crowded into their cells. The guards stood and sat in the space between the cells. All awaited the moment of the Scythians' arrival.

Then the massive strike came, which had trapped Cherry in the elevator at the Leader's Residence and snuffed out thousands of lives in one stroke. The jail would have been rocked by the impact. Perhaps the prisoners or guards had panicked, perhaps they had been shocked to silence.

Either at that point or soon afterward, the Guardian had moved to the bars of its cell, grabbed one with its remaining hand, and bent it wide. Then it had grabbed the neighboring bar and bent it in the opposite direction. By this time, it would have attracted everyone's attention. The guards may have shot it, but regular weapons had little effect on the Guardians.

The escaping prisoner stepped through the bars. A brave guard ran up to it, ordering the creature back into its cell. The Guardian grabbed the man's head and wrenched it around, killing him instantly. Horrified and terrified, the other guards had shrunk backward, none of them daring to approach the Guardian. What point would there be in summoning the courage to face this indestructible opponent?

The Guardian strode along the central section to the steps, mounted them and threw open the hatch, and then disappeared. In the general pandemonium, no one had reported the prisoner's escape until after the attack was over. The prisoners and guards had been forced to share the basement with the brave guard's corpse until the decision was taken to free everyone and let them save themselves.

The scenario fit what Cherry saw before her. What she didn't know was where the Guardian had gone next. The burned up figure would be easy to miss among the many burned and injured individuals roaming around, seeking treatment, in the aftermath of the attack. Cherry had certainly not heard any reports of sightings of it. She had no clue to go on in that regard.

She climbed the steps to the first floor of the destroyed prison. The sun had set and shadows had engulfed the place. Leaving on her helmet light, she walked through the wreckage of the building and went outside. Except for the switch to monochrome due to the faded light, Oceanside's remains looked the same.

Cherry sought and found a smooth piece of rubble on which to sit—after she had come so far, it would be a pity if a simple cut in her haz suit allowed in the biocide and killed her. She surveyed the devastation but only absently. She focused on trying to figure out her next move.

Where would a Guardian go? Or, if the thing was an agent of the Scythians, what would it do? Its masters were already billions of kilometers away, leaving their deadly chemical to finish off the destruction of Concordia. They had abandoned their inorganic, sentient creation to endless confinement on a dead planet. Would it seek out a starship to escape on? If it had accessed the colony's data it would know that nothing of the kind existed on the surface, save, perhaps, for the shuttlecraft that conveyed passengers to the *Opportunity*. As they belonged to the Fila, Cherry had no idea where the small, slim vessels were kept, except they were no doubt somewhere in the oceans or rivers where the Fila had resided.

On the other hand, what if the escaped prisoner really was Faina, last survivor of the crash of the *Mistral*? Where would the android head to in the wake of the battle? Unless the damage it sustained while crashing into Concordia had affected its programming, Faina would be carrying out its mission to save the colony at all costs. But what did that mean?

Cherry shook her head. She was getting nowhere. She got up from her seat and set off in no direction in particular. Though night was falling and she knew she really should be heading back to the refuge site if she wanted to sleep in a bed that night, she didn't want to give up her search. She'd learned the escaped prisoner was dangerous and violent. Concordians had already seen enough death and destruction to last them several lifetimes, they didn't need a homicidal android on the loose too. Finding and destroying the creature was the least she could do after her terrible mess up.

She wandered through the deserted ruins, occasionally recognizing the remains of familiar places but mostly not knowing exactly where she was or where she was headed. The dusky sky turned dark and stars appeared between the patches of scudding clouds. It became difficult to see where she was going despite the gleam from her helmet's light, and she had to slow down to avoid tripping and tearing open her suit.

Eventually she reached an area of Oceanside that hadn't been affected by the Scythian attack. The buildings were untouched, only abandoned. Doors stood open where the occupants had left in a hurry, fearing the encroaching biocide, and dropped belongings littered the sidewalks and roads.

Suddenly, it occurred to Cherry that her suit's

filtration system would only work for a limited time. How much longer did she have? Her visor had no HUD. She guessed she was supposed to know how long the suit would protect her, but she'd missed that piece of information.

She was about to search on the public files when she turned a corner and saw she'd reached the harbor. The ocean spread out in front of her, starlight reflecting from the moving water. Boats bobbed against in their moorings on the swell. Mercifully, no Fila corpses were visible.

Cherry leaned against a wall, watching the scene. Boats that used to gather the tiny creatures of the sea which had become a staple of Concordians' diets mingled with leisure cruisers. The quayside was crammed with vessels. All boats and cruise ships had put into the nearest port after the announcement of the Scythian's return.

Slowly, Cherry stood upright. What if...?

She began to walk along the line of boats.

What if the escaped prisoner had wanted to go to Suddene? If it was working for the Scythians, perhaps they had told it to go to their ancient city, now buried beneath the desert sands. Perhaps there was something there they wanted it to retrieve. Or if the creature was Faina, perhaps it had another reason for making its way to the site where humanity would survive longest on Concordia.

All the helis had been flown out of Oceanside and Annwn when the cities were abandoned. None of the aircraft would be easily accessible to unauthorized personnel. But a boat would be easy to obtain, and the android would have had its pick of the fastest.

Cherry scanned the ranks of vessels, but there was no way of telling if one had been taken. A gap in the line meant nothing. But there was one avenue of information she hadn't explored.

She accessed the governmental data on shipping. Her security clearance meant everything was open to her. She prayed that Concordia's single remaining satellite first launched from the *Nova* soon after Arrival was still functioning.

She halted, waiting. The comm system had slowed to a crawl. Cherry looked up at the stars, wondering which of them was the old satellite, if it was visible at all.

"C'mon," she said softly. "Tell me what I want to know. Tell me where it's gone."

Her interface pinged. The data was arriving. The screen was bright with figures in the dark night. Names of ships were followed by their recent movements. Cherry's gaze ran down the numbers. All followed the same pattern. After the Scythian attack, all the ships had remained in the same position, moored either along the coast of Oceanside or Suddene. The information fed up the screen.

Then the anomaly jumped out. The movements of one ship, the *Astrea*, were vastly different from the others. The vessel had put out to sea from Oceanside after the fateful date. Cherry input its current coordinates into a map of Concordia. The *Astrea* rested at Suddene's only port.

In the days since the battle with the Scythians, the android had sailed from Lyonesse to Suddene. She was sure of it. No human would have dared pass over an ocean filled with biocide. Cherry didn't know the creature's motivation but she did know it could not be good.

She had to get to Suddene too, and find it. But the journey would take too long by boat and her suit's filter would not last. She would have to travel all the way back to the refuge and find a pilot to fly her to Suddene.

CHAPTER NINE

Kes was dreaming. He knew everything he was seeing and hearing and touching wasn't real, but he couldn't wake up. Or maybe it was only that he didn't want to.

He was at his home in Annwn and everything was normal. He'd made it home early from work for once, and he was playing with Miki in the living room while Izzy fixed dinner. His little girl had invited him to a tea party at her playhouse, but unfortunately he was too big to fit in it. He was forced to sit outside the window while the other guests all crammed around a small table inside, perching lopsidedly on three-legged stools.

Teddy was one of the guests, though his rotund tummy indicated he'd been to a few too many parties in his time and eaten far too much cake. Giraffe was there too, her head poking out of the top of the playhouse. The third guest at the table was Miki's best friend, a rag doll called Dotty after the patterning on the dress she always wore. To be fair, the dress was sewn onto her so focusing on her failure to change clothes was unjust.

It had always bemused Kes that Concordian children's toys were nearly identical to the ones he had grown up playing with, and had been the same kind of toys for many generations of children. Dolls were understandable, but teddies and giraffes?

When Miki grew older, he would have to explain to her that teddies were based on real animals called bears, and that neither they nor giraffes were mythical creatures but had once lived—and perhaps still lived—on humanity's origin planet, many light years away.

The problem was there were no equivalent animals on Concordia to be copied into plush playmates for small children. Kes couldn't imagine a furry sluglimpet having tea with his daughter, or any of the other native creatures. They were all fairly monstrous to human eyes, though he was curious about the creatures Wilder had mentioned as her pets. He guessed the creatures were probably cute if Wilder had adopted them.

The only non-Earth creature he had ever seen fashioned into a toy was the non-native, many-tentacled Fila. Miki didn't have a toy Fila, but one of her friends had brought a huge example to Miki's second birthday party. Kes recalled the boy's mother complaining the child insisted on taking the toy everywhere with him though it was twice his size and had tens of long tentacles that constantly got caught on things.

The boy had been fascinated with the Fila ever since he'd seen his first live example in the lake out at the farming district. The Fila had approached the toddler while he was learning to swim and taken him for a ride around the lake. *It was love at first sight,* the mom had said. *Now he can't get enough of them. I wouldn't be surprised if he got a job as a diver when he grows up, just so he can spend as much time as he can with them.*

There was something in his memory of the woman's words that made Kes feel sad, but he didn't know what it was. Things were getting hazy. Perhaps he would wake up soon.

"Tea for Daddy," said Miki, passing out a cup through the window of the house.

"Thanks, Miki. Mmmm. Looks delicious."

"Drink," Miki urged, apparently annoyed that Kes wasn't following the rules of the party.

Kes dutifully took an imaginary sip from the empty cup under Miki's watchful gaze. Satisfied, she poured more imaginary tea for the other partygoers and placed their cups in front of them.

"Daddy like some cake?" Miki asked Kes.

"Yes, please."

Miki gave a small, secret smile, turned toward the kitchen corner of her playhouse, and lifted a toy piece of cake onto a plate.

"What kind is it?" Kes asked as he took it.

"Um, sweet potato. No! Walnut."

"Sounds yummy." Kes pretended to take a bite.

Walnut? That was a new one. He hadn't been aware the colony even had walnut trees, though it made sense. Many nut trees were wind pollinated. A moment of wistful sadness hit him. Miki would never taste so many of the delicious fruits that grew on Earth. Nothing that required bees to pollinate the flowers. No strawberries, no blueberries, no oranges or melons or hundreds of others.

Though it had been years since he'd eaten any of them, Kes could still remember the flavors and textures of his favorite fruits. Sometimes, when the longing for food he would never taste again grew bad, he wished the ecologists had not made the decision to exclude bees from the colony. Their reasoning had been that the risk the insects might throw the local ecology out of balance was too high. He guessed the scientists knew their stuff and their caution had been correct, but that didn't make him miss strawberries any less.

"Is it nice?" Miki asked.

"Delicious, sweetheart," Kes replied. "Could I have some more?"

"Uh uh." His daughter shook her head. "Dinner soon." She sat down at the table and pretended to eat cake. Then she held the pieces to the toys' mouths.

Kes watched the little girl contentedly. Miki was one of the best things that had ever happened to him, as much as Isobel was. Like always when he arrived home from work in time to see her before her bedtime, he was glad he'd made the effort and puzzled as to why he didn't always manage it.

Miki was a very special kid. Kes knew all parents thought the same about their children, but he also felt that, deep down, he was objectively correct. The same as all parents. But her vocabulary seemed to grow bigger every day, and she already understood simple arithmetic and recognized many words by sight. She was also *such* a pretty child. The red tinge to her black hair really made her stand out.

Isobel appeared in the living room doorway. "Dinner's ready, guys. Time to wash up."

Miki picked up her doll. "Dotty come too, Mommy?"

"Sure, Dotty can come too. Hurry up and wash your hands, though, or your dinner will get cold."

The door to the playhouse opened and Miki came out, clutching her doll upside down. Dotty's head hit the door frame as she was carried out, but it didn't seem to bother her.

"Daddy carry me," said Miki. She held up her free arm to Kes.

"Miki," Isobel admonished, "you're only going to the bathroom."

"I'm tired," Miki said. "Daddy carry."

As Kes stooped to pick up his daughter, Isobel said, "You really shouldn't encourage her." Kes paused.

"She can't continue expecting to be carried everywhere," said Isobel. "I can barely manage to carry her now as it is, and when the baby comes I definitely won't be able to carry both of them."

Kes said, "Miki, how about if Daddy *cuddles* you instead?"

Miki beamed and jiggled, holding up her arm higher. Kes lifted her and then said to Isobel, "Move out of the way. We're coming through!"

Isobel sighed and rolled her eyes as she backed out of the doorway.

Miki had one arm around Kes' neck and the other around the upside-down Dotty. Kes swooped through into the hall with her and into the bathroom, where he deposited her on the little stool she used to reach the basin.

Miki dropped Dotty on her head and reached for the faucet. As she turned the lever, she gave a slight cough. She squeezed soap onto her hands and rubbed them together under the stream of water. Miki coughed again as she turned off the faucet. She jumped down from the stool and took a step to the towel rail. She dried her hands and coughed for the third time, this time deeper and noisier, as if mucus was gathering in her throat and chest.

"Are you feeling okay, honey?" Kes asked. When Miki didn't answer and only bent down to pick up her doll, Kes put a hand to her forehead. Her skin felt warmer than it should.

"Izzy," Kes called, "has Miki been coughing a lot lately?"

"I didn't notice," Isobel called back from the dining room.

Kes squatted down and studied his daughter closely. She was holding Dotty's arms over the sink, and Kes managed to stop her from turning on the faucet and soaking the doll's hands only just in time.

"Miki, look at me."

She turned to face him. Her cheeks seemed redder than usual and her eyes were exceptionally bright. Kes brushed her bangs away from her face and held his hand on top of her head. Seeming to sense the change in mood, Miki became still and stared gravely into her father's eyes.

"How do you feel, sweetheart?" Kes asked. "Do you hurt anywhere? Do you have a pain here, in your head?"

Miki slowly shook her head while maintaining eye contact with Kes.

"How about here?" asked Kes, moving his hand to Miki's abdomen. "In your tummy."

Miki hesitated, then gave one sharp nod. Suddenly, she coughed again, right into Kes' face. He flinched as the barrage of saliva spray hit him.

"Gee, thanks for that." Kes stood up and ran water into the basin. He splashed his face clean, and then reached for a towel. As he moved, something in the corner of his eye caught his attention. Miki's face looked redder and slightly distorted. He blinked, thinking it was only an effect of the water on his vision, and wiped his face dry.

When he turned his attention to his daughter again, he gasped. Miki's face *had* changed, drastically, and it continued to change as he stared at it, disbelieving the evidence of his eyes. Miki's face had turned bright red, and it was swelling up. Her entire head was swelling, and her body too.

"Izzy," he yelled, "call an ambulance!"

"What?" she replied. "Why?"

"Just do it! Miki! Are you okay?" Kes knelt down and grabbed his daughter's shoulders.

She didn't reply.

"Miki!"

She was growing larger under his hands, and her red face was taking on a different hue. Her skin was becoming purplish shadowed with black, as if she were undergoing sepsis at a fantastic rate. Kes picked up his daughter and ran out into the hall. "Izzy!" Where was she? Had she called an ambulance? He couldn't see her anywhere.

There was a hospital in Annwn. It was only small but

it dealt with medical emergencies. It wasn't far away. Kes estimated it would be faster to go there by autocar than wait for an ambulance. He turned toward the front door and took a step, but his movements were slowing down. He tried to take another step, but the air had turned into some kind of resistant force field. He forced his other leg forward, straining against the invisible barrier.

He wanted to look down at Miki but his head would not budge. He was frozen, fighting with every muscle he possessed and entirely failing to move even a centimeter.

He awoke. Kes leapt to a sitting position and cried out. Then he remembered where he was and he relaxed a little, softly panting. The lights in the refuge remained dimmed. It was still nighttime.

"Kes?" asked Isobel, turning over. "What's wrong?"

The specter of the dream still clung to his mind. Kes peered over Isobel and saw Miki sleeping deeply. She looked entirely normal and healthy. His panic and dismay eased.

"Could you keep it down in there?" came a disgruntled voice from the next cubicle.

"Sorry," said Kes. He lay on the mattress and took Isobel in his arms.

"Bad dream?" she asked, snuggling into his shoulder.

"Yeah."

"What was it about?"

"You don't want to know."

How long had he slept? It was hard to tell. He felt refreshed, so it was probably quite a while. He debated if he should get up and go back to the lab. *Just another few minutes*, he decided. Holding Isobel, he was warm and comfortable, and his nightmare hadn't yet entirely faded. He felt afraid to let his wife and daughter out of his sight.

The dream had taken him back to Annwn, before

everything had gone to hell. At one point he'd known he was dreaming but then he'd forgotten and had sunken into the false reality of the dream. Usually, his dreams were far weirder than that. The nightmare had seemed a facsimile of normal life. It was very strange—perhaps a reaction to the circumstances. Perhaps his subconscious had been anticipating the biocide reaching Miki.

"Are you okay, honey?" Isobel asked softly.

Kes realized his grip on her had tightened. He purposefully relaxed his arms. "Uh huh. I'm getting up soon."

"Just a little longer," said Isobel.

Usually, when Kes dreamed of people and places he knew, he dreamed of Earth and of people long dead and places that probably no longer existed. But he hadn't dreamed of Earth in a long time.

What would their lives be like if they were on Earth and not Concordia? Very different, he guessed. Maybe survival there was now nearly impossible. And Isobel would not be Isobel, descendant of the Gens who'd lived out their lives aboard a starship.

But what if...? Kes daydreamed an impossible scenario. He was back home, working as a researcher at the local college. He lived with Isobel and Miki in the little cottage on his parents' land. On the weekends, they would drive to the lake. Life would be predictable. Boring in some ways, but in others it would be just perfect. And he wouldn't have to worry about Miki getting sick because—

Kes sat bolt upright, for the second time. *"Shit!"*

"Kes, what's wrong?" asked Isobel.

"Would you *please* keep quiet," exclaimed the irritated neighbor.

Kes climbed out of bed. "I have to get back to the lab." He groped for his clothes in the semi-darkness. His hands touched textile and he pulled the garment closer for inspection. He'd found his pants. He began to put them on.

"Did you think of something?" Isobel asked.

"I did. Or rather, my subconscious did, I think." Kes was pushing his feet into his shoes. "I have to go." He'd located his shirt. "I love you." He stooped and kissed Isobel on the lips and then awkwardly leaned over her to kiss the still-sleeping Miki on the cheek. The normal temperature of his daughter's skin was reassuring. The tendrils of his nightmare still clung on inside his mind.

Kes pulled on his shirt and felt for the opening in the curtains. "When Miki wakes up, tell her Daddy loves her." He'd found the gap between the two curtains. He pulled them apart and stepped into the passageway. Fastening the buttons of his shirt, he strode toward the lab.

CHAPTER TEN

The first light of dawn suffused the eastern sky as the group of storage warehouses came into view from Cherry's autocar. It had taken the rest of the night to walk back to the vehicle on the outskirts of Oceanside and then return in it to the refuge. Cherry's eyes ached with tiredness but she was determined to set out for Suddene as soon as possible. The android already had a head start on her of several days. Who knew what it had gotten up to already?

The autocar was approaching the warehouses from the east, the approaching sunrise behind it. The group of buildings sat on flat land at the side of the road, hulking and dark. Some of their occupants were already awake. Cherry could see figures passing along the paths that led to the latrines.

More importantly, she also saw all the helis that had been flown over from Annwn remained on site, sitting in a section of the truck parking lot. She counted eight. One would be enough for her purposes, but she also needed a pilot.

She knew just the person, but was he at the refuge?

He might be stuck at Cerberus along with Aubriot and the other military personnel who staffed the silo. It was early, but Cherry had no time to waste. She comm'd him. When he didn't answer she tried twice more and then finally activated his alarm. She was one of the few people allowed to invade someone's quiet and privacy in that way.

Zapata's voice was heavy and husky with sleep as he answered, "Yes, ma'am?"

"I need you to fly me to Suddene." She asked if he was at the warehouse refuge. He was.

"Okay, meet me at the helis as soon as you can. I'm on my way there now."

"Yes, ma'am."

"I told you not to call me that."

"Yeah...I'm not at my sharpest when I've just woken up."

"Sorry about that. See you soon." Cherry closed the comm.

Ordering pilots around and having access to high security information were among the many privileges of her position. How much longer would they last? Cherry hadn't met face to face with Meredith since the battle and she didn't know the Leader's attitude toward her, but she guessed it was not good. Cherry had deliberately ignored Meredith's wishes and unilaterally launched a counterattack against the Scythians.

Technically, she had committed treason and should have been immediately stripped of her position. Cherry didn't know why that hadn't happened yet. Perhaps it was only that Meredith was too busy with other, life-and-death issues. Whatever the reason, Cherry intended to exploit her position as long as she could, particularly regarding the mysterious android. If there was one more thing she would butt heads with the Leader on, it was that. With luck, Zapata would get them both into the air and on their way to Suddene before Meredith even woke up.

The autocar rolled to a stop outside the main warehouse gates and Cherry got out. She had taken off her haz suit's helmet on the way back at the first sight of green she'd seen. The suit's filter already seemed to have stopped working. The smell of vomit had entirely faded. She reminded herself to collect a replacement before meeting Zapata at the heli. She would get him a suit too. They might need to enter areas affected by the biocide. The morning wind thrust itself through the fabric of her clothes as she crossed the space between the autocar and the first warehouse. She shivered. Fatigue tugged at her legs and feet after her long walk around Oceanside.

The warehouse door stood ajar. She slipped inside and had to halt for a moment while her eyes became accustomed to the darkness. Even at that early hour a hum of soft voices filtered through the space. Cherry walked across the entrance to the glass-walled room that stored the haz suits, and dumped hers onto the 'used' pile.

She grabbed two more suits, wedging them under her arm.

"Gotta shower first," said a voice.

A man had appeared in the doorway. He was one of the refuge coordinators.

"I'm not going inside," Cherry replied. "I'm going out again right now."

"If you come into the warehouse from outside, you have to shower now. Those are the rules."

"But...That makes no sense," said Cherry. "If I had a molecule of biocide on my skin I'd be dead."

"Leader's orders."

Cherry dropped the suits. There was no point in arguing or trying to avoid the requirement. That would only delay her.

The door through to the showers opened

automatically. Cherry was already stripping as she walked through it. She dumped all her clothes on the floor and stepped into the cubicle. A hot water spray hit her forcefully.

"Make sure you get all the nooks and crannies," came the coordinator's voice from outside the stall. He'd followed her into the shower room. *Asshole.* In a couple of minutes Cherry was done. She turned on the dryer and let the warm air dissolve the water droplets that clung to her skin. Another minute later, she stepped out of the stall.

The floor was bare. Her clothes were gone, and the coordinator was nowhere to be seen.

"Hey!" Cherry yelled. "What did you do with my clothes?"

The coordinator either didn't hear her or refused to answer. Cherry scanned the room. In a corner stood a rectangular wire receptacle that contained folded clothes. Next to it was a large box of shoes. She had a closer look. The clothes seemed clean. After riffling through them she found some that were about her size and put them on. She also found a pair of boots that fit her.

When she returned to the haz suit room, the coordinator was waiting for her.

"The biocide's getting closer," he said. "We can't afford to take any chances with people who've been off site."

"Fine," said Cherry. "*Now* can I take two suits?"

"Be my guest," said the man. As he left, he remarked, half to himself, "I hope you're allowed in when you get back. We might begin refusing entry altogether."

Cherry picked up the fresh suits. As an afterthought, she grabbed four additional filters. Her arm weighed down with her new possessions, she crossed the warehouse entrance again and went outside.

Walking quickly, she made her way around the

warehouse in the direction of the truck parking lot. Zapata was probably waiting for her. As the helis came into sight, Cherry was surprised to see not only the distant figure of the pilot in his uniform, but four more people standing near the helis too.

She sped up her pace to a trot, wondering if a new obstacle to her hasty departure had arisen.

It had.

Zapata and the four other people were arguing. Cherry couldn't make out the words properly, but tempers were flaring from the tone and volume of their speech. Zapata had his back to her. When he noticed the others' gazes switch to Cherry approaching from behind him, he turned.

"Great," he said, turning to face his antagonists, "I'd like to see you refuse the General's order to her face."

"What's the problem?" asked Cherry, panting a little from her exertion.

"They won't allow me to board a heli," said Zapata. "They're saying it's Leader's orders. That isn't right, is it?"

"Uh…" Cherry handed Zapata the haz suits and filters. "What orders are those?" she asked the assembled men and women. They were not military, as far as she knew. They were wearing civvies. But they had an air of authority about them, as if they were confident in their position.

"No helis are to be taken under any pretext," said a short, skinny woman with a severe haircut. "The evacuation is to begin at dawn."

"Evacuation?" asked Zapata. "No one said anything about an evacuation."

Cherry was similarly flummoxed. "When did you hear about this?" she asked the short woman.

"Not that it matters," the woman replied, "but we were informed late last night. We were told to keep an eye on these helis and make sure no one took any.

We're going to need them all when the evacuation begins. The Leader wanted to make sure they were all on site when she made the announcement. I guess she didn't want anyone cutting the line." Her eyes narrowed as she looked from Cherry to Zapata.

"Right," Cherry said. Meredith seemed to have put together a plan to move the population sheltering within the warehouses to another, less dangerous, site. But that would be a very long-winded operation. Even if she deployed all the helis, only sixteen people at a time could be transported. The warehouses held thousands.

"Where's the new evacuation site?" asked Cherry.

The woman looked at her colleagues, as though seeking their opinion on whether she should answer the question. Two shrugged and the other gave no response.

"Suddene," the woman said. "We're all going to Suddene. It's safe there."

Suddene? Where the android had gone? Cherry wasn't sure the continent was safe at all, not with that thing roaming it. But how would she convince Meredith?

CHAPTER ELEVEN

Kes burst into the lab, accidentally slamming the door against the temporary wall. All the scientists pivoted and stared at him.

"Everyone, stop what you're doing and go to the meeting room immediately. I want you all there in two minutes."

There was a moment of stunned silence, and then all the women and men began to move, quickly putting down their instruments, equipment, or interfaces.

Kes strode through the scientists, organizing his thoughts as he went. On his way to the lab, he'd been joyous. He'd finally made the breakthrough they needed. If he was right, the colony stood a chance. On the other hand, he'd also cursed himself for missing the answer for so long. But he hadn't been expecting it to be so simple.

Now that he was faced with explaining it to the others, however, his optimism was waning. None of the others had grown up on Earth. They had no experience with what he was about to tell them. What he wanted to propose might sound like magic or the ravings of a madman. And if he couldn't convince them he was right, they would be back to square one, faced with the impossible task of defeating the biocide before it killed them all.

Kes pushed open the door to the meeting room, went inside, and sat down in a spot where everyone would be able to see him. Two people followed him in and also took seats. While he was waiting for the others to arrive, he opened an interface and began to search for files on medical practices on Earth.

They were difficult to find. If Kes had been looking for them soon after coming out of cryo aboard the *Nova*, he would have found them in a jiffy. Since then, as the information in the colony's data banks increased, the older files had become more and more difficult to locate. More than five decades of files now filled the system. Kes doubted the ancient information he was seeking was no longer traceable, but he needed more time to find it than the two minutes' notice he'd given for the meeting.

The room was filling quickly and an anticipatory hum was building up. Kes interlocked his fingers and rested his joined hands on the table. He would have to rely on his own powers of explanation to convince his colleagues. There was nothing else he could do.

In a few moments the room was nearly full. Kes gave the stragglers another thirty seconds, counting down in his head. Sure enough, two more scientists came in and took the nearest empty seats.

"Thanks for dropping what you were doing and coming here so quickly," Kes began.

"I think we're all guessing you have something important to tell us," said Tricia.

"I do," Kes replied. "But as I've been sitting here waiting for you, I've realized how strange what I'm about to say may seem to you."

"Now you really do have our undivided attention," Dean said.

"Okay, here it goes," said Kes. "At our last meeting I

commented that the biocide's method of transmission indicated that it might be attached to a virus, and Thom commented it might actually *be* a virus, not the toxic agent we were imagining. If it is, and if we can isolate it, then we have a very simple solution to our problem." Kes paused and took a breath. "Has anyone heard of vaccination?"

The silence was deafening. Blank looks passed between the assembled scientists and returned to meet Kes' gaze. His resolve sank a little. He was hoping *someone* might know about the ancient practice.

"Okay." Kes pulled his hands apart and lay them face down on the table. "This will take some explaining, but hear me out. You all know I'm one of the Woken, right? I was born on Earth, grew up there, and worked on the *Nova Fortuna* Project before traveling here in cryonic suspension." Kes' words had begun to sound somewhat far-fetched even to himself.

"I think we all know that," said Tricia, casting glances around the room. No one contradicted her.

"All the Gens—the generational colonists who were originally chosen to live on the ship—were virus-free when they came aboard. They'd been treated with anti-virals and anyone who didn't have a clean bill of health after treatment was denied entry to the ship. The same was true for me and the other project scientists. If we weren't free of all viruses we couldn't go.

"And during the trip to Concordia, no viruses emerged. Bacteria, yes. It was impossible to make everything sterile and it would have been foolish to try. We need bacteria to survive, even though some cause infections. But no measles, no chicken pox, not even the common cold. In a sense, it's a miracle. Humanity has been plagued by viruses all the millennia of its existence, and in the end it was a virus that destroyed civilization on Earth. But not here. Not on Concordia. No Concordian virus has ever infected a human as far as we know.

"But what that means is, you don't know about vaccination. I'm not an immunologist, but I'll do my best to explain. You know how if bacteria enter a wound and cause an infection, the body's antibodies rush to the spot to destroy the invading microorganisms? A similar thing happens with viruses, only, in the majority of cases, the body *remembers* the virus and if the body detects it again, it already has antibodies to deal with it. Most humans can only be infected by a virus one time. After that, they can't suffer the same infection again. In fact, it's a little more complicated than that, but that's the gist of it."

"And this process is called vaccination?" Tricia asked.

"No. Vaccination is the process of priming the body to recognize and destroy the virus before it can do any harm."

"By infecting the person with the virus?" asked Tricia. "That seems self-defeating."

"Just listen, and then we'll do questions," said Kes, worried that Tricia's innocent inquiries would sow doubt about his proposal. "On Earth, most children were vaccinated against viruses when they were babies and toddlers to prevent them from catching certain serious childhood diseases. Or, rather, the practice *was* commonplace until the Natural Movement got going and put an end to widespread vaccination. But for a couple hundred years the practice worked. It saved countless lives and...My point is, I don't see any reason why we can't try to do the same here."

"You mean do this vaccination thing on us?" asked Thom.

"If I'm right, it means our bodies will fight off the biocide and we won't even notice it tried to infect us."

"*If* it's a virus," Thom said.

"If it's a virus," agreed Kes.

The mood in the room was skeptical. Kes knew he could simply order them to do what he wanted, but he didn't want that. It was important that everyone understood what they were doing and believed in it. He didn't want to force his colleagues or their skepticism would be apparent to the rest of the Concordians, who then might refuse their vaccination.

"If we had more time," said Kes, "I would find and show you the files from Earth that explain the phenomenon, but we don't. I have to ask you to believe me and to trust me."

"We do trust you, Kes," said Tricia. "It just seems so weird. I've never seen this happen in Concordian life forms. I've seen them die of viral illnesses, but—"

"We've barely broken the surface of understanding viruses here," Kes said. "In fact, we've been extremely lucky that no Concordian viruses have infected humans or the food we grow. In coming centuries, one may mutate and we could have an epidemic on our hands, but that isn't our problem at the moment. If this biocide is a virus, vaccination could be the way we defeat it: by harnessing our immune system."

"I'm happy to try anything," said Dean. "It isn't like we have a choice, is it? The biocide will be on our doorstep soon. What do we have to do?"

"Right," said Kes. Introducing the concept hadn't gone too badly. His colleagues hadn't outright rejected it. Now came the hard part. "To trigger the immune system response, we have to give it something to recognize as the enemy."

"Like what?" asked Tricia. "Surely the only way the immune system can recognize the biocide is by introducing the biocide to it."

"Yes," said Kes, "that's right."

"You *have* to be kidding," Tricia said.

"That's insane," Dean said. "Anyone who encounters that stuff dies before they take another breath. A corpse's immune system isn't going to respond to anything."

"I know how it sounds," Kes said. "But bear with me. Vaccination entails injecting a weakened form of the virus or the dead virus into the blood system. Sometimes the recipient experiences a reaction—a low fever, for example—but in nearly all cases the reaction is minor and the recipient develops immunity to the virus. I have to tell you, however, that the process isn't perfect. A small percentage of recipients don't develop immunity and a handful of cases out of a million experience a serious reaction."

"So this vaccination you're proposing could make some people very ill and for others it won't work at all?" asked Tricia.

"That's my prediction, according to what I know."

"And this is a solution?" someone asked quietly.

"Even dead biocide..." said Thom. He shook his head. "I don't know. I wouldn't like any of that stuff injected into me."

"What other options do we have?" asked Dean. "What else have we turned up? We haven't made any real progress in days. We have to try *something*. And the basic idea...It does make sense. I'm sure I recall stumbling across the process when I was an undergrad doing research for an assignment. I didn't understand it at the time, but now...I don't see a reason why it wouldn't work."

"I do," Tricia said. "If it works for viruses, why doesn't it work for bacteria?"

"The immune system responds differently to viruses compared to bacteria," said Kes. "Or we could treat the biocide with antibiotics. But we know the biocide isn't a bacterium. If it was we would have found it days ago, and it wouldn't act so fast."

"Did Earth viruses act that fast?"

"No, or I never heard of one that killed that fast,

anyway," said Kes. "But, talking of speed, are we agreed that we move our work in the direction of vaccination? We don't have time to prevaricate. I plan on searching the files to find out all I can about creating vaccines. Unfortunately, we won't have much time for testing, if any. What I need you to do is examine the tissue samples for anything that resembles a virus. I know that immunology is an obscure area of study these days, but —"

"I've studied it a little bit," interrupted a young man. He didn't look old enough to have graduated. A beard was trying and failing to grow on his upper lip and chin. Kes didn't know his name.

"You have?" Kes asked.

"I thought it seemed interesting, and I thought there might be practical applications in the future if native viruses began to infect our crops."

It was a serendipitous moment. Everything seemed to be coming together at last.

"Right," Kes said to the young man. "You're going to give us all a crash course in everything you know about isolating viruses from infected tissue,...?" He looked questioningly at the man.

"Drew. My name's Drew. I'll do my best," Drew continued. "I'll prepare some equipment for a demonstration." He rose and left the room.

No one moved for a moment. Kes waited. He'd done all he could to sell the idea. Now it was down to the others to run with it, or not. If he faced downright refusal, he didn't know what he would do.

Finally, Tricia said, "Come on, guys. Let's get to work." Her words seemed to break the spell, and the other scientists began to stand and shuffle toward the door.

As Tricia stood up she leaned toward Kes. Under the noise of the departing attendees, she said, "I hope you're right."

"So do I," he replied. "So do I."

CHAPTER TWELVE

Cherry hovered outside the cubicle assigned to the Leader, composing herself before she went in. She knew she would not be able to look Meredith in the eye without reliving that fateful moment she'd taken the destiny of Concordia into her own hands and issued the order to engage in battle with the Scythians.

How many times had she gone over that moment in her mind? How many times had she wondered if she'd done the right thing? On the face of it, it seemed her decision had been entirely wrong. Millions of Fila had died, thousands of Concordians too, and the planet was set on a path toward utter barrenness.

But if she hadn't given that order, what would be happening now? The Scythians had given a vicious demonstration of their attitude toward the human population of the planet, entirely unprovoked. They had sought to crush any thought of refusal or rebellion in the minds of their prospective slaves. But they had also given Cherry a picture of what Concordians could expect to endure if they agreed to the Scythians' demands.

What kind of life would that have been? All their hard

work and resources would have gone to supply a growing population of Scythians, living in idleness on their origin planet, unable to leave their environment-controlled domes. What was the point of that kind of existence for humanity?

All the work and preparation that went into building and supplying the *Nova*, all the thousands of people who lived and died on its long journey across the galaxy, all the effort that had gone into building a civilization on their new home planet—all of it would have been for nothing if they'd given up their freedom and self-determination.

She had no doubt that Meredith disagreed, and fervently. Their Leader had been all for capitulating, kowtowing to the Scythians who had just murdered thousands of her people. Even as she thought back to that moment and Meredith's cowardly response, disgust and fury rose up in Cherry. But she had to keep it under control if she was to persuade the Leader to agree to her request to take a heli to Suddene.

An unbidden memory popped into Cherry's mind. She was in the shelter she'd constructed after the first Scythian attack, when they had razed the settlement. She could recall the damp, the hunger, and the desperation so vividly. Ethan was there. Garwin, too. Poor Garwin. He'd died too young and broken-hearted.

The colony had needed a leader who would take them forward. Someone pure-hearted, brave, and tenacious. Everyone except Ethan knew *he* was that person. But he'd suggested that she should do it. *I don't have the patience*, she'd replied. How true that was. Her snap responses had worked against her so many times, not least when she'd alienated Wilder.

Cherry reflexively closed and opened her fist. The regret she felt for her decision to fire on the Scythians was inescapable and enormous, but in honesty it was more regret for what had happened as a result, and less regret for the decision itself. She wasn't sure if, given identical circumstances and knowing the terrible outcome, she would not have done exactly the same thing again.

If Meredith brought up the subject, what should she say? Should she lie to her, tell the Leader she'd been wrong? Tell Meredith that they would all be better living as slaves because any kind of life was better than none? No matter how expedient the response might be, Cherry knew she could never say it. The words would refuse to leave her mouth.

The only other option would be a shameful skirting around the truth, which was not something she had any practice with. That time in the shelter with Ethan and Garwin, she'd been right. She would make an awful Leader.

There was nothing for it. She would just have to go in and wing it. Lacking a hard surface to knock or a doorbell to ring, Cherry went to announce her presence, but Meredith said,

"Cherry, are you going to come in or are you going to stand out there all morning?"

Cherry opened the curtain. Meredith was sitting on a camping chair at a small table. The only other furniture in the room was a low cot.

"I could see your boots at the bottom of the curtain," said Meredith.

Cherry stepped into the cubicle and let the curtain fall closed behind her. "These aren't even my boots. How did you know it was me?"

"The people I asked to keep watch on the helis comm'd me that you were coming over."

"Right. I need to take one of them to Suddene."

Meredith looked at Cherry with Ethan's eyes. It was the first frank look that had passed between them since the battle. Reproach, resentment, and rancor exuded from Meredith's gaze, yet fatigue and defeat were also there. Perhaps the latter two had been prominent in the Leader long before the Scythians returned. A stab of pity hit Cherry. Meredith had been expected to fulfill a role she was unsuited for and to live up to impossible expectations, based on Ethan's legacy.

The Leader seemed to have aged ten years in the past week.

"And?" Meredith asked coldly.

"And what?"

"I believe it's customary to state a reason when requesting the use of government property. Or do you think you're above that too?"

Cherry chose to ignore the bait Meredith offered. An argument about what she'd done would only delay her trip to Suddene. Besides, what was done was done. There was no undoing it, however much they debated the wisdom of her decision. Cherry also suspected that Meredith wanted to be worked into such a state of heightened emotion that she would do what she should have done in the first place: sack her general. Incarcerate her, even. She'd committed treason and, in the Leader's position, Cherry would not have tolerated it.

But Meredith was not Cherry. She was weak, Cherry realized with a flash of insight—weak, tired, and way out of her depth.

"Is it okay if I sit?" Cherry asked.

Meredith sighed. "Be my guest."

Cherry perched on the edge of Meredith's cot. "I went back to Oceanside, into the dead zone. I wanted to find out what happened to that thing that calls itself a Guardian."

"That seems the least of our worries now."

"I don't know. Maybe not. Meredith, I'm no scientist. I can't figure out a way to stop the biocide. All I can do is continue to try to protect this colony as well as I can for as long as I can."

"You don't seem to have done a very good job so far."

Cherry grimaced. Again, she refused the bait. "The Guardian has gone to Suddene. It took a ship and it arrived there days ago. It has a purpose, a job it has to do. What that is, I don't know. But I suspect it isn't anything that's for our benefit. It may be trying to finish us off faster than the biocide will."

"I don't understand why you're suspicious of that thing. The Guardians' sole purpose was to protect us. That was what they were made for."

"We don't know that it is what it says it is, and even if it is a Guardian, the situation is way more complicated than that. Believe me, Meredith. I know them far better than you. More than once I was at the wrong end of a Guardian's weapon, and it would not have hesitated to shoot me if its electronic brain decided my death was justified. *That* is what Guardians are. Not the colony's saviors."

Meredith looked unconvinced.

"What if it's working for the Scythians?" asked Cherry. "Don't you think it's a good idea to go after it and find out what it's up to?"

"The Scythians have finished us off already," Meredith said. "They can't hurt us more than they already have."

"I haven't given up hope yet, and neither should you. You're the Leader. If anyone needs to believe we can survive this, it's you. People are looking to you for the will to carry on. You have to stand firm, Meredith. The colony is counting on you." Cherry was about to say more but she bit back her words. Referring to Meredith's father wouldn't be helpful, though it would have been true to say that without Ethan's faith they could make it the colony would never have survived.

Meredith's head sunk low. She said nothing for several moments, and eventually Cherry realized the woman was crying. Her teardrops dripped from her eyes onto the dark concrete floor.

Shit. Cherry wondered if she'd said too much. Meredith was under tremendous pressure. Cherry scooted closer and put her arm over the Leader's shoulders. They sat together like that for a while in silence. Cherry didn't know what to say. She was terrible with that kind of thing.

Finally, Meredith sniffed and rubbed her eyes with her sleeve. "Not very dignified for a Leader, huh?"

"It's okay," Cherry replied. "Leader or not, you're still a human being. I know it must be hard for you to be in the position you're in. I couldn't do it."

Her head still hanging low, Meredith said, "When the Scythians returned and I wanted to agree to their terms, you told me that my father would be ashamed of me."

Cherry winced. "I have a habit of saying the wrong thing at the wrong time. I'm sorry."

"Did you mean it?" Meredith asked. "Do you think it's true? You knew Dad from when he was young. You probably knew him as well as Mom did. Do you really think he would have been ashamed of me?"

Cherry thought for a moment. She recalled Ethan as she'd known him. "No. He wouldn't have been ashamed of you. That was a dumb thing for me to say. He would have been proud of you for doing the best you could with the shitty, impossible circumstances that were handed to you. He would have been very proud of you. I'm sure of it."

Meredith slowly nodded. She straightened up. "Thanks for saying that. It means a lot to me. More than you know."

"I'm not saying it to make you feel better. It's the truth."

"I believe you. Take a heli to Suddene, Cherry. I hope you do us some good out there. We certainly need it."

"Thanks. I'll keep you updated."

Meredith nodded again, absently.

CHAPTER THIRTEEN

Kes was taking a short break, hastily eating a meal of pasta and seaweed as he stood outside the lab doors. Inside, his colleagues were working hard. Renewed energy had invigorated the scientists. The fraught, quietly despairing atmosphere of the lab had been replaced by dynamic vitality. It would have been an exaggeration to call the atmosphere hopeful, but it was clear the scientists were now working with a strong sense of purpose.

The desired breakthrough had arrived. They had found the virus. Rather—Kes reminded himself so that his optimism didn't grow out of bounds—they had found **a** virus. Something viral in origin had infected the Fila tissue samples, and it seemed to have been responsible for the majority of the cells bursting and dying.

No one had managed to isolate any virions from within the cells that remained whole, which indicated they had died not due to viral infection but due to the entire organism suffering extensive and devastating damage that was incompatible with life.

Kes had sent all the data up to Quinn along with

several questions. He hoped the Fila would confirm that his species was not routinely infected by one or more viruses. Kes recalled there had been a handful of viral diseases on Earth that chronically infected a portion of the population. If the same was true of the Fila, it could mean the scientists hadn't found the biocide at all, but something irrelevant.

Even if they had found the biocide, it was only the first step in protecting the colony. They would have to create a vaccine from the dead virus. Kes only knew the basics of the process, and that was only because he'd finally managed to locate the relevant files in the recesses of the databases. And if they could create a vaccine, there was no guarantee it would work. It could be fatally dangerous.

If the biocide wasn't dead but only in another state it could reactivate when introduced to live cells. They would test it on living human cells first, but eventually they would have to test it on a human subject. The person could die—instantly if the biocide followed its usual pattern.

And assuming they managed to jump all the hurdles that stood in their way and they created an effective, harmless vaccine, they could still be too late. The human immune system did not move at anywhere near the speed of the deadly biocide. It could be days or weeks before the colonists built up sufficient antibodies to deal with the powerful virus the Scythians had created.

Kes had also not forgotten the concept of herd immunity. Vaccines on Earth had never been one hundred percent effective. A minority of the vaccinated did not develop an immune response. Providing a substantial proportion of the population was vaccinated these individuals were protected anyway, because the virus was prevented from circulating. But on Concordia the biocide was everywhere. When it reached the refuges, every living thing would be a vector. The people whose immune systems had not been triggered by the vaccine would die, and there was nothing Kes could do about it.

It was an awful, sobering thought. Kes' appetite disappeared. He put down his half-finished plate of pasta on a nearby table. Through the window in the lab doors, he watched the energetic movements of the scientists as they worked.

Even if they succeeded in making a vaccine, there were colonists whose fate was already decided. The biocide would arrive at the refuges and pass through them without effect except for the unlucky individuals.

What if Miki or Isobel didn't develop immunity? Kes was sure that pregnant women's immune systems behaved differently, though he didn't know any details. What if *he* didn't develop immunity? At least it would be a fast death, and he would die knowing that he'd helped to save many others.

Kes fastened his lab coat. It was time to get back to work.

As he pushed open the lab door, a scream rang out. Kes froze, the cry arresting his movement. The scream was filled with horror and dismay, and it echoed from the corrugated roof of the warehouse and bounced from wall to wall.

The scientists in the lab heard it too, through the open door. They paused in their conversations and actions, their eyes widening.

"What the...?" asked Tricia. She walked to the door and looked out, but the wider view of the warehouse was blocked by rows of curtained cubicles.

In the distance, a commotion started up. Kes could hear shouts, cries, and exclamations, but he couldn't make out what people were saying.

"Go back inside," he told Tricia through the door comm. "I'll find out what's happening and let you know.

Hopefully it isn't as serious as it sounds, but we can't afford to waste time on it, whatever's happened."

It wasn't difficult to find the location of the disturbance. Kes only had to head toward the growing noise of people in shock and distress. Had the biocide already arrived and begun to work its way through the refuge? He didn't think so. The last report he'd heard had said it was still far distant, though working its way steadily nearer. Unless a canister of the stuff had landed nearby during the attack and hadn't opened until now, Kes couldn't imagine how it could have traveled to the warehouses so quickly.

As he drew nearer to the epicenter of the disturbance, he could make out what was being said.

"I can't believe it. I just can't believe it," said one voice.

"She seemed all right," said another. "Didn't she seem all right? I mean, if anyone had known..."

"Ugh, I can't look," said someone else. "I'm leaving. I can't deal with this. Not along with everything else."

People were running past Kes, heading toward the same spot. Others were coming in the opposite direction, their heads down. When they were asked by the newcomers what had happened, they wouldn't answer and only hurried away.

Kes saw a crowd of people gathered around something on the ground. They seemed transfixed in horrified fascination. They were clustered so tightly in the narrow space between two rows of cubicles, Kes couldn't see what they were looking at. A horrible dread overcame him anyway. Something terrible had happened. Something devastating.

Kes slowed his pace. He almost didn't want to find out the source of the horror on the faces of the onlookers. He wanted to turn around and head back, go to find Isobel and Miki and hug them and protect them from yet another appalling event to befall the colony.

But his feet carried him forward.

A comm request arrived from Tricia.

"Have you found out what's happened yet?" she asked.

"No, but it's bad."

"An awful rumor's reached us. I wanted to check if it's true."

"Give me a minute." Kes pushed gently through the throng of people. They didn't resist. They were in a state of shock, he realized, and not in control of what they were doing. The onlookers parted and Kes saw what they were looking at.

He saw two feet first. Splayed apart. A woman was lying on her back. Kes didn't recognize who it was from her feet. They could have been any woman's. Her slim legs were also splayed, as if she were sleeping, casually at rest, perhaps after a vivid dream.

Kes could not see the upper half of the woman's body because it was obscured by the back of the man who crouched beside her. The man was working energetically, pumping on her chest. He was trying to resuscitate the woman.

Kes still did not guess who it was.

Inexorably, he was drawn forward, as if pulled by a string attached to his torso. He felt compelled onward against his will. Someone had suffered a heart attack, probably. It was morbid and an invasion of privacy to gawp at the poor person. But he couldn't help himself.

He stepped closer, and the woman's head came into view. Kes' strength left him. He recognized Meredith, though her face was deformed. Kes could hardly bear to look at it.

The belt around her neck had been loosened, but it remained there. The man—presumably a doctor— pounded rhythmically on her, jerking Meredith's body as if she were a marionette operated by an unskilled puppeteer.

But there was no life left. To Kes' eyes at least, the doctor's efforts were heroic but hopeless.

Overburdened with responsibility for the colony, or perhaps for another reason, Meredith had taken her own life.

CHAPTER FOURTEEN

Suddene was a yellow strip on the horizon. The ocean surged below, deep blue and scattered with the foamy crests of high waves. What effect would millions of rotting Fila corpses have on the water? Every other marine organism had died, too. If Kes and the other scientists managed to neutralize the biocide, would the ocean ever recover from the massive disturbance to its chemical balance? Would any surviving Fila ever be able to return to it?

At least Quinn had survived, Cherry reflected. By a lucky stroke of fate, her decision to stand up to the Scythians hadn't resulted in his death too. Compared to the numbers of anonymous Fila who had died, her friend's survival was only a minor consolation, but she would take it. She needed every small comfort she could get.

"Looking hot over there," Zapata remarked.

Cherry's eyes rose to the band of yellow. It had grown larger while she'd been contemplating the fate of the Fila.

Zapata threw a glance at her. They were both wearing the haz suits. The attire wasn't particularly suitable for desert traveling.

"Do you know the temperature at ground level?" Cherry asked.

"Forty-two C."

"It shouldn't be a problem. I'm going underground as soon as I arrive."

"So we're heading to Chimera?" asked Zapata. "I thought I recognized the coordinates as the same place I flew you before."

Cherry said, "We're heading to an excavation site. That's all you... Uh, I guess it's a little late for that kind of thing. Yes, we're heading to the site that would have become Chimera, Concordia's fifth missile silo. Is there anything else you want to know?" she added, ironically.

She liked the large, bearded man. He didn't try to make small talk to fill the silence on long flights—his comment about Suddene's desert had been his first in hours—and he exuded calmness and reassurance with his presence. Cherry was tempted to ask him to remain with her after they arrived. She was not afraid to go after the Guardian alone, but navigating the underground Scythian city would not be easy and her lack of a limb would hamper her.

But she had promised Meredith that she would send the heli and its pilot back to Lyonesse to help with the evacuation.

"I'll understand if you don't want to tell me," said Zapata, "but I'm wondering why you're going to Suddene. I know it isn't to escape the biocide."

Cherry thought for a moment. It wouldn't hurt to tell the pilot the reason for her mission. She outlined the sequence of events that had led up to her decision to travel to Concordia's second continent. "I have a feeling it's gone to the Scythians' city," she concluded. "I don't know why, but I plan on finding out. At the very least, if I discover it has gone there, that means it's working for the enemy. If it really is Faina, the last surviving

Guardian, it wouldn't know anything about the city's existence, let alone where it is."

"That's some story," Zapata said. "I learned about the Guardians at school. It's hard to imagine one of them might still exist. What'll you do if you find this thing in the city?"

"Kill it, of course. Destroy it, rather. It's a machine, not alive."

"But you haven't brought any weapons with you. How do you plan on killing it?"

"Even the Guardians' own, high tech weapons had no effect on them. I won't be able to destroy it by shooting at it."

"Wait a minute," Zapata said. "You said if it's in the city it isn't a Guardian."

"Well, it could be. Another possibility just occurred to me. The Scythians might have picked one of them out of the wreckage of the *Mistral* and reprogrammed it for their own purposes." Cherry blinked. What if she was right? Her guess fit the facts. The damaged android did look like Faina, but if it was Faina, Cherry predicted the Guardian would have followed the human survivors to a refuge rather than going alone to Suddene. Unless Faina knew something or was trying to do something Cherry had no knowledge of. "Whatever it is, I'm going to destroy it."

"Even if it's a Guardian?"

"If it's a Guardian that hasn't been tampered with and it can demonstrate that to my satisfaction, maybe I'll give it fifteen seconds to explain itself. Maybe. I understand this might seem odd to you according to what you learned at school, but the colony is better off without them."

"Right. I suppose you know what you're talking about. So, how will you destroy it if it isn't affected by weapon fire?"

"I'll figure something out."

***

Someone had built a perimeter fence around the Chimera excavation site. Tall, chain link fencing attached to metal posts encircled the dark opening of the tunnel. Heavy metal gates barred the single dirt road that led to the tunnel entrance, and the excavation workers' giant trucks sat inside the fence. The fence, gates, and tunnel roof were only small anomalies in the vast expanse of desert, but they were foreboding and entirely unexpected.

Zapata had to have seen them too, but his only comment was, "Do you want me to land inside or outside the compound?"

It *was* a compound, Cherry realized. The only reason for the fence was in order to protect something or some people within it. The citizens of Suddene must have relocated to the Chimera excavation site, hoping to avoid the biocide as long as possible. But why the fence?

"Did you know about this?" Cherry asked the pilot.

"Uh uh. But I think it means trouble. I'll fly you inside if you want, but..."

"It might be more diplomatic to ask for admittance."

"Yep."

"You're right. Set her down fifty meters from the gates."

Cherry's stomach moved rapidly upward into her throat as Zapata lowered the heli out of the sky. He landed on the highway, predictably lifting clouds of sand.

As the landing skids touched down, Cherry reached for the door, but Zapata said, "Wait a minute." He turned off the engine, and the heli's circling blades slowed to a stop. The sand began to settle. "A weapon might not work against a Guardian, but it might have been handy to deal with scared colonists."

The fence around the Chimera site was beginning to

make sense to Cherry too. Whoever had put it up wanted to keep out everyone else—anyone who wasn't already inside it might be contaminated with the biocide.

"Weapon or not, I have to talk to them," said Cherry.

"I'll come with you."

Cherry was grateful. She wouldn't have asked Zapata to take the risk on her behalf, but the large man had an intimidating presence that might come in handy.

The desert and the distant fence were becoming visible as more of the disturbed sand settled. Zapata opened his door. Cherry did the same and they both climbed out of the craft. She recalled her previous visit to the site, when a gale had been blowing and the light heli had not even been able to land. Now, the air was still and the desert baking. As Cherry stepped out of the shadow of the heli, the blazing heat of the sun immediately began to warm the inside of her haz suit.

They walked toward the metal gates in silence. No movement stirred within the fence. It was possible the gates were unmanned. Standing outside in the desert heat for any length of time would be brutal. She hoped they would not be forced to stand and holler to be let in.

"Stop where you are," a voice shouted. The sound had come from the gates, though Cherry couldn't see its source. The effect was odd, as if the words had been discharged by the shimmering desert haze. "Non-Chimera residents are not permitted to enter," the voice continued, faintly. "Turn around and go back. You aren't welcome here."

Cherry and Zapata were still forty meters from the gates. Zapata continued to stride onward, but Cherry touched his arm, signaling him to halt. Something had rung a bell in her mind. She knew that voice. It was a man, but not Alun, the Chimera site supervisor. What had the other man's name been? The one who had lost the game with Pearl and remained behind while she went with Cherry into the Scythian city.

She had it. "Laurie?" Cherry called, straining to make her voice as loud as possible to counteract the muffling effect of her suit's helmet. The biocide clearly hadn't made it that far. She removed her helmet. "It's me, Cherry. We met when I came to—"

"I guessed who you were," Laurie yelled. "There aren't many one-armed women on Concordia. Go away. You're not bringing that poison in here to kill us all."

"I'm not bringing..." Cherry looked at Zapata and rolled her eyes. "We aren't carrying any biocide. We're only wearing haz suits because I thought it might have reached here already. We can take them off if you want."

"Doesn't matter," Laurie shouted. "We aren't taking risks."

Cherry went to speak but then closed her mouth. He had a point. The safest thing for anyone to do in the circumstances was to remain as isolated from other living things as possible, even other human beings. No one knew the exact details of how the biocide was transmitted. It was conceivable the poison could be carried on clothes without affecting the wearer, which is why she'd been forced to change into clean clothes at the refuge.

The dry desert air and all the shouting was making Cherry hoarse. "Can I come up to the gate to talk about this?"

"No. If you move a single step in this direction I'll shoot."

The reply was exactly what Cherry had feared. The people in the compound had weapons. Where had they gotten hold of arms on Suddene?

"I hate to suggest it," Zapata said, "but they might allow you to come closer if you strip off your clothes."

"If I...? Cherry's shoulders drooped.

"I'll turn around," said the pilot. "I promise."

The idea didn't appeal, but it might work. *"Shit."*

But if that was what it took... Cherry called out, "What if I take off all my clothes? If I had biocide on my skin, I'd be dead, right?"

This drew a pause from Laurie. Was he thinking over the proposal or discussing it with someone else? The shouted conversation must have attracted the attention of others within the compound.

"If you strip butt naked," yelled Laurie, "you can approach the gate. But we're still not letting you in."

Great.

Zapata turned his back but not before Cherry detected his eyes creasing in amusement.

She pulled open her haz suit and unzipped it. As the suit crumpled to the ground she stepped out of the legs. She quickly unfastened the buttons of her shirt and shrugged it off before stepping on the heels of her boots to remove them. Finally, she pulled down her pants and took off her underwear. The sun coated her naked skin in broiling heat.

Angry and embarrassed, Cherry didn't wait for the okay from Laurie. She set off toward the gate and after a few steps she broke into a trot. The hot sand burned the soles of her feet and the sun's rays felt as though they were cooking her skin. Cherry had heard of people going to the beaches to lie in the sun simply for the pleasure of it, but the idea had never appealed to her. She didn't think she'd ever exposed her body while outdoors. What an occasion for a first experience.

The shadow cast by the gate was a welcome relief the moment she set foot into it. The sand felt cool under her feet and her skin ceased to burn.

"I'm here," Cherry said, her nose against the solid metal of the gate. "Open up."

"I said, we're not letting you in." Laurie's disembodied voice came from the other side of the gates. There was no hole or window but it was clear he could see her. Cherry looked upward, craning her neck to see along the lengths of the posts on each side of the gates. The black, glass eye of a camera reflected the bright sunlight.

"Then what was the point of all this?" Cherry asked.

"You wanted to come closer to the gate."

"This is ridiculous!" Cherry exclaimed. "Open up, dammit. I'm the general. I go where I want. Do you want me to give a command to blow these gates apart?"

"Concordia doesn't have a military anymore," said Laurie. "The Scythians destroyed it. And now they're destroying the planet, but we'll last the longest in here. We might even last forever if the biocide burns itself out. We have seed and everything we need to start again. So, no. I'm not letting you in. I'm sorry. You seemed like a good person. It's nothing personal. But we can't take the risk. So go back to your heli and return to Lyonesse. It was nice knowing you."

Everything we need to start again? If the biocide burns itself out? Was it possible the people holed up in the Chimera site were on to something?

Even if they were, that didn't help Cherry with her immediate problem. She rested her forehead on the cool metal. Then she had an idea.

"You haven't asked me why I'm here," she said.

"I know why you're here," Laurie replied. "You want to escape the biocide. But we're full. We can't take any more people. I'm sorry, but we just can't. So go home, and tell the others if anyone tries to break in we'll shoot to kill."

"No, you're wrong. I'm not here to get away from the biocide. And hardly anyone on Lyonesse even knows about this place. The project was secret, remember? No one knows about your plan to hide out here. No one is going to try to join you. I guarantee it."

"I don't believe you. What other reason could you have for coming?" asked Laurie.

Here was Cherry's moment to explain. The man was finally going to listen to her. But before she could speak, another voice rang out from behind the gate.

"Laurie, what are you doing?" It was a man's voice.

"Alun?" asked Cherry.

"Who's that?" Alun asked. He uttered an expletive then said, "Why the hell is there a naked woman out there?"

"Alun, it's me, Cherry. You helped me investigate the Scythian city."

"Open the gate, Laurie," ordered Alun.

Laurie protested, but Alun cut him off, saying, "Open the gate, you damned idiot!"

Locks rattled, and one door of the gates opened a few inches. An arm holding a jacket appeared through it. Cherry took the jacket and put it on. The hem reached low enough to cover her modestly.

"Thanks," Cherry said. "Can I please come in now?"

CHAPTER FIFTEEN

Wilder was going crazy with boredom. Her confinement aboard the *Opportunity* reminded her of her trip to the Galactic Assembly space station. The weeks and months of that journey had dragged by, with little to stimulate her mental faculties except her studies of the Fila, and the strange interpersonal dynamic between Cherry and Aubriot.

But at least then she'd had other humans to keep her company. At the time, she would have given a lot to get away from them and the close, sweaty proximity of other people with their loud voices and boring conversations. Now, she would give a lot to have just one of them aboard the ship with her. Even that asshole Aubriot would be better than no one.

Wilder idly pressed the button on the a-grav machine. It turned on and immediately moved slightly toward the ceiling, which faced away from Concordia. The movement was barely noticeable but in micro-g Wilder couldn't expect any more. It was enough to tell her the machine was working.

When she'd first made it work, she'd been overjoyed. She'd hollered and bounced around the living quarters, rebounding from all its surfaces and sending Piddle and

Puddle scampering into their sleeping pouches. But then she'd been sad she had no one to share her success with. She'd contemplated trying to comm the surface to let one of the secret team working on the project know what she'd done, but she'd realized how crass and tactless it would be. Whoever she spoke to would have been in fear of their imminent death, assuming they'd even survived the battle with the Scythians. Her news, from the safety of the *Opportunity*, would seem extremely self-centered and would probably be meaningless to them.

For the first time in her life, she'd felt lonely. She'd been alone plenty of times, and it was her preferred mode of existence, but she'd also known there was always someone she could comm if she wanted. She'd had the choice. Her circumstances were different now. Soon, she might be the only human being left alive, and no matter how much she craved human company, she would never see or hear another person again.

From then on she'd tried to keep herself occupied to stave off the sense of loneliness and her intellectual boredom. She had taken apart the a-grav machine and put it together again twice. The thing worked like a dream. She couldn't have asked for a better result from her and others' years of toil. What a waste that no one except Quinn and the other Fila crew might know about it.

She turned off the machine. It sank a few centimeters and floated, like her, in midair.

She had to talk to someone. She liked Quinn. Perhaps she even loved him. But he wasn't human. Talking to him wasn't the same as talking to someone who thought in a similar way to her. Someone she could relate to. Heck, Quinn didn't even perceive time the same way she did.

As the days had passed, the prospect of remaining alive after all the other Concordians died had appeared more and more bleak. Wilder had begun to regret her promise to Kes.

He'd said she could talk to him whenever, but he was racing against time to try to halt the progress of the biocide. She had no right to interrupt his work or the precious few hours of rest he would be allowing himself. Not for something as trivial as a chat. Yet even thinking about hearing the sweet man's voice made her tear up.

Kes hadn't gotten back to her about the people she'd asked him to check up on. He was too busy, of course. Maybe she could do the sleuthing herself.

"Quinn, can I comm the surface directly from here?" she asked.

"I can arrange it so you can," the Fila replied, "but I warn you the network is very slow and most individuals have no direct access to comm. The connections must be made via coordinators at each refuge."

Wilder suddenly realized she didn't even know the real name of the person she wanted to speak to, let alone which refuge he'd gone to. "How about the public records? Are they still available?"

"I believe so. They haven't been updated since the battle, however, except for a list of known refuges. No one has recorded the deceased or the locations of the survivors, if that's what you want to find out."

"I actually want to find out something different. Can you connect me to the surface now?" Wilder reached out and grabbed a handhold. Her head turned downward toward Concordia, she searched for information on inhabitants of a certain address. She remembered it from the time she'd gone there with Tycho to pick up the spare a-grav machine parts.

The information wasn't available to the general public but Wilder used a couple of hacks she'd devised years ago to access far more sensitive data. In moments she had the names of the family members, including that of a fifteen-year-old boy. She was surprised by the boy's age. When she'd seen him she'd thought he was about twelve.

Her task had been easy so far. Now came the hard work. She had to locate Niall Cully among tens of thousands of displaced Concordians. One fifteen year old kid, who could be anywhere. There was nothing for it except to comm each refuge, one by one, and hope that the coordinators had a local database of residents.

Wilder worked her way through the list of refuges. Each time it took ages for the comm to go through, and then even longer for the brief conversation with the local coordinator. Some did have lists of people living in the refuge that the coordinator was fairly confident was complete. None of the lists contained the name Niall Cully, or anyone who had the same surname. Wilder was sure Niall would have remained with his family when Oceanside was evacuated. He was only a kid.

The names of the refuges gave no indication of the number of people who were sheltering there so Wilder couldn't comm the largest ones first. An hour from when she began, she'd spoken to five coordinators and she had eleven more refuges to contact. Though she didn't know how large the refuges were, sometimes she recognized a place name that would all but rule the refuge out from her search. Cerberus, for instance, was an unlikely destination for Niall's family. The missile silo was far from Oceanside and who in their right mind would head there when the planet was under attack?

Wilder moved to the sixth refuge on her list. A place called simply Highway 1 15 k. She guessed that meant a spot near the highway fifteen kilometers from Oceanside. In fact, it had to mean that. It was a smart choice of name. The refuge would be easy to locate. She placed a comm to the center coordinator and waited.

The deathly silence of the ship reigned in the living quarters. Except for an extremely faint, possibly imaginary hum from the engines, Wilder was surrounded by the silence of space. The lack of noise seemed to encroach and press into her ears. Her sense of loneliness, hundreds of kilometers from another human being, grew almost too great to bear. Wilder was about to ask Quinn to play some music when the coordinator replied.

"Hello, Highway 1 15 k."

"Hi, I'm looking for someone. Can you help me?" asked Wilder. She waited many seconds for the reply.

"I can try," said the coordinator. "Who are you looking for? I need their full name and the person's rough age if possible."

When she had first heard the coordinator's voice, Wilder had felt a tinge of familiarity, but it was too faint to draw her full attention. But the second time the coordinator spoke, the bell rang louder. She thought she recognized the speaker, but she couldn't quite believe it. Was her loneliness causing her imagination to play tricks on her? She didn't want to look like a fool by stating her suspicion.

"I'm looking for a boy who's about fifteen years old. His name's Niall Cully."

Long seconds later, the reply came. "Uh..." The coordinator hesitated. "That's me." He sounded confused, as well he might. He probably had all his family with him and maybe his friends too. No doubt he was wondering who this stranger was who was looking for him.

Wilder was about to attempt to explain herself when the coordinator continued, "Is that...? Are you Deadly After Midnight?"

"Yes!" Wilder exclaimed. "It's me. Did you recognize my voice? Hello, Jamie Bond. You'll never guess where I am." Excitement at talking to her friend from the secret a-grav machine group was making her giddy.

But she had to wait many frustrating seconds for Jamie Bond's reply.

Surprisingly, he sounded a little annoyed. "How come you know my real name? We aren't supposed to snoop on each other. What did you hack into to find out?"

"It was easy," Wilder replied. "I came to your house, remember? I knew your address and your rough age. There was only one occupant at that address of around the right age. Anyway, don't you think we're a little past sticking to the rules and regulations?"

"Agreeing not to snoop on each other isn't a rule or regulation. It's a part of the honor code."

Wilder paused and swallowed. The conversation wasn't going at all how she'd hoped. "I'm sorry, okay? I'm glad you survived the attack. I only wanted to find out how you are and I-I wanted someone to talk to."

The lag before Niall's reply was longer than usual. He was pausing too, perhaps thinking about what to say. Wilder hoped he didn't close the comm on her. Eventually, he said, "I'm sorry. I didn't mean to be so hard on you. Things aren't easy right now. I guess the stress is getting to me. Hey, now you know my real name, you should tell me yours."

Smiling, Wilder told him. Then she told him where she was, in the interest of full disclosure. She didn't want to delude Niall into thinking she was in the same predicament as him, even by omission. In anticipation of his inevitable question and to save time, she also told him how she'd ended up on the *Opportunity*, the sole Concordian who wasn't at risk from the biocide.

At the end of the intervening silence came Niall's low whistle. Unsurprisingly, the section of her story of most interest to him was the part where she'd gotten the a-grav machine to work. "What a shame the people who rescued you let the machine go."

Tell me about it, thought Wilder.

"So that's why you wanted the spare parts," Niall continued. "You wanted to take them up to the

Opportunity. Have you had any success repeating your process?"

Trying not to sound too proud, Wilder replied in the affirmative. "I have a complete working machine in here with me right now. I wish I could send you a vid, but it would be frivolous in the circumstances." She didn't want to take up any more of the precious network bandwidth.

"Oh, I believe you," said Niall. "You wouldn't lie about something like that. I'm green with envy and full of admiration at the same time. Well done, Wilder. Well done."

Not wanting to dwell on the a-grav machine, which she was honestly finding less interesting now, Wilder asked, "How are things where you are? And what's happened to your coordinator? I was surprised you answered on their behalf."

"I *am* Highway 1 15 K's coordinator," Niall replied. "There are only thirteen of us and I kind of took charge. No one else wanted the job. We may have to change our name to Highway 1 20 k pretty soon. Someone went on a scouting mission the other day and saw the biocide has spread in our direction. It's unpredictable. Sometimes it spreads in one direction but not another. Sometimes it races through the ground faster than a man can run. That was how it got my mom."

Niall's tone had turned soft and quiet.

"Niall, I'm so sorry." Wilder blinked as her vision blurred with tears. In micro-g the water didn't run down her face. She had to wipe her eyes with her sleeve. "Here I am talking about stupid a-grav machines when your mom has just died."

"That's okay. I don't really like to talk about it, but the short story is, we were evacuating from Oceanside like we'd been told to when Mom remembered she hadn't brought any food. We'd just grabbed what we could and left. I told her not to go back, that we would find food or the government would supply it, but she went anyway. I saw her coming back…" A long pause followed in which Wilder said nothing. What could she say?

"She didn't make it," Niall finished.

Wilder still didn't know what to say. "I'm sorry," she repeated.

"I don't know where my dad is," said Niall, answering her unasked question. "Haven't seen him for a few years." His tone had lapsed into utter misery.

"I wish you could come up here with me," said Wilder. "It would be cool to show you the a-grav machine."

"Thanks, but I would never leave these people. They depend on me. We all depend on each other. We're going to wait it out. Keep moving. Until they figure out how to stop the biocide. Then I'll go home."

"Don't do that. When this is all over I want you to come and live with me. I have a cool place…" Wilder realized her forest home was probably a tree graveyard by now, assuming it had survived the battle. "I *had* a cool place, and I'll build another one. We can live together and work on interesting projects. What do you say?"

"I like the sound of that," Niall replied, sounding happier.

"Great. Let's do it. When this is all over and I can return to Concordia."

"When this is all over," said Niall.

There didn't seem to be a lot else to say and Wilder didn't want to take up any more network time. "I guess I better let you go."

"Yeah," said Niall. "It's been great talking to you, Wilder."

"You too, Niall. I hope we can meet up soon."

They said their farewells and Niall closed the comm.

Wilder repeated her wish to herself, that she would

see Niall soon, but she feared it would not come true. Not ever.

CHAPTER SIXTEEN

The death of the Leader had dimmed the already dark mood in the warehouse refuge by several notches. Kes could feel the morose, despondent atmosphere among the scientists as they worked quietly on developing a vaccine for the biocide. Even the mild banter that had gone on between the tired workers had disappeared. Speaking at a normal volume seemed intrusive and extravagant.

The reason for the change in attitude was clear and didn't need to be stated: the loss of their Leader when they needed her most was bad enough, but the fact that Meredith had committed suicide was way worse. What greater testament was there to the hopeless state of the colony than its own leader giving up on it?

It was more important than ever that the scientists announced some good news. Something to indicate that all hope was not lost. Without a boost of that kind, Kes feared there would be copycat suicides. Meredith, in her sad, desperate act, would have sowed the idea as a quick way out of the dreadful situation.

Kes recalled the Second Scythian Attack, when the

colonists had been hiding in Sidhe. Cherry's thought processes had been similar: if death was inevitable, better for it to be fast and under your own terms. Rather than waiting for the Scythian spiders to cut their way to her, she had run out to face them. It had been a rash, brave, and perhaps foolhardy act. A typical Cherry thing to do, like this new task she'd set herself of chasing down the escaped Guardian.

He didn't harbor the same suspicions about the android. His first encounter with them had been when Cariad had reactivated them to help defend the colony against the return of the Scythians. He'd only ever known them to be helpful and self-sacrificing in the extreme. Cherry's experience had been different and Kes understood why she hated them, but he also wondered if her new undertaking was mostly due to the enormous guilt she felt.

The outcome of her decision to fight back against the Scythians had been devastating but unforeseeable. No one could have guessed that their enemy would choose to destroy all life on Concordia in preference to another intelligent species inhabiting their origin planet. It was yet another example of what Kes' colleague, the long-dead Vasquez, had always said: they couldn't expect to understand how an alien species would think or act.

But Kes doubted that Cherry would ever be able to forgive herself for what she'd done. If she was successful in her effort to track down the Guardian and then discovered her suspicion about it was correct, she might be able to live with herself—just.

He thought it more probable that the android was only malfunctioning. After the damage it had suffered on its re-entry to Concordia, he was surprised it was working at all. At least finding it would keep Cherry occupied for a while. He wondered if she knew about Meredith's suicide yet, and if she didn't, should he be the one to tell her?

A comm arrived from Isobel. She rarely comm'd him while he was at work, and then only if it was about something important. Kes' stomach muscles clenched. The only reason he could think for Isobel to comm him would be if she'd gone into labor. She wasn't due for another three weeks, but an early labor wouldn't be unusual, especially for a second baby.

"Hey, honey," Kes said. "Is everything okay?" As he spoke, he was mentally listing the doctors he knew were living at the warehouse. They had set up a clinic already. One of them had been working on Meredith when he'd found her. Kes was sure there was a nurse living only a few cubicles along from their own, too.

"I'm fine," Isobel replied in a reassuring tone. "Miki's fine too, but we're leaving for Suddene. I thought you might want to come and see us off. We have to be at the helis in a few minutes. That's all the notice I got."

"That's great news," Kes replied. "Yes, I'll come to see you. I'll be there as soon as I can."

He stood up and strode to the door, telling the nearest person where he was going. As soon as he was outside the lab, he jogged along the pathways between the cots and cubicles until he reached his temporary home of the last few days.

Isobel was pushing clothes into a bag. Miki was bouncing on the mattress, something she hadn't been allowed to do previously, clearly enjoying the freedom afforded by her mother's haste and distraction.

After briefly hugging his wife, Kes said, "I didn't realize the coordinators would go ahead with the evacuation to Suddene so soon after Meredith's death, but I have to admit it's a relief to know you and Miki will be safe. I'll help you pack. What do you want to take?"

"We're only allowed one bag per person," Isobel replied. "The weight the helis will carry is pretty low. But it'll be warmer on Suddene so we won't need as much clothing. I'm packing summer clothes and a few of Miki's old baby things for the new baby when she comes."

Kes felt as though the wind had been knocked out of him. If Isobel gave birth soon he would miss it. He'd been there for Miki's birth and it had been the most emotional moment of his entire life, with the exception perhaps of marrying Isobel.

"Is something wrong?" asked Isobel, studying Kes' expression carefully.

In answer, he put down the bag he was holding and wrapped his arms around her. "I'm going to miss you."

"I'll miss you too."

"If the baby comes while we're apart..."

"Aw, honey. I hope she doesn't but if she does, I'll think of you."

"You'll have other things to concentrate on," Kes said, "but I appreciate the sentiment."

"We'll have our whole lives together with this child, and Miki, and any more that come along. That's the most important thing."

Kes squeezed his wife tight, carefully avoiding putting pressure on her bump. "You're right. And I'd rather miss the birth than have you and Miki spend a moment longer here with that biocide creeping nearer every minute. Come on. Let's get you packed."

"I think we're done. It's time to go out to the helis."

When Miki realized they were going somewhere, she immediately raised her hands and said, "Daddy carry."

Kes stole a glance at Isobel.

"Go ahead," she said, smiling. "She's going to miss you while we're gone."

Kes slung both bags over his shoulders and lifted Miki up.

"I can carry a bag, you know," said Isobel.

"It's no trouble," Kes replied. "Let's hurry. You don't want to lose your seat."

They stepped out into the corridor and went quickly toward the exit of the warehouse. It was obvious to everyone who saw them that Isobel and Miki were two of the chosen few about to be transported out of immediate danger. Kes didn't detect any jealous or angry looks, but the situation was not yet dire. When the biocide drew near, people might begin to panic. Then, those who were lucky enough to escape via heli might attract more—hostile—attention. Moving the thousands sheltering in the refuge to Suddene would take far more time than they had and it was inevitable that the majority would be left behind.

Kes would be one to remain at the warehouse. He was sure of it. He would never willingly take the place of another person, even if it meant leaving Isobel a widow and Miki and his baby daughter fatherless.

He pushed the morbid thought to the back of his mind. If he was right about the vaccine, he would only die if he was unlucky and his body didn't develop immunity, or didn't develop it in time for the arrival of the biocide.

As they stepped out of the warehouse, the wind hit him like a wave of cold water. He squinted in the sunlight. How long had it been since he was last outside? As far as he could remember, he hadn't set foot outside the warehouse since arriving there after evacuating from Oceanside.

"It's cold, Daddy!" Miki exclaimed, clutching her father tighter.

"It certainly is," Kes replied. "Do you have her jacket for the heli ride?" he asked Isobel. Though the weather would be warm in Suddene, Isobel and Miki faced an hours-long flight at altitude, and the heli heaters were inadequate at staving off the low temperatures.

"Yes, I packed that first," Isobel replied. "And I have mine too. Quit worrying."

They walked quickly around the perimeter of the

warehouse toward the section of the parking lot reserved for the helis. Kes spotted people in the far distance, doing something to the land.

"Do you know what's going on over there?" he asked.

"Uh huh." Isobel raised her voice to reply as the stiff breeze threatened to drown out her words. "The coordinators put together teams of workers to construct a defense against the biocide. A last resort, I guess. I'm sure you and the other scientists will figure something out before it comes too close."

"What kind of defense?"

They had rounded the corner of the warehouse and the helis were in view at the far corner of the lot, past the ranks of autocars. Some colonists were already gathered there and the distant figures could be seen already boarding the aircraft. Kes had a sudden presentiment he might have to fight for Isobel and Miki's place. He told himself he was being irrational, while at the same time steeling himself for conflict. He would do whatever it took to get the two—almost three —most important people in the world to him onto a heli.

"I'm not sure," Isobel replied. "I heard two different stories. Our neighbor told me they were sinking plastic sheeting four meters deep, but someone else told me they were digging a trench four meters wide and filling it with sand. I guess whatever they're making, the dimensions are four meters."

Kes was skeptical. Bacteria and other microorganisms could be found way deeper than four meters, even in bedrock, and life of one kind or another would quickly colonize a stretch of sand, even if it was sterile when the workers put it in. That was the problem with life: once it got going, it was very hard to stop. It would colonize the most unlikely places, even the exteriors of deep space starships, clustering around venting ports.

The Scythians' plan to render Concordia was doomed

to fail in the long run. If a planet could support life, life would evolve. And space-faring intelligent species would find the world and settle there eventually. But perhaps the Scythians knew this and the death of humankind was enough for them, for now. Either way, it made no difference to the colony.

They were getting close to the helis. Kes lifted an arm and waved to attract attention. One of the pilots seemed to be waiting for them. She waved back and beckoned urgently, telling them to hurry up. Some of the helis' rotors were already turning and their doors closing.

When Kes arrived at the vessel that would transport Isobel and Miki, he was out of breath. The pilot checked Isobel's name.

"You realize she'll have to sit in your lap the whole way?" the pilot asked, glancing at Isobel's protruding belly.

"I know," she replied. "Don't worry. I'll manage."

The pilot nodded in reply. "Stow the bags behind the seats," she told Kes. As he moved to do as she directed, she said, "Wait a minute. Give me those." She took each bag from him and lifted it, judging its weight. "Okay, go ahead." She returned the bags to him.

While Kes was putting the bags in the craft, the pilot gave Isobel and Miki pairs of ear protectors. She smiled as the little girl's eyes widened with amazement at the effect of the mufflers.

"Hop aboard and strap in," she said, and left them to go around the heli's body to her door.

"This is it," said Isobel. Her eyes suddenly shone wetly.

"Yup, this is it," said Kes. His throat was closing up. He kissed Miki on the cheek and told her he loved her.

The little girl sensed the emotion of the moment and began to wail. Then she noticed she couldn't hear herself and was distracted by her ear protectors again.

Kes held Isobel close. "Stay safe," he said into her ear.

"You too."

Time would not wait for a longer goodbye. They broke their embrace. Isobel climbed ungracefully into the heli, and Kes passed Miki to her. Their gazes did not break from each other while Isobel closed her door and Kes stepped backward as the rotors started up.

The heli lifted up into the sky and still he held eye contact with his wife. Too soon, she was swept out of his sight. He stood and watched until the machine was a speck in the sky. When even the speck of the heli had disappeared from sight, Kes turned and walked slowly back to the warehouse. The wind had cut through his clothes and chilled him, but there was an even chillier place in his heart.

Fifteen minutes previously, Isobel and Miki had been only a few tens of meters away from him. Now they were gone and he didn't know when he would see them again.

CHAPTER SEVENTEEN

Alun offered to carry Cherry across the sand between the fence and the tunnel entrance to the Chimera excavation site to protect her feet. After weighing up the level of indignity, she declined.

"It's hot, but it's bearable," she said. "As long as I run, I should be okay."

"You could wear my boots," Alun said. "Or his." He swiped Laurie around the head and relieved him of his weapon.

The younger man cringed a little, possibly feeling ashamed. Now that he was face to face with Cherry, he avoided her gaze.

Cherry looked from her bare feet to Alun's large, worn, dusty work boots. "I'm sure I'll be fine, thanks." She clutched the supervisor's jacket around her.

"What were you *thinking*?" Alun admonished Laurie for the fourth or fifth time. His subordinate had given up on trying to justify his behavior.

"Look, let's forget about it, okay?" said Cherry. "Is the comm network working here on Suddene?" she asked.

"It is. I just heard some bad news from Lyonesse, in fact," Alun replied.

He was about to tell her more but Cherry was already comming Zapata. "As you can see, they let me inside."

"Right," Zapata replied. "I didn't see, actually. I'm still facing the other way. Listen, I have to return to the refuge. While you were running around naked in the desert I received a comm asking me to come back. They're beginning the evacuation to Suddene."

"Okay, go ahead," said Cherry. "I have plenty to do here while you're gone. Wait a minute. Where are you supposed to take these people after you collect them?"

"To Port City, the coordinator said."

The "City" part of the place name was a misnomer, though it was based on what the Port City had been expected to become. The collection of buildings around Suddene's only port was the closest thing the continent had to a town.

Cherry looked thoughtfully at the dark hole that led down to the man made cavern. "I might have a better idea," she said to Zapata. "Return to the refuge for now. If there's a change of plan about where to transport your new passengers, I or someone else will be in touch."

"Got it. I hope you find what you're looking for."

"Alun," Cherry said as she closed the comm to Zapata. "I have a proposal for you. But let's get out of the sun before we discuss it."

***

The excavation that was to have become Concordia's fifth missile silo looked very different from how Cherry remembered it. The large, brilliant lights were the same, but the area they illuminated now held an array of tents and shacks, where people sat or walked, casting glances at her.

She was quite the sight: entirely naked under Alun's

jacket, thanks to Laurie's paranoid, exclusionary tactic. Alun had told him to go and find her some clothes, while she stood and waited at the entrance to the cavern.

Cherry was relieved that Alun didn't share Laurie's sentiment about 'outsiders' entering Chimera, but she was unsure who held the majority's viewpoint. In truth, she hadn't been shocked by Laurie's attitude. It was understandable. No one wanted to die, and the encroachment of the biocide was putting everyone in fear for their lives.

"How long have you all been down here?" Cherry asked Alun.

"We excavation workers never really left," he replied. "As soon as we heard about the return of the Scythians, it seemed the safest place to wait out the battle. We brought our spouses and kids down here. When the fighting stopped, we thought we'd won, but then we heard about the biocide. Dead Fila started washing up in the bay. It was then the people living in Port City and out at the solar farm asked if they could come here too. We said yes, of course. We weren't about to turn anyone away. I don't think any Suddeners were hurt by the biocide in the end. That stuff moves slowly through the desert."

"You really didn't mind the others coming down here too?" asked Cherry. "You weren't worried they might bring in the biocide?"

"We aren't all like that idiot," said Alun. "As I understand it, once that stuff touches you, you're dead. How would anyone who'd been in contact with it make it all the way in here?"

Cherry didn't mention the possibility that the biocide could theoretically be carried on clothing without immediately killing the wearer. "Then why the fence?" she asked.

"There are desert animals who could bring the biocide in," Alun replied. "Mostly nocturnal. The fence is just a precaution, and an excessive one in my opinion."

"If it's going to get inside here, it'll enter through microorganisms in the sand and rock," said Cherry.

"My thoughts exactly."

Laurie was approaching from the far side of the cavern, carrying an armful of donated clothes over one arm and a pair of donated boots in his other hand.

Cherry wanted to make her proposal before he arrived and was present to voice an objection. "Alun, when I spoke to my pilot just now, he said he'd been recalled to Lyonesse to begin transporting some of the most vulnerable people here, to Suddene."

"I thought that was what your conversation was about," said Alun. "You're about to ask me if they can come here."

"You read my mind."

The older man rubbed his stubbly chin and narrowed his eyes as his gaze roved the vast underground chamber. "Space is no problem," he answered, "as you can see. We don't have an infinite supply of water or food, though. How many do you think will come?"

"The helis can only transport one person at a time, or one person and a small child. We're only talking tens of people per day, at the most." How many those tens might add up to, Cherry didn't know. But Alun was no fool. He knew what she was asking. The new arrivals from Lyonesse were likely to put a strain on the resources at Chimera, if not immediately, then eventually.

He shrugged. "We're all Concordians, right? Tell them to come here and we'll do our best to accommodate them."

"Thanks," said Cherry. "You're a good man. But is it likely to cause tension? Do many people here hold the same views as Laurie?"

"I don't think so, and if they do, I'll soon talk them

around."

Laurie arrived. "I don't know if these will fit." He handed the clothes and boots to Cherry, still not making eye contact. "I did the best I could."

Cherry took them without comment. It would be a long time before she would forgive the man. "I'm going to walk back into the tunnel a bit," she said to Alun, "to get dressed."

Under the cover of darkness, in the cool air of the access tunnel, she put on the borrowed clothes. They didn't fit well, but Laurie had included a belt, which she fastened tightly to hold up her pants. She rolled up the pant legs and the sleeves of the sweater. The boots were only a little too large but were bound to chafe without socks. Her attire would have to do.

When she emerged into the light of the construction lamps, Laurie had disappeared, but Alun remained, waiting for her.

"I guess you're wondering why I'm here," she said.

"You aren't here to find new refuges?" asked Alun.

"No, that's just a coincidence. I'm on the trail of someone, or rather, some*thing*. Has anyone noticed someone who looks injured or burned around here?"

"Injured or burned? That's an odd kind of question. No, I don't think so. I haven't heard about anything like that anyway. I can ask around if you want."

"I don't have time for that. This thing has several days' lead on me. I guess it might have arrived and gone down to the city without anyone noticing. Do you turn out the lamps at night?"

"We turn them down, pretty low, but enough to see by. What is this *thing* you're talking about? And how did it get burned?"

"Have you heard of the Guardians?"

"The Guardians? Who hasn't? They're in every history textbook in school."

"This thing claims it's a Guardian, returned from

outer space. I'm sorry, I don't have time to explain properly. I want to find it. I think it may have come through here and gone down into the Scythian city. Is it possible it could have done that without anyone noticing?"

"This place has been occupied since the battle," said Alun. "I would be surprised if—" His eyes widened. "The ghost! Now, when was it? Three nights ago, I think. I was woken up by some kids screaming. Then it all went quiet and I fell asleep. The next day I heard the kids had snuck out of their parents' tents at night to have some fun playing ghosts, and they claimed they'd seen a real ghost, or a monster, running across the open space in the center of the cavern. No one believed them, of course. A kid who's up past his bed-time and playing a scary game is bound to start seeing things. Mine were like that when they were young. But now I'm wondering if it was your Guardian that they saw."

"Do you know if these children said where the monster went?"

"No, I didn't hear anything about that and I didn't ask. It was only a piece of gossip. I can try to find out for you."

"It doesn't matter. If the children saw what I think they saw, I know where it was heading. I need to get down into that city, Alun. The Guardian's been down there three days already from the sound of it."

"You want to go back down there? Are you sure? Rather you than me."

Cherry did not want to return to that strange place, where everything was in pitch darkness and the edges of drop-offs were marked by scents she could not detect. But she had no choice. "That's the plan. Can you help me? Can you lower me down, the way we did it before?"

"That won't be a problem. We have everything we need down here already."

"Great," said Cherry. "But can you ask someone other than Laurie to lower me this time?"

CHAPTER EIGHTEEN

Kes didn't know how long he'd been working. He'd lost track of time. He'd thought that Isobel and Miki going to Suddene would bring him peace of mind, but the opposite was the case. When his wife and child had been only tens of meters away from him, it had been easy to reassure himself they were okay. Now their safety was a mental concept, not a physical fact. He didn't regret their transfer to Suddene, but he knew he would never be comfortable until he was reunited with them, preferably before the baby came.

He comforted himself that, with the way things were going in the lab, his hope might be fulfilled. With the threat of the end of the colony hanging over them, the scientists were working faster and more efficiently than Kes had thought possible. Not only that, with the exception of Drew, they were all working within an unfamiliar field and so having to learn as they went along.

If they produced a vaccine that defeated the biocide it would be nothing short of a miracle, yet Kes thought they might just do it.

However, they faced a major stumbling block. On Earth, the process of creating a vaccine included animal testing to assess the vaccine's safety before the final human trials. From beginning the development of a vaccine to administering it on a wide scale would take years. They had days and no animals to use as test subjects. Even if they'd known they would need them, there would have been no point in collecting some before evacuating Oceanside. Concordian animals would be next to useless for their purposes. Their anatomy and cell structure were vastly different from humans'.

What the scientists needed as a minimum were mice —specially bred lab mice—and the only mice in the galaxy were light years away.

Kes rubbed his temples. They had no mice, specially bred for experiments or otherwise. They had no rats, rabbits, or monkeys either. Not even a cockroach. Inevitably, at some point in the very near future, they would need to test the vaccine on a human subject. They would have to inject 'inactive' biocide into a human being. Who would they choose? Would one of the scientists volunteer? That wouldn't make a lot of sense considering that currently scientists were what the colony needed most. Yet who among them would nominate someone else to take the risk?

Waiting for death to arrive was one thing, taking the chance of walking into its arms was another.

Thump! Kes looked up from his work. The noise had come from the lab's outer door. Kes walked over to see what had caused it and saw an angry face in the further window of the two sets of double doors. The outer doors jumped as something hit them from outside. All the scientists froze as they realized what was happening. Someone was trying to get into the lab. The person must have tried the outer doors and found they were locked.

Kes had asked for a security device to be installed when the lab had first been set up, only to prevent children or clueless colonists from wandering in by accident. The lab was a dangerous place. But Kes hadn't imagined security would be needed to prevent someone from *forcing* their way in.

"Open up!" shouted the person outside, though his voice was faint and muffled.

Kes couldn't see much more than the man's red, sweaty face and his gaping mouth as he shouted again. "Let me in! Give me that biocide treatment! I want it. Now!"

A few scientists were walking over to the door.

"Go back to your benches," Kes said. "I'll talk to him." He opened the inner door and began decontamination.

This stalled the angry man for a time, but then he struck the outer doors again and they jumped on their hinges. The walls and the entrance to the lab were all temporary structures, not particularly strong. Anyone could get inside if they had enough determination.

Kes comm'd one of the refuge coordinators. "We have an emergency situation here," he said. "Find some CED officers if you can and send them over." He went to the outer doors and stood face to face with the would-be intruder. "Settle down," he said to the man through the triple-paned plexiglass. "You can't come in here. It isn't safe for you."

Kes didn't recognize the man. He looked a mess, but then again, so did they all. Everyone was just getting by in the spartan and distressing conditions.

"Open up!" the man repeated. "I know what you're doing in there. You've made a cure and you're keeping it to yourselves. You're gonna wait for everyone to die and then you'll divide up the planet between yourselves!"

Kes had to force himself to not roll his eyes. As conspiracy theories went, this one was one of the most outlandish he'd ever heard. But pointing out the stupidity of the man's statement was not going to get him anywhere. It would only entrench his mind further in his ridiculous notion.

"Look," said Kes, "I understand you're frightened. We all are."

The man lifted both of his sizable arms and brought his fists down on the door with such force, Kes took a step backward. He feared that if the assault on the door continued, it would soon give way.

"Please calm down!" Kes exclaimed, stepping close to the door once more. "If you calm down, I'll come out and explain what we're doing. It isn't a secret."

Kes still hadn't made an official announcement about the proposed vaccine, but that was only because he'd been concentrating on his work. Meredith's suicide had been a major distraction too. Perhaps the announcement was way overdue. People needed to hear something positive. The tension was clearly driving some of them crazy.

Kes saw movement in his narrow field of vision behind the man's head. He thought he'd glimpsed a couple of people running toward the lab door. Kes kept his gaze fixed firmly on the man's eyes to avoid giving him a clue about what was happening behind him.

"I don't want an *explanation*," the man snarled. "I want a cure! For myself and the rest of us out here. And I want it now!" He raised a fist to hit the door again, but before he could make contact, he disappeared.

Kes leaned forward and peered down through the glass. The man was on the floor and two more men were wrestling with him. One of them had his arm behind his back. The other pressed down with a knee to his kidneys.

Kes released the lock and put a hand on the door to push it open. Feeling an obligation to help fix the situation, he went outside.

Thom was there among the gathering crowd, arriving

for his shift.

"Thank the stars for the good old CED, huh?" he said. "What a lunatic."

"Oh, I don't know," said Kes. "We can't really blame him. Everyone's feeling nervous right now. It's bound to tip some people over the edge."

"Nervous?" Thom asked. "More like desperate and terrified."

"Yes, that too. I think I'll talk to that guy, now the officers have him subdued. News of this incident is going to spread through the refuge like wildfire. It's already attracted considerable attention." A circle of curious onlookers continued to form to witness the angry man's struggle with the CED officers. "I don't want anyone to think what he's saying might be true. Then I'll make an announcement about what we're trying to do here and the progress we've made."

"Hmm," said Thom. "Yes to the second, no to the first. I wouldn't waste my breath on talking to him if I were you. There's no reasoning with someone when they're in that state."

The man who had tried to force his way into the lab was resisting arrest. One of the CED officers had managed to fasten handcuffs around his wrists but they were struggling to get him to his feet. The man was kicking out at them. Kes felt somewhat responsible for his aggression and rage. If he'd explained to the residents of the refuge what the scientists were trying to do, the man might not have acted as he had.

His appearance from the lab had drawn the interest of the growing crowd away from the fight on the ground and onto himself. The stares of the onlookers were hard and unforgiving.

Second-guessing his decision, Kes nevertheless side-stepped the tussle of the officers and the large man they were trying to apprehend and moved out into the open space. He raised his hands. "I want to explain what we've been doing in the lab. I have some news I'm sure you'll be interested to hear."

The gazes that rested on his face suddenly shifted to a spot at his rear and everyone's eyebrows rose.

"Watch out!" shouted Thom.

Reflexively, Kes quickly crouched down, concluding from the various clues that the angry man had broken free and was coming for him.

A figure sailed over his head and crashed to the ground. The man had launched himself at Kes and flown over him when he met no resistance. The crowd gasped and drew back.

His hands secured behind his back, the man struggled to rise to his feet, but he managed it. His teeth were bared in fury and his eyes were bloodshot with rage. Kes had no chance of escape. The man came at him, so Kes did the only thing he could in the circumstances and punched the man on his jaw with all the strength he could muster.

His attacker was out cold long before he hit the floor. Kes stood over the fallen figure, a little bewildered by the speed of events.

"Thanks very much," said a CED officer. "I've been trying to do that for the last five minutes."

The two officers grabbed the large man under his armpits and began to drag him away. The crowd remained, their expressions now less angry but more cautious. Kes rubbed his aching hand with the other.

"I'm going to broadcast an official statement in a moment," he said, "but I'll give you all a synopsis now as you're here and clearly anxious about what we've been doing to halt the spread of the biocide. That's perfectly understandable and I apologize for not saying something earlier. First of all, what you have to understand is that it's going to be impossible to prevent the biocide from spreading."

This statement drew expressions of dismay. Kes

raised his hands. "Please, let me finish. The biocide spreads through contact between life forms, and Concordia is a living planet. The poison will continue to spread until it reaches a point where nothing living remains to sustain it, and then presumably it will die. But we may have a solution. Though I don't think there's anything we can do for any other species on the planet, we may be able to save human life."

Kes then gave a brief explanation of the principle of vaccination, putting it into layman's terms as well as he could. "I know most of you won't have any idea what I'm talking about, but I can assure you that vaccines saved millions, possibly billions of lives on Earth. The only reason you haven't heard of them is because until now we haven't needed them. We're making the biocide vaccine right now. I wish I could give you a one hundred percent guarantee that it will work, but I'm a scientist, not a politician. I only deal in facts, and the fact is, we won't know for sure until the moment of truth arrives. When the biocide reaches us, then we'll be sure. But I am confident that this is our best shot."

"If you're so confident," a voice yelled, "why did you send your wife and kid to Suddene?"

It was a good point, and Kes could only speak from his heart in reply. "My wife is pregnant. I love her and I want her and my daughter to live as long as possible. They qualified to be transferred to Suddene, along with all the other vulnerable people in this refuge. In my position, what would you do?" He paused. "But one thing you're forgetting is that *I* am here. I and the rest of the scientists are doing our damnedest to save you and every other Concordian. We're doing our very best. We aren't hoarding a biocide cure as that man alleged. As soon as we've made a vaccine and tested it, we'll begin immunizing everyone in the refuge and then everyone on Concordia. After that, we wait."

Kes had said all he had to say. In the silence that

followed, the assembled men and women muttered and grumbled, but they appeared mollified by his words. The crowd began to break up. From somewhere at the back, an old man walked through the widening gap. He looked vaguely familiar, but Kes couldn't place him.

"Do you want to know more about the vaccine?" Kes asked.

"You don't remember me, do you?"

"I have to admit I don't," Kes replied. "I'm sorry."

"No need to apologize," said the man. "It's been longer than a hundred Concordian years since we met. I'm one of Wilder's friends."

"Oh, damn!" Kes exclaimed. Wilder had asked him to check up on some of her friends and he'd entirely forgotten.

The man was looking quizzically at him.

"I'm sorry," Kes said again. "I realized I'd forgotten to do something important. What's your name? I believe Wilder might have been worried about you."

"I'm Tycho. But I'm not here to talk to you about Wilder. I came here to see what all the commotion was about, and I heard you mention this thing called a vaccine you've been working on. It's supposed to help us defeat the biocide, am I right?"

"Yes, that's right."

"I also heard you mention that you have to test this medicine. I figured you're going to need people to test it on. Well, I want to volunteer."

"You want to...? I'm not sure—"

"Don't you need people you can test with it?"

"Absolutely, but we can't—"

"I've lived a long, good life. It's going to end soon, one way or another. I can't think of a better way to go out than by helping my fellow Concordians. And, to be honest, it would be preferable to waiting on that horrible stuff to creep up on me. What do you say?"

What *could* he say? The main objection that sprang to

Kes' mind was, if Tycho died, how would he explain to Wilder what he'd done? But the old man was entirely in charge of his senses and they did desperately need test subjects.

"I say that, with the deepest gratitude, I accept your offer."

CHAPTER NINETEEN

Pearl was going to lower Cherry down to the Scythian city. Cherry remembered the woman well, and not only due to her blonde hair, green eyes and pale skin. When it came to actually entering the city, Pearl had backed out, saying the place gave her the creeps. Cherry knew exactly what she meant. It wasn't that the place had once been inhabited by aliens—Cherry had spent plenty of time in the company of the Fila aboard the *Opportunity*, and had eventually overcome her prejudice against them—there was simply something about the Scythian city that made her skin crawl when she came in close proximity to it. The Fila had never affected her like that.

It was a feeling she was going to have to get used to as she spent who knew how long searching for the Guardian. On her previous visit, she and Alun hadn't gotten far inside before the announcement of the return of the Scythians had forced her to abandon her investigation. There was no telling how deep or wide the metropolis of Concordia's former occupants stretched. This time, she could be inside for days.

Cherry stood at the overhang, looking down into the dark abyss. Behind her, Pearl sat at the controls of one of the massive excavators, preparing to use the giant spiraled borer to unwind the line attached to Cherry's harness.

"If we'd had a bit more notice, we could have put together a proper winch for you," said Alun. "There's a few of us who are handy with that kind of thing. If you could wait another day or so..."

"No," Cherry replied. "I can't afford to waste any more time." She adjusted her backpack to make it more comfortable. Despite the short notice he'd mentioned, Alun had gathered an impressive array of equipment to help Cherry in her search. Night vision goggles, a pathfinder to prevent her from getting lost, several lightweight lines and two small grapnels, a full water bottle and an attached device for drawing moisture from the air, emergency rations, an extremely sharp knife that contained a heating mechanism in the handle, and a small rectangular device with a square display screen. Alun had called the last item an 'electronic canary' and said it could detect poisonous gases.

"What's a canary?" Cherry had asked.

"No idea," had been Alun's reply. He'd also given her Laurie's weapon, insisting she take it with her.

"No weapon on Concordia will have any effect on a Guardian," Cherry had said.

"Maybe not. But maybe you'll find something other than a Guardian down there," was Alun's reply.

Could a Scythian have survived hundreds of thousands of years on a planet with an atmosphere that no longer supported its metabolism? Cherry had known Woken who had been revived from cryonic suspension after a hundred and eighty years of frozen sleep. But hundreds of thousands of years? Cherry didn't think it was possible, but then, what did she know? Perhaps there were Scythians down there who could wake up and attack her. If they did, she hoped the oxygen in the air would do its work before she was forced to fight them.

"All set?" asked Alun. Pearl waited patiently at the excavator's controls, watching for the moment Cherry stepped over the edge into empty space.

"Yeah," said Cherry. Yet she didn't step forward into darkness or lower her night vision goggles over her eyes.

"Have you considered the fact that it's unlikely there's another way out of the city?" asked Alun. "Not after all this time. Any other exits will lie beneath tens of meters of sand or soil. Unless this Guardian has done whatever it came here to do and already left without us noticing, all you have to do to catch it is sit here and wait for it to try to leave."

"I did think of that," Cherry replied. "But if it's doing something in there, I want to find out what. If I catch it on its way out, empty-handed, I'll never know. What if the Scythians left behind a gigantic explosive device, a kind of booby trap for the entire planet, and the Guardian starts up the self-destruct sequence?"

"Then we're truly screwed," said Alun. "Unless you imagine you can figure out how to deactivate it. And what are the chances you'll be able to do that?"

"Okay, bad example. But you understand what I mean, don't you? If we survive the biocide and manage to start again—though I admit that's a big *if*—the Scythians are bound to find out and return to finish us off properly."

Her statement was a depressing fact that had haunted Cherry for days. As long as the colony remained on Concordia, and as long as the Scythians had ships to attack them with, the battle for the planet would rage on. Concordians would remain under constant threat of attack, down the generations. But though the situation appeared dire, they'd survived thus far. They would continue to battle on.

She continued, "Anything I can do to find out more about them, including why the Guardian has gone to their city, is going to help us. And to achieve that, I have to go down there and try to find out where it's gone."

"I can see there's no arguing with you," said Alun. He paused, clearly expecting Cherry to say her goodbye and begin her journey into the strange city.

Yet still she did not. Something was niggling at her, holding her back. She'd denied the impulse for a long time. Now she knew she had to give in to it before she could take another step on this road from which she might not return.

"Is there a comm connection in here?" she asked Alun.

"I don't think you'll be able to use it in here, but if you return to the main chamber, it's set up with relays to the surface."

"I just want to speak to someone quickly before I leave."

"Go ahead," said Alun. "Pearl and I aren't in a hurry."

Cherry walked through the tunnel dug by the original excavator that had broken through to the city. She pulled down her goggles to see better in the darkness until she reached the cavern. As soon as she entered the vast space, she tried to connect to the comm network. She had to wait long seconds for the comm to go through.

"Hello again." Aubriot's tone was dour, as usual.

"You're still alive," said Cherry.

"You too, from the sound of it."

"What's happening out at Cerberus?"

"Honestly, it's not good. The ground's damp and fertile around here. Plenty of microorganisms for the biocide to travel through. No one's looked outside for a while, but at the last check it was pretty close."

"But down there in the silo, it might never reach

you," said Cherry. "How deep are you? There has to be seventy-five meters of dead metal and concrete between you and the nearest soil. You might last indefinitely."

"Doubt it," Aubriot said. "The air's full of bacteria. The metal and concrete won't save us, though it'll slow it down a bit. Where are you? Still at the refuge?"

"No, I'm on Suddene, at the Chimera excavation. The Guardian came here, and I'm going after it. I think it's in the Scythian city."

"Hmpf," was Aubriot's laconic reaction. Then, "Wish I were there. I could help. I'd give a lot to pay back those machines for what they did to me."

"You would be a big help, but never mind. I'll have to deal with it myself."

"Did you hear about our illustrious leader?"

"Meredith?" Cherry asked. "What about her?"

"You don't know? I guessed you might not. Not if you've been traveling for most of the day."

"Are you going to tell me or are you going to keep me hanging?" Cherry asked.

"Unlucky choice of words there, Cherry. Meredith topped herself this morning. Must have been not long after you left."

"She...?" Cherry's legs suddenly weakened. She put a hand on the bare rock wall for support. "She *killed* herself? Stars, I had no idea. I don't think the news has reached here yet either. No one's said a thing."

She recalled the last few things Meredith had said to her. *It means a lot to me. More than you know.* The Leader must have been planning her suicide even as Cherry spoke to her. That was why she'd asked what Ethan would have thought about how she'd acted. Poor, poor Meredith. It had all been too much for her. The responsibility for the colony had been too great a burden.

"You okay?" Aubriot asked.

"I spoke to her just before I left. I had to...It doesn't

matter now. She didn't give any sign of what she was planning. Or maybe she did and I missed it. I don't know. Stars, I feel terrible. I wish I hadn't been so hard on her. I was so critical. I didn't have to be. Shit. Why do I always have to be such a bitch? That poor woman."

"I thought I was the egotist around here," Aubriot said. "It isn't always about you, you know."

"But this is. If I hadn't—"

"You couldn't have known. No one knew. If they had, they would have stopped her. And whatever you said to her, it was because you care about the colony and you were trying to protect us all. Like you're doing now."

Cherry was silent. The news of Meredith's death weighed heavily on her shoulders, no matter how much Aubriot might want to reassure her it was not her fault. If she could take back her angry comments to the Leader over the years, she would, in a heartbeat. What would Ethan think? She was glad he hadn't survived to see this terrible turn of events.

"Cherry," said Aubriot, a new sternness in his tone. "Snap out of it. You've got a job to do. Stop wallowing and go and do it."

Anger rose in Cherry's chest in response. Who was he to tell her what to do? But then her shoulders sagged. He was right.

"All right. I'm going," she said.

"Good," said Aubriot. "Catch that Guardian and cut its fucking head off for me."

"You got it," Cherry said. She closed the comm. In the distant edges of the cavern, on the fringes of the glare cast by the lamps, the Suddeners were going about their daily lives. Soon, they would discover their Leader was dead, and that, rather than lead the colony toward overcoming the challenges it faced, she had abandoned it.

The news would destroy whatever morale they had remaining. *All* Concordians would need a reason to continue on, to try to win despite the terrible odds that were stacked against them. Cherry would do whatever she could to help, and right now that was catching the Guardian. Perhaps if she could prove the android was sent by the Scythians and she had prevented it from fulfilling its purpose, that would demonstrate that the aliens were not invincible; that the colony had a chance, if only it had the determination to try.

It was the least she could do to honor Meredith's memory.

CHAPTER TWENTY

"Wilder," said a voice.

She was in her forest home, trapped against the ceiling by the a-grav machine. How long had she been there? Days. It was early morning, and the new day's sun was shining through the window and the gaps in the woven, dried leaf fronds of the walls.

It hurt so much. She couldn't feel her feet or hands, and she couldn't remember when she'd last been able to move her limbs. But worse than all that was the dreadful thirst. Outside her window, dew sparkled on the vegetation. The glittering drops looked more precious than gemstones. If only she could lick them. To lick just one leaf would be bliss.

"Wilder," the voice repeated.

She opened her eyes and saw the blank face of a starship's bulkhead. She was aboard the *Opportunity*. The ghost of the pain and thirst of her dream remained, however. It had been so vivid. She felt as though all she had to do was close her eyes to return to that time and place.

She realized someone had been calling her name.

"Quinn? Did you want me for something?"

"I am sorry to wake you," said Quinn over the ship's comm.

"No problem. You did me a favor. I was having a horrible dream." Wilder unzipped herself from her sleeping bag and pushed off from the wall toward the food and drink station.

"I thought you might be," Quinn said. "Your facial expression indicated you were distressed and you were making some slight movements."

"You can read human faces now?" Wilder asked. "I'm impressed." She removed a water bottle from the store and sucked on the straw. She'd long gotten over the fact that she was drinking her own recycled urine and sweat. If it hadn't been for the *Opportunity's* water conservation system she would be in the same state she'd been in her dream, or dead.

If only the ship recycled food too, she thought, assessing what remained of her rations. Then she grimaced as she realized what recycling her food would entail.

She was already a light eater, yet even so she was down to half of what she'd brought aboard. How long could she make the food last? Would the scientists on Concordia halt the spread of the biocide by then? She might have to choose between starvation and death by poison. At least the latter would be quick.

"I would say I can read some expressions of the humans I am most familiar with," said Quinn. "I would not describe myself as an expert."

"Still, that's quite an achievement in my opinion," said Wilder. Her stomach growled. Hunger was beginning to bite, but she decided she would try to wait a few hours before eating.

"I imagine you must find us very easy to read," said Quinn.

"Uh, in what way?" Wilder asked.

"When Fila are in a state of heightened emotion, such as fear or joy, we can't help but express it in our movements. You must have noticed."

"Ummm." Wilder sucked another mouthful of water as she tried to remember seeing anything akin to what Quinn was talking about.

"You mean you don't see the way our tentacles quiver when we're angry or stressed? But it's obvious to the most casual observer."

Wilder chuckled with embarrassment. "I'm so sorry. I guess I must be very unobservant."

"Nonsense," said Quinn. "You are the most observant human I've met, and humans as a species are more observant than my own, in my estimation."

"In that case, I can't explain it. I confess I have no idea how you're feeling most of the time, and all the translation equipment conveys to me is the bare meaning of your communication." Had she offended him? Would she ever be able to tell? Unless Quinn told her so, she would never know. She made a mental note to watch his tentacles more carefully in the future.

A pause followed. Perhaps she had offended him.

"I woke you for another reason than your apparent agitation," said Quinn. "I had an idea regarding your a-grav device."

"You did?" Wilder pushed off from the wall and glided over to Piddle and Puddle's sweater pouches. Peering inside, she saw that both her pets remained asleep. They'd been sleeping for longer periods lately and she was getting worried about them.

"I'm not sure if you're aware," Quinn said, "but no other galactic species has invented this type of device. As far as I know, it's unique."

"Seriously?" Wilder eyed the machine, which she had tied to the floor to prevent it from floating around and bumping into things. "Cool." Her invention had begun to lose her interest, but Quinn's information had given it a new shine in her mind.

"Ever since you managed to repeat your earlier success and make the machine work here aboard the *Opportunity*, I've been in contact with Assembly members, checking if my impression was correct."

"You didn't tell me you were doing that," Wilder said. "I didn't even know you were talking to them."

"But of course I am. How else did you think they would know about the attack on Concordia?"

"Yeah, I guess I've been distracted by everything that's happening down there."

"That's natural. Wilder, you must understand that the a-grav device is a sensitive topic. My communications with the rest of the Assembly have been under the tightest security."

"You mean because of what it can do?" The possibilities the a-grav machine opened up were vast, not only for planet-based transportation but also for interplanetary and interstellar travel. With a flick of a switch a deep space vessel sitting on the surface of a planet could achieve escape velocity almost immediately.

"Exactly. This invention comes with vast implications. I believe it signals the beginning of a new galactic era."

Wilder hadn't considered that humans were the only species ever to have invented a-grav. Quinn's earlier reference to the machine as *her* device made her feel a little guilty. "You know my work was based on the information in the Guardians' data? A-grav was invented on Earth hundreds of years ago, but it seems it was only used in the flitters. Then the Natural Movement became too strong and the invention wasn't developed any further. I had a lot of help, too, from all the other Concordians who were working on it. It was a team effort." Her sense of guilt increased. The way these kinds of things worked, it would be she who was forever associated with a-grav. Her name would be listed as the inventor, and not anyone else's who had contributed to the work.

"I feel you're missing the point," said Quinn. "What I am trying to tell you is, this new invention puts you in a position of great power."

Wilder was holding onto a cupboard handle and floating gently in midair. Her hair, which she always cut herself to save time, was in a messy array around her head, and her ship's suit was wrinkled and fitted poorly on her skinny body. She was hungry and she missed her friends, about whom she was deeply worried.

She didn't feel like someone in a position of great power.

"How's that?" she asked, though as she spoke, the logic of what Quinn had said was becoming clear. Any intelligent galactic species would give a lot—would *do* a lot—for the knowledge of how to build a-grav machines.

"The Assembly members I've spoken to are very interested in your device."

As the realization hit, Wilder's grip on the cupboard handle relaxed. She began to float free. On the edge of her vision, she saw the outline of Puddle stirring inside his pouch. The enormous implications of what Quinn was telling her pressed on her brain like a crushing fist, but it was a good feeling. A very, very good feeling. Only it was a little too much to deal with all at once.

Wilder recalled the vast Assembly space station she'd visited, with its thousands of inhabitants of many galactic species. She recalled the gigantic alien organizers of the station, and the equipment that could read minds and simulate scenarios that were indistinguishable from reality. She recalled the strange starships of the Assembly members who visited the station.

At the time of her mission, Wilder had felt awed by all that she'd seen, and grateful that the Assembly had allowed such an insignificant species as Homo sapiens into its society. But now, things were changing. Now, humanity had something valuable to offer. It was no longer a beggar at the door of the great galactic powers.

Then her heart sank. "I almost wish you hadn't told them about the a-grav machine, Quinn. If the Assembly members demand that I give it to them in return for helping us, I can hardly refuse, can I?"

"I think they would have more integrity than to *demand* anything from you," Quinn replied.

"Maybe, but..." Wilder sighed. "I have to give it over. It's the least I can do. There are several ships coming to Concordia now, right? That takes fuel and a crew, not to mention their ships are probably needed elsewhere. I know! I should give the machine to the Parvus. If it weren't for them we would never have beaten off the last Scythian attack."

"These are noble sentiments," said Quinn. "But, if I may say so, you're thinking like a human."

Wilder wondered what species she was supposed to think like.

"By which I mean," Quinn continued, "you're confining your speculations to your own extremely short life span. Galactic time is much longer and wider and deeper than your species' imagination seems capable of grasping. I'll try to put this in terms you are able to comprehend. The Assembly does not view your contribution and value as a member only within Concordia's next few hundred orbits of its star. It views you as an intelligent, compassionate species with all the potential those attributes imply. Your notion of 'owing' the Parvus the a-grav machine as 'repayment' for their help is simplistic in the extreme."

Wilder was not at all used to condescending tones, not from Quinn nor anyone else, not since she'd decided that school wasn't for her and had stopped attending. Annoyance flared up inside her but she tried to mask it as well as she could. She had to concede that Quinn's understanding in the matters he was explaining was way superior to hers.

"Well, what do *you* think I should do?" she asked.

"I think, as an opening to discussion, you should state your willingness to share your invention with the Assembly. When we hear what they have to say, and perhaps to offer, we can think further on how to turn this fortuitous event to humanity's long-term advantage."

"Okay. That sounds good. Send them that message."

"In my opinion it would be better for you to tell them yourself, face to face. We should set out now and meet them on their journey to Concordia."

"Leave planetary orbit? I don't want to! I don't want to abandon my friends or anyone else down there. I might still be able to help them."

"The greatest help you can offer your planet is to wield the influence you have with allies who can actually help them."

Wilder sighed in frustration. "I guess so. I don't like it, but I can't argue against it. Let's go meet some aliens!"

"You must recline in your safety seat while we accelerate."

"Ugh. I'd forgotten about that. I hope Piddle and Puddle will be okay." Wilder pushed herself in the direction of the living quarters' exit. She wasn't looking forward to the hours of acceleration she was about to endure.

CHAPTER TWENTY-ONE

When her feet touched the ground at the bottom of the drop, Cherry unfastened her harness. Way up above her, the lights from the excavator glared out, brilliant white in the view through her night vision goggles. The harness and the line it was attached to would remain there until she returned from the Scythian city. Alun had set up a relay so a comm from her current position would be received within the Chimera cavern.

Cherry saw a figure lean out over the edge high above and wave at her. The figure was only a small silhouette against the brilliant beams of the excavator, but she guessed it had to be Alun. She waved back, uncertain if he could see her. She hadn't brought along any flashlights or head lamps, concerned that visible light would alert the Guardian to her presence, though in truth the android probably had superior visual and audio capabilities. It would know she was coming from a kilometer away.

"Thanks for everything, Alun," she comm'd.

"No need for that," he replied. "Come back, with android or not. That'll be thanks enough for me."

A second dark figure appeared at Alun's side and also

waved.

"Be careful," said Pearl. "Don't take any dangerous risks."

"I'll try not to," said Cherry, which was a lie. As far as she was concerned, this was a do-or-die mission. She had screwed up, badly, and in more than one way. The news of Meredith's suicide had dealt another blow. Her final memory of the woman kept replaying in her mind. No matter what Aubriot said about it not being her fault, she couldn't help but think there was so much she could have, and *should* have, done differently.

Capturing the Guardian was the one chance she to do something right, for a change. She would take whatever risks that entailed, dangerous or not. She was fighting for her own future: her ability to look at herself in a mirror, to sleep at night, and to live with herself for the rest of her natural life. This wasn't only about the survival of the colony. This was personal.

"I'm going in now," she said to Alun and Pearl. "I'll comm when I return."

If I return.

Cherry had elected not to take one of the survey vehicles in with her for transportation. Prior experience told her that a car moved too fast to safely navigate inside the city, where deep fissures dissected the pavement. If any markings warned of the fissures' presence, they were not easily perceived by human senses.

She walked toward the high boundary wall surrounding the city. The night vision goggles gave some indication of color, though the hues were more muted than they would have been in regular sight. Yet Cherry could still make out the greens, purples, and pinks she'd seen before, in an irregular pattern over the wall's surface. Which of the colors had been so soft that simply pushing would enable her to pass through it?

Cherry strode quickly closer, wondering if the

Guardian might be watching her approach. Had it guessed it would be pursued? Was it lying in wait for her?

No sign of anything else in that place appeared to her. Finally, she reached the wall. Whichever color material was the softest, it clearly didn't retain the impression of earlier passages through it. The wall was smooth and unmarked. It bore no sign of the vehicle Alun had driven through it or of the Guardian's entrance.

Cherry pressed a pink and then a purple section of wall. The surface gave somewhat under the pressure, but she quickly realized the green section must be the softest. She approached the wide area of wall and paused, checking the tightness of the straps of her backpack.

Ever since stepping off the drop that led down to the city, she'd been grasping her knife. She lifted the blade and held it in front of her but slightly to one side, so that she wouldn't cut herself on it as she entered the city.

She stepped forward, forcing her foot into the spongy substance. It slipped in quite easily. Immediately, she pushed the rest of her body into the wall, wishing to minimize the time she was blind and vulnerable. The green material parted in front of her like thick paste. A beat later, she was through.

The first time Cherry had entered the area directly surrounding the Scythian city she'd been without the benefit of night vision goggles. All that she'd been able to see had been within the scope of the survey vehicle's headlights, and that had been a whole bunch of nothing except empty space and openings in the floor. This time, what she saw took her breath away. The stench of the place made her gasp too. She'd forgotten the resemblance of the atmosphere's odor to feces. Her electronic canary swung from her belt. The device would warn her if it detected dangerous gases, but she checked it nonetheless. The only thing she had to fear from the air so far was puking from the smell.

The path the survey vehicle had followed was about the only straight line in the place. She and Alun had been incredibly lucky to enter the city where they had. A crazed labyrinth of black lines patterned the floor, each an opening to an unknown depth. Beyond the maze, which looked like the production of a demented mind, tall edifices rose upward. The structure of the buildings reminded Cherry of the serried ranks of mountains that ran through central Lyonesse, only the edges of the constructions were steeper and more jagged. Arched openings stood black in their sides, though none sat at ground level.

She wondered what kind of creatures the Scythians were if they didn't enter their buildings at the bottom. Did they climb up the sides? With a shiver, she recalled the speed and agility of the mechanical spiders the Scythians had sent to find and kill the Concordians. The spider that had sliced through the bone of her left arm with the same ease she had used to push through the green mush at the city's edge had ascended a tree to reach her with ease. Had the Scythians modeled their spiders after their own forms?

Cherry scanned the expanse thoroughly before she took another step. The floor was black, a marginally lighter black than the abysses that ran through it. The structures dotted with openings were the same range of colors as the boundary wall: green, purple, and pink, though the sections were not so clearly defined and in some areas the colors merged as if the soft substances had mixed together.

Nothing moved in that ancient place. If the Guardian was watching her, it gave no sign of its presence.

Where to go first? The place was kilometers square. Cherry corrected herself—it was kilometers *cubed*. The vertical dimensions of the city were significant, and she didn't even know how deep the fissures went.

She walked to one floor opening and, after slipping her knife into its sheath, she knelt down at its edge. Holding onto the side, she leaned forward and peered down. Smooth, black walls ran out of sight. Spots of darker black signaled similar arched openings to those in the city's buildings.

How would she locate the burned-up android in this enormous place? The challenge of the task she had set herself was daunting, but she pushed her doubts to the back of her mind. She stood up.

Should she go upward or downward to look for the Guardian? The black walls that fell away below her didn't seem to hold any protrusions or anything else to grip. And climbing one-handed was hard, as she had discovered when climbing the ladder out of the elevator shaft after the Scythians attacked.

Upward it would have to be. Cherry walked quickly along the single straight section of pavement, toward the towering constructions. Soon, the straight section branched out, and then quickly branched again and again, each new pathway narrower than the last. Cherry was forced to follow the slim surfaces as well as she could to move forward toward the buildings, while at the same time avoiding falling into a void.

After many frustrating twists and turns and doubling back—once taking a chance and vaulting over one of the openings—Cherry finally made it to the base of a building. She gazed upward at the steep surface, which leaned slightly inward as it rose toward a distant peak. The arched openings she'd seen from the distance of the boundary were higher than she'd guessed. Way too high above for her to reach without climbing and, like the openings in the floor, the walls didn't seem to hold anything that would help her climb.

Frustration niggled at her. Had she come so far only

to fail at this simple obstacle to her progress? If she'd been able to bring climbing equipment, she would have, but such things were not easily found on a desert continent or at short notice.

Cherry thumped the wall in annoyance. Her fist sank into the green material. Of course! Putting her hand out in front of her, she pushed into the wall and stepped through it.

And immediately she found herself buried in debris. Cherry flailed, trying to find purchase in the dusty fragments of matter. She couldn't breathe. Her nose and mouth were blocked by dry flakes. She backed up, intending to push through the wall again to get out, but her back didn't meet anything like a solid surface, only more of the soft stuff that was choking her to death. The substance pressed against her goggles, rendering her blind.

Fighting down her rising panic, Cherry lifted her hand and scooped away the material in front of her face. More didn't take its place and she found she'd created an empty space. She sucked in air gratefully as her heart rate and breathing slowed. She was not about to suffocate. But the stuff surrounded her in a claustrophobic fashion. She had to find her way back to the wall. It couldn't be far away. She was sure she'd only taken two steps, or three at most, since emerging from it.

The cocooning material was a homogeneous light gray. Cherry couldn't guess what it was, or what it had originally been hundreds of thousands of years ago when the Scythians had abandoned their city. For all she knew she was trying to move through the remains of dead Scythians themselves. Perhaps she'd entered a graveyard or crematorium.

Cherry waded forward slowly, clearing space in front of her face as she went. She breathed shallowly, worrying about the dust motes she was taking into her lungs. The electronic canary would sound an alarm if it detected poisonous gases but she doubted it was any use at checking for dangerous particles.

Before she'd moved more than a couple of meters, she knew she was heading the wrong way. If she'd been going in the right direction she would have hit the wall almost straightaway. She turned and tried a different direction. Again, she encountered nothing except the maddening, choking debris. Cherry turned another ninety degrees and made a third foray into the congested fragments.

She scooped soft detritus from her face, and as her hand moved forward, it hit solidity. At last, the wall!

But on further exploration, she found the surface she was touching was not spongy, but hard. And it was not flat. Cherry moved her hand higher and lower and felt a flat object about ten centimeters thick. She moved closer to it and cleared more space in front of her to try to get a look at it. Eventually the edge of the object came into view. The white, smooth surface didn't look like much of anything, but it was wide enough for her to climb onto and perhaps rise out of the fragments. Cherry climbed onto it but as she tried to straighten up she hit another solid surface.

This seemed a copy of the platform on which she was kneeling. She felt for the edge. It was easy to reach and only a little way inward from her position. She climbed onto the second surface and encountered a third just above her. Cherry moved blindly upward, holding her breath to avoid wasting time on removing the material from her face. It seemed to be lessening in density anyway.

At the fourth platform, her head broke free. A light gray sea stretched out around her. Above, the series of platforms continued to rise, spiraling. A few meters behind her stood the wall she had pushed through. An arched opening gaped in its surface, revealing the darkness outside the city.

She'd done it. She was the first human being ever to set foot inside the ancient metropolis of the self-exiled Scythians. Somewhere in that place, the Guardian was doing something or searching for something. Now all she had to do was find it.

***

Cherry woke up, turned over, and groaned. She wasn't unaccustomed to sleeping on the floor—Scythian attacks had destroyed her abode more than once—but there was something about the hard, black surface that they'd used through much of their city that was particularly uncomfortable. The lightweight sleeping bag Alun had given her offered little protection against the heat-sucking, bone-bruising material.

She pulled back the cover that lay over her face. Pitch darkness greeted her. And silence. Utter silence. Over the last two days, the absence of any sound except her own breathing and the slight noise of her movements had begun to grind into her consciousness like the heel of a boot crushing an insect. Several times she'd been tempted to speak just to hear a voice, even if it was her own, but she couldn't afford to do anything unnecessary that might alert the Guardian to her presence.

She was deeply outclassed by the machine as it was. Despite the damage it had sustained, the android remained stronger, faster, and more agile than she was. The twisted neck of the corpse she'd found at the Oceanside jail was a testament to the fact. Surprising the Guardian would be about the only advantage Cherry had.

But she didn't only want to destroy it. She also wanted to know what it was doing.

Cherry pulled on her night vision goggles and a gray ceiling came into view. If there were any colors in the interior of the Scythian constructions, the goggles were not picking them up. Apart from the oddly sectioned and colored walls, everything else she'd seen had been white, light gray, mid-gray, dark gray, or black.

She sat up and reached for her backpack, pulling out ration strips to chew on and water to sip. As she ate and drank, she opened the pathfinder to check her position. The device had mapped each section she'd passed through in her search and gave distances, along the level and perpendicular. She had climbed and descended through structures as she'd traveled. Outside the map of her route everything was blank, but from the total distance and her extremely rough estimate of the size of the city, she guessed she was about one-quarter of the way into it.

She was heading for the center. Important places tended to be in the center of metropolises, in Cherry's limited experience. The Guardian must have gone to the city for the purpose of doing or retrieving something important, so it made sense it would go to the center. Cherry knew there were probably thousands more possibilities, but that one conclusion of her reasoning was the best she had.

On her hunt for the Guardian, she had moved through many strange places—places that had left her confused and disturbed somehow. The sea of dusty fragments she had encountered upon entering the city had spread more than a hundred meters wide, and spiraling 'steps' like the one she'd happened upon rose out of it everywhere. Slim cylinders protruded from the walls, and the same arched portals opened in them that she'd seen in the outer walls.

Navigating the city was difficult. The problem she'd encountered after passing through the boundary wall, when she'd had to cross the crazed pattern of fissures, was multiplied the deeper she moved into the metropolis. The place was clearly designed to accommodate creatures larger than humans. Everything seemed too large: the rooms, the buildings, the openings that led from one space to another. The Scythians could also climb walls. No opening was ever at ground level. Cherry had been forced to use a line and grapnel more than once in order to access a construction. Managing the feat one-handed had been no joke.

She hadn't encountered any roads. The Scythians didn't seem to use or need them. Each building abutted the next, with perhaps a few openings joining them. The rooms inside were taller than they were wide. In one room, curved, concave hemispheres lined the walls and the same kind of debris Cherry had first encountered in the city lay thick on the floor.

She'd also seen what had once been equipment of various kinds, but they were barely distinguishable. Most were little more than heaps of rust. Anything she touched immediately dissolved into particles, puffing dust as it imploded. One wall had held long lines of shelves. Slim, dark gray flakes and light gray puffs of a fibrous substance were all that remained of whatever the shelves had held.

The extent of the decay, though predictable given the time that had passed since the Scythians left, had left Cherry wondering what could possibly have survived for the Guardian to seek out. Had the original inhabitants of the planet had the foresight to prepare something that would last for eons? It seemed the only conclusion to draw from the Guardian's behavior, but Cherry couldn't guess what that thing might be.

The stench of feces seemed to have gone away, though she suspected it only appeared that way and she'd gotten used to the smell. What she hadn't gotten used to was the aridity of the atmosphere. The air was painfully dry. It drew moisture from eyes and mouth, and though she'd been careful to always have her water condenser running, the amount the device managed to draw in was worryingly small.

If the Scythians needed water to live, the liquid had long since disappeared from their former habitation. Thirst was already a constant companion. Cherry had soon realized that lack of water could be her downfall in her search for the Guardian. Her determination would not overcome her body's needs, no matter how strong it was.

She took another small sip of water and checked the level in the bottle. Only two hundred and thirty mils remained of the water the condenser had drawn from the atmosphere in the eight hours she'd slept. She pushed the straw into the bottle insert and climbed out of her bag, ready to face another long day of hunting.

After quickly repacking her backpack, leaving out a line and the attached grapnel, Cherry lifted it onto her back and tightened the straps. Facing away from the boundary wall and into the city, she set off. The place where she'd chosen to sleep was small and only two portals stood in the walls. Both were too high for her to climb through.

She swung the grapnel and threw it through an opening. Gently, she pulled the line until the grapnel caught on the farther side of the opening. She tugged on the line to check the grapnel was holding—twice the previous day it had slipped while she was mid-climb and she'd fallen to the floor. It hadn't taken much imagination to see herself incapacitated with a broken leg or ankle, beyond hope of comm'ing for help, dying of thirst.

Cherry walked to the base of the wall, shortening the line as she went. When she was standing below the portal, she put a foot on the wall, braced herself, gripped the line hard in her only hand, and began her climb upward.

Ever since losing her arm to a Scythian spider, Cherry had gotten used to using her teeth as another hand. After some trial and error on her first day in the city, she'd put this habit to good use when she devised a method of climbing. She would 'walk' up the wall, pulling herself as high as she could with her arm, and then bite the line to hold her place while she let go with her hand to reach higher.

It was strenuous, ungainly, and painful, but it worked.

She reached the bottom of the opening, reached over it, and clambered onto it. Straddling the gap she looked into the next room. This one had no roof. Cherry had seen many similar rooms but she was none the wiser about their purpose. For the first time, however, she saw a series of ledges running around the walls. The floor of the room was some distance below—a fatal distance if she fell.

One ledge was within reach. Cherry touched it. She guessed it was about fifteen centimeters wide. If she turned her feet sideways she could stand on it easily. She mentally debated with herself, stowing her grapnel and line as she considered her options. Which way to go? Should she try to cross the room or return the way she'd come and take a different route?

The situation with her water would soon become dire. She couldn't afford to take many diversions. And she might encounter similar or more difficult obstacles to her progress. She might already be looking at her easiest path.

Directly across from her at the same level was another opening, and the nearest ledge ran right around to it. Cherry made her choice. She didn't have time to waste dithering. Traversing the room should be easy providing she kept her head.

She rose to her feet, holding onto the edge of the opening for balance. She would have to face the wall as she made her way along the ledge. Her backpack protruded too much for her to have her back to the wall.

She turned around, and then carefully placed one foot on the nearest ledge.

Cherry paused. Would the ledge bear her weight? It looked solid enough, but it was hundreds of thousands of years old. It was a miracle that any of the Scythian city remained standing after all the time that had passed, let alone the ledge. If the place hadn't been enclosed by the dome, it would have been dust.

She stamped down, hard. The ledge remained solid.

"Well, here goes," she murmured to herself, and stepped out.

Her hand flat on the wall, Cherry shuffled sideways. Her heart began to race and her breathing sped up. The distance around the perimeter of the room to the other opening was about ten or twelve meters. Not far at all. She took some deep breaths and exhaled slowly to calm herself. All she had to do was walk a few meters then she would be through the opening and into the next room. Nothing could be easier.

She'd reached the corner. The space was too narrow for her to remain close to the wall as she went around it. She was forced to step over a gap. Bracing herself against the vertical surface with her only hand, she made the crossing, letting out a whoosh of expelled air as she reached the other side. She would have to do the same again at the next corner. Then it would be a straight run to the other opening.

Cherry set off shuffling to her left again. As she went, she wondered what was happening on the surface. Had Kes found a way to neutralize the biocide? Was Aubriot okay out at Cerberus? How was Wilder coping with being cut off from the rest of Concordia aboard the *Opportunity*? Cherry hoped they would all make it out of the crisis alive, along with the rest of the Concordians. The colony had been through so much, had come so far with so many sacrifices, it deserved to survive.

As the toes of Cherry's left boot touched the next

ledge, it crumbled. She tried to back up but it was too late. She overbalanced, cried out, and clutched the wall. But her hand only met a flat surface. There was nothing to grip. She tried to force herself forward, tried to shift her weight onto her other foot, but the weight of her backpack was pulling her backward, pulling her down.

Cherry fell.

CHAPTER TWENTY-TWO

The biocide was getting closer. Kes studied the latest satellite images as he sat in the lab, waiting for a special person to arrive. They showed that the patches of brown, dead vegetation spreading out from the landing site of each of the Scythians' canisters were growing wider and in some places they had grown so large they'd joined up. Sometimes, a tongue of poison would suddenly run out, as if following a rich seam of life in the ground. As soon as biocide encountered water it would run rapidly through it, massacring all aquatic life the water contained. Cerberus was hemmed in on all sides. The biocide was creeping up the mountain slopes toward the mines and adjacent settlements, and soon it would reach the Vimur, the last major refuge of Concordia's Fila.

What could humans do to stop its progress? The best they could hope for was to slow it down, such as by the efforts that were currently taking place around the warehouse refuge. The idea had been put forward by a farmer, but Kes recognized it as a technique that had been used to prevent the spread of wildfires on Earth. A fire break, only for all living things, not fire.

The men and women of the refuge had dug a deep trench all the way around the site. It had been a monumental effort, but the work had also been a welcome distraction from Meredith's suicide and the fear of impending death that threatened the refuge with panic and chaos.

Next, they had sprayed the interior of the trench with a powerful agricultural pesticide stored at one of the warehouses. The reasoning was that if the biocide hit an area where no microorganisms remained alive, its progress would halt. With nothing to feed it, it should die. That was the reasoning, and Kes could see the logic in it, though he suspected the trench was not sufficiently deep and the pesticide would not penetrate the soil and rock enough to destroy all life in the vicinity of the encroaching biocide. The trench and pesticide might slow it down, but eventually it would breach the fire break and then move swiftly on toward the warehouses.

But perhaps, by then, they would be ready for it. Perhaps the fire break would buy them enough time.

"He's here," said Thom.

Kes looked up. Wilder's friend, Tycho, could be seen waiting outside the lab. A feeling that had become familiar over the previous couple of days—guilt mixed with gratitude—returned in full force.

"This is it, then," said Drew, the young scientist who had educated the team on all he knew about creating and administering vaccines.

Kes cast the young man a sympathetic look, guessing he was dreading what would happen in the next ten or fifteen minutes. They all were, of course, though perhaps Drew felt especially responsible.

"Isn't anyone going to let him in?" asked Tricia, striding toward the door.

Tycho stepped into the lab.

"You know," said Drew quietly, "I wouldn't mind volunteering myself."

Kes put a hand on his shoulder. "You wouldn't be the first scientist to experiment on himself, but it's a stupid idea. If the vaccine doesn't work, who do you think is best equipped to continue to work on it, you or Tycho? No one doubts your bravery, Drew, or thinks that experimenting on another human being is a cop out. These are extraordinary times."

For a man who might only have a few more minutes of life left, Tycho looked extremely calm and relaxed. As he walked up to Kes and the others who were awaiting him, everyone else in the lab stopped what they were doing and watched him.

"I'm ready," he announced. "Stephie and I said our goodbyes, just in case. Though I hope I will be seeing her again, and living another few years at least. But if not, so be it. Where do you want to do it?" He looked around the lab.

"I'm afraid we have to draw out the suspense a little longer," said Kes. "We need to measure your vitals, height, weight, that kind of thing. Any information we can gather may be useful, whatever the outcome."

"Right, I understand," said Tycho.

Kes thought he detected nervousness creeping into the man's demeanor, which was entirely understandable. He had probably steeled himself for this moment and hadn't expected to have to wait. Kes wasn't sure he could retain composure himself in such circumstances. Tycho wasn't only staring death in the face, he was going up to him and shaking his hand.

"If you wouldn't mind following me," said Drew. He led Tycho to the station he'd set up with basic medical equipment he'd borrowed from the refuge's doctors. The older man obligingly and patiently did as he was instructed, taking off his shoes to have his height measured, standing on the scales, and rolling up his sleeve to have his blood pressure and a blood sample taken.

Though most of the scientists continued with their work as if nothing special was happening—they could not afford to waste time, whether the experiment with Tycho was successful or not—the atmosphere in the lab was stretched as taut as a bow string. Kes tried to tell himself that if the vaccine didn't work and Tycho unfortunately died, plenty remained for them to do to continue with their efforts. Nevertheless he couldn't help hoping that, unlikely though it was, they had gotten it right the first time.

He wouldn't allow himself to imagine the other possibilities: that Tycho wouldn't die but would suffer unbearably painful complications or would end up a shell of a man, his mind gone but his body living on. After Kes had accepted Tycho's offer to play lab rat, he'd backtracked and tried to explain to the old man that what he was volunteering for could be worse than death. But Tycho had refused to listen, only repeating, *I want to do it.*

The long, awkward minutes had passed. Drew had taken all the measurements and samples they needed. It was time.

"We've prepared a bed for you to lie down on while we give you the vaccination, and we'd like you to stay here at least another day for monitoring," said Drew. "I hope that's okay. Things have been rushed around here. I'm not sure if anyone informed you about what we had in mind."

"Oh, I didn't know that," said Tycho. "Someone will have to find Stephie and ask her for my pajamas and toothbrush."

Drew smiled. "That won't be a problem, sir. Please step this way."

The small party set off once again, this time toward the meeting room. One corner of it had been curtained off. Thom brought up the rear, pushing the monitor that measured blood pressure, blood oxygen saturation, heart rate, and respiration. As they administered the vaccine, all these vitals would be measured, and for around a day afterward.

"How soon will you know if it's worked?" Tycho asked Kes as he pushed open the meeting room door.

"We'll check your blood every hour or so," Kes replied. "I'm hoping to see a response within twenty-four hours if not sooner. The window for an adverse reaction should have passed by then too. I should tell you, though, we won't know anything about the long-term effects."

The fact was, they could vaccinate the entire colony and save them from the biocide, only for everyone to develop cancer five years hence. What they were doing was incredibly risky, but no other options were open.

They had reached the curtained section of the meeting room. Tricia pulled back the drapes, and Thom pushed the trolley holding the medical equipment through the gap.

"Should I lie down or sit up?" Tycho asked, arriving at the bed. His calm poise had returned. He looked relieved, in fact, to be finally getting to the point of no return.

Kes was wondering, as he had so many times, if Tycho died, what he would say to Wilder.

"I think it would be best if you lie down," said Drew.

The young man hooked Tycho up to the medical equipment. "I want you to know," he said, softly, "that we have many medications on standby if anything goes wrong. The last thing we want is for you to suffer. I hope you understand what I mean."

Tycho looked into Drew's eyes. "I'll try to bear it for as long as I can so you can get your information. If it gets too much, I'll give you the signal. The only thing I ask is, don't tell Stephie I suffered. Tell her I went peacefully."

Drew nodded. He turned to face Kes. His eyes were bright. "Can I speak to you outside, just for a moment?"

Kes said, "I'm sorry, Tycho. We won't keep you waiting long."

When the two men had left the curtained area, Drew whispered, "I can't do it." He held up the injector. It shook in his hands.

"I'll do it," Kes said. "Don't worry. I know how hard this is."

He did know. Now, if Tycho died, Kes would have killed Wilder's friend with his own hands.

They returned to the bed. "Ready?" Kes asked Tycho.

"I'm more than ready," the older man replied. "Let's do this."

Kes pressed the injector against Tycho's withered bicep and fired it.

The vaccine contained a refined form of the dead, inactive biocide they had collected from the Fila tissue. When they had tested the vaccine on living human cells, there had been no response. They had also assessed the effects of introducing it into a sample of human blood. Again, the cells hadn't been affected.

But injecting the vaccine into a living human being was something different entirely. They could only guess how the subject's immune system would react. It might mount a massive response that would manifest as anaphylactic shock. Though they had an adrenaline shot available, Tycho could still die, not from the biocide but from his body's reaction to it. Or his immune system might show no response at all, in which case, Kes' idea was probably wrong and they had no alternative to try, or any time left.

A sound from behind Kes distracted him from watching Tycho. The sound had come from outside the drapes. He pulled them back and saw the meeting room door crammed with scientists, unable to contain their curiosity about the results of the vaccination test.

Kes returned his attention to Tycho. "How are you feeling?"

"I don't feel a thing," the old man replied. "Should I?"

"No," said Drew. "If it's working, or not harmful, you shouldn't feel anything. The literature I read stated you might experience some soreness at the vaccination site and maybe a low grade fever. But those signs are good. They mean your body's immune system is reacting. We won't know that for definite for a few hours at minimum."

Seconds ticked past, drawing out into minutes as Drew monitored Tycho's vitals.

"Everything looks normal," Drew said. "I hope I'm not speaking too soon, but…" He grinned, embarrassed. "I don't dare say it."

"I'll say it, then," said Thom. "Tycho, if the biocide vaccine was going to kill you you'd be dead by now. I think you're going to be okay."

Tycho firmly shook his head. "This isn't over yet. If you think my body's learned to fight off the poison, I want to be certain. I want to prove it. I want someone to drop me in a dead zone with no protection."

"No," said Drew, aghast. "We couldn't possibly—"

"I insist," Tycho said. "It's the only way you'll know for sure if your treatment works."

The old man was right, though it pained Kes to admit it to himself. If they were to have any confidence in the vaccine it would require a field trial, though they would have to wait some days to give the old man's system time to develop the antibodies to fight off the virus. Did they even have that long?

They didn't know if the vaccine was effective, but they *did* know it wasn't deadly. They had passed the first, critical stage.

CHAPTER TWENTY-THREE

When Cherry came to, her mouth and nose were covered up and she could hardly breathe. Panicking, she thrashed about. Then the familiarity of the sensation hit her: she was covered in the debris fragments she'd encountered when she first entered the city. Wiping the dusty bits away from her face, she tried to stand. The back of her head and her back hurt like hell. She guessed she must have landed on her backpack, which had softened the impact as she hit the floor. She was lucky she hadn't broken her back.

Cherry made it onto her hand and knees. She pushed away the fragments from her mouth and nose, creating a gap to breathe in. How would she get out of the detritus? Unlike the first time she'd been submerged in the debris, there were no spiraling platforms in the room. Nothing but straight walls.

She clumsily rose to her feet and her head broke through the surface of fragments into fresh air. The layer of debris was only as deep as her shoulders. That was something. Now how would she get out of the room?

The openings were high above and they looked identical. Cherry couldn't figure out which one was the one she'd been moving toward. She picked the left one to try to reach. She wouldn't mind too much if it was the wrong one as long as she got out.

Would her line reach the distance? One on its own might not, but if that were the case she could tie two together. She gave an inward groan. Her thighs, buttocks, arms, and abs were already sore from her first climb that morning, and it hadn't been even half the height of the one that now faced her.

But there was nothing for it except to begin. The longer she delayed the thirstier and less able to make the climb she would become. She payed out the entire length of one line and stood on its end. If the line was too short and the grapnel caught on the opening, she wouldn't be able to reach it.

Cherry aimed, and threw. The grapnel bounced off the wall just below the opening, tugging on the end of the line under her foot. It was just long enough. She took her foot off the rope to allow enough length for the grapnel to reach the opening, aimed, and threw again. This time, the grapnel bounced off the wall above the opening.

She gathered the fallen heap of line and the grapnel from the debris, wiping them free of the fragments, before trying again.

At her third attempt, the grapnel disappeared through the opening. *Shit.*

She winced, waiting for the grapnel to fall down the other side, taking the line with it. The lightweight rope slapped against the wall, and began to slide down it, pulling up the grapnel at the other end. *Phew.*

Cherry waded through the debris to the wall and the hanging line. Hoping the grapnel would not slip from its precarious position on the farther edge of the opening— she wasn't sure she would survive a second fall from that great height—she began to climb.

A second strenuous climb so soon after her first that day quickly set her muscles complaining. Each step up the wall, each shift of her hand to a new position while she gripped the rope in her teeth, was a great effort. Sweat stung her eyes and made her palm slippery. She could feel her body's precious moisture soaking into her clothes. Meanwhile, her mouth and throat remained dry as the dusty debris beneath her.

About halfway up the wall, she rested, locking her elbow to take some of her weight from the screaming muscles of her arm. She psyched herself up to complete the second half of her endeavor. She told herself that she'd made it that far so she could climb the rest. If she failed she would only have to do it again, and it would be twice as hard the second time around. Once she got to the top she would be able to rest as long as she wanted.

It was time to move.

Cherry moved her head toward the rope and bit it, clenching the slim line firmly between her teeth. She released the rope from her grasp, reached upward to grab it higher up, and—

There was something in the opening.

Cherry gasped. The line slipped from her mouth. At the last split second, she clutched at it and gripped it. But her boots had lost their traction on the wall. She swung free and then slammed into it. The impact knocked the breath from her. She hung on for her life, only her grip on the rope preventing her from falling, drawing in great lungfuls of air.

What had she seen? She could have sworn a figure had appeared in the opening and looked down at her. Or had she imagined it?

Her arm felt like it was being slowly ripped from its socket. She had to regain her purchase on the wall. She scrabbled with her feet against the vertical surface, pushing out her body until it was level again. She had to let go before her arm seized up entirely. She opened her mouth, bit the rope, and looked upward.

Dread froze her heart. Something *was* in the opening. Dark, disfigured, the hairless head looked down at her impassively.

The android had found her, while she was in the most vulnerable, precarious position possible.

Cherry transferred the line to her hand. "Hey!" she called. "Help me up."

It was an insane, desperate measure, but it was the only one available. The android had claimed it was a Guardian. And the Guardians' prime directive was to help the colony. Everyone knew that. And Cherry was part of the colony. Perhaps the android would attempt to maintain the masquerade, despite the odd, suspicious situation it was in.

The android did not move. It did not answer. The gaze of its remaining eye was fixed on Cherry's.

"Help me up, dammit!" Cherry called again. "That's what you're supposed to do, isn't it? Are you a Guardian or not? Help me. Now!"

What thought processes were whirring in the creature's electronic brain? Was it thinking at all? Or was it only waiting to see if she died, or if it would have to kill her itself?

Cherry couldn't afford to waste any more breath or effort. She had to reach the opening before her strength gave up, and take whatever fate awaited her there. She resumed her climb, grunting and panting, working her way slowly upward. While she climbed, she tried to convince the waiting android there was no reason to kill her.

When she could spare the breath, she released staccato sentences. "I figured I'd better come after you...Something's gone wrong with you, right?...You're confused...Understandable, after the attack...I'll take you out of here…We can go back and help the others."

The android didn't move a centimeter. It remained so still Cherry wondered if its power supply had happened to give out at that very moment, fortuitously. But she knew her luck wasn't that good.

She had only three meters to go. Then a couple more meters. If the android didn't do anything, she might actually make it. Then she and the Guardian could sort out their differences.

The thing looked just as horrible close up as it had in the hospital. Half its face was missing, and, as if a macabre mirror image of herself, its right arm too.

Cherry drew closer to it. Relief that her trial was nearly over was sending adrenaline pumping through her body, easing her pain. Or was it not relief, but fear of what the android might do when it could reach her?

The thing finally moved. Without taking its gaze from Cherry, it lifted its remaining hand to its mouth, bit on its forefinger, and tugged. To Cherry's horror, the finger parted company with the hand, revealing a small dagger only as long as the first joint.

"No," Cherry breathed.

The android placed the edge of the tiny dagger against the line where it stretched below the opening, and sawed. The thing regarded Cherry without expression as its remaining arm moved backward and forward.

Cherry grunted and took another step upward. She gripped the line in her teeth. She reached for the opening. She was almost there. Another step…

The line snapped.

Again, she fell.

This time, she was ready. She curled up, tucking her head into her chest, and allowed the backpack to absorb the impact. As soon as she hit the floor, she rolled through the debris, trying to lessen the impact further. In another beat she was on her feet and brushing fragments from her face.

All of a sudden it hit her: things weren't as bad as they seemed. She'd been trying to find the Guardian, and now she'd found it. Though, strictly speaking, the Guardian had found her. It had probably heard her yell the first time she'd fallen and homed in on the sound in the silent city. But the result was the same.

She hadn't caught it in the middle of doing whatever it had come there to do, but perhaps there was still a way she could find out its reason for being in the city, *if* she had the creature under her control. And despite the apparent imbalance in their physical abilities getting it under her control wasn't as impossible as it might seem.

Since beginning her quest to find the Guardian, Cherry had remembered a snippet of information Cariad had told her long ago. Knowing her dislike, bordering on fear, of the androids sent from Earth, Cariad had told Cherry of a weakness the Guardian called Strongquist had once revealed.

If she could keep the android from killing her just long enough, she knew how to subdue it.

The thing remained in the opening, staring at her. It was probably processing the fact that she was still alive and deciding what to do next. Should it take the time to finish her off, or should it allow nature to take its course while she was trapped without food or water?

"You know what?" Cherry called up. "I have something in my pack I bet you'd like to see." She dropped her backpack from her shoulders. It thumped on the floor, sending up a cloud of choking dust. Cherry coughed and wiped the dirt from her eyes. She swallowed, dryly. Squatting down and pushing the debris layer to one side, she opened the pack and took out a line and her other grapnel.

"Look what I found," she shouted hoarsely. "Thank the stars for that. I'll be able to climb right out of here, when I've had a rest. Isn't that great? I bet that pleases your human-safeguarding, metal heart."

The android's gaze had switched to the line, which Cherry was casually tying to the grapnel. Just the thought of making that climb again sent her muscles into spasms of protest, though in fact she had a much harder task ahead.

The android moved into the opening.

Good!

It was crouching, grasping the edge.

"C'mon!" Cherry softly exclaimed.

The android remained still, apparently stuck in a whirr of conflicting commands.

A great hatred rose up in Cherry. Ever since the Guardians had raised their weapons against innocent Gens, she had loathed them. She hated their false faces and twisted motivations. To other colonists they had been Concordia's saviors, but she knew what they really were: machines with the potential for murder. Robotic psychopaths. And here was the last one. Once it was destroyed the Guardians would never plague the colony again.

"C'MON!" she screamed.

The Guardian jumped.

As the android fell through the air, Cherry swung the grapnel and ran backward. She wasn't hoping to draw the creature closer to her—it would do that itself—but she wanted to unbalance it. If she could just reach...

The android hit the floor in a crouch, sinking into gray debris. As it rose, Cherry threw the line. But the creature was too fast. The grapnel sank into the dust, useless. The Guardian ran at Cherry.

She feinted left and then dived right, sliding through soft fragments and scattering them. A hand fastened around her ankle with a steely grip and yanked her back. Cherry turned onto her back and kicked. Her boot heel caught the Guardian under the chin, snapping its head backward. Cherry kicked again, landing her next blow on the android's chest. But it was like kicking a wall.

Cherry twisted violently to her right, spinning right around, and managed to break the android's hold, though it felt like the skin of her ankle had been ripped off. She kicked side of the creature's knee, momentarily unbalancing it.

She'd bought herself a second in which to rise to her feet, but then the android's hand was around her throat. It lifted her off the floor and walked, carrying her suspended by her neck, to the wall, thrusting her into it.

The Guardian leaned in, and pressed.

Cherry had less than a second to live. The Guardian's superior strength meant it wouldn't even need to choke her to death. Its hand could probably squeeze right through her neck.

Already weakening, she reached behind its ear. Where was that place? That special spot Cariad had mentioned, marked by a mole?

The android's hand was hard and smooth. All its fake human skin and flesh had been burned away. Cherry's airway was shut. Pressure was building up in her head, forcing blood into her tongue, squeezing her eyeballs from their sockets.

Her fingers desperately scrambled around the android's remaining ear. Had the pressure point been on the other side of its head? The incinerated side? Or had Cariad lied to her, seeking to calm her fears?

Cherry was dying. The strength was draining from her arm. Her vision was closing in.

A pleasant euphoria began to overtake her. She hoped the colony would survive. The colony would survive. It always had. And she'd done her best to help it.

The Guardian released its grip. It glared into Cherry's eyes. It had realized what she was trying to do. It released its grip on her throat. Cherry's feet touched the floor. The android reached for her arm.

And then Cherry felt it. A tiny bump, a small, raised spot in the well behind the android's earlobe.

She pressed.

It was like turning a switch. It *was* turning a switch. The android was immediately, utterly still.

Cherry slumped to her knees in the detritus, nursing her agonized throat. For several long moments she couldn't move.

When she could breathe properly again, she looked up at the Guardian, frozen into position. Its arm bent at the elbow, it had been a centimeter from grabbing Cherry's arm and preventing her from reaching its deactivation switch. If it had succeeded, everything would have been over for Cherry. She would have had no second chances.

Shakily, she got to her feet. What next? Should she continue to explore and try to find out what the android had been doing in the city? She might be able to follow its trail, especially if it had passed through debris layers like the one they were currently in. Even without the debris, the dust that lay over everything would have been disturbed wherever the android had passed.

But her water was low and she was exhausted.

Perhaps she could somehow force the android to tell her why it had gone to the city. Or maybe a techie could access its data storage.

A realization hit her, and Cherry stared up at the two arched openings in the walls high above. She would have to complete her nearly impossible climb again, but not only that, if she wanted to take the android with her, she would have to find a way to drag it up too. Then she would have to carry the thing all the way through the city and back to the Chimera excavation site.

Cherry wrapped her arm around the strange, burned mannequin's waist and tried to lift it. It was surprisingly heavy for its size. She doubted she could lift it off the floor even with two hands. *Dammit.*

She would have to leave it behind. And she was too weak to search farther into the city and discover the reason for its mission. *Dammit. Dammit. Dammit.*

Cherry closed her eyes. After all her effort, she'd failed, again. She would never find out why the android was on Concordia or what it might have done in the city. Two pieces of information that could be vital.

Then, out of nowhere, something Aubriot had said popped into her mind.

Catch that Guardian and cut its fucking head off for me.

Smiling grimly, Cherry unsheathed her knife.

CHAPTER TWENTY-FOUR

Wilder lay in the acceleration seat and calculated the time that had passed as the *Opportunity* journeyed to meet the Assembly ships. By her reckoning, based on ship's time, an entire day had gone by, but the effect of time dilation meant that more time had passed on Concordia. To work out the duration of her journey from the perspective of the Concordians, she would need to ask Quinn the distance and speeds the ship had traveled. Her Fila friend was forced to regularly slow down the ship to allow her to recover from the effects of acceleration. Traveling continuously at its top speed was more than any human body could endure.

By figuring out how long it took her to reach the Assembly ships, she hoped to estimate the time the Concordians would have to wait for help to arrive—the Assembly ships would have to traverse roughly the same distance at about the same speed, she guessed. But the question was too difficult to answer, and asking Quinn wouldn't be any help. He struggled to think of time from a human perspective.

Leaving Concordia's orbit meant she could no longer

comm Kes. She could send him a message, but his reply would take so long to reach her there was little point. Knowing she would be to all intents and purposes cut off from him and every other fellow human being, she had tried to comm him one last time before Quinn engaged the engines, but he hadn't been available.

It was to be expected. He was busy trying to save everyone on the planet. He didn't have time to chat with teenage girls. But Wilder couldn't help feeling sad and lonely. She'd wanted to speak to Niall instead, but she could sense that Quinn was anxious to set off, so she left Kes a short message, briefly telling him where she was going and why.

She found the latter part of her message hard to explain. What could she hope to gain from the Assembly in return for gifting them the secret of a-grav? The members were already coming to Concordia's aid as fast as they could. What greater gift could they give? Measured against the scale of other galactic civilizations, humanity's was insignificant. It had destroyed its civilization on its origin planet and for all Wilder knew it might even have destroyed its planet's ecosystem, like the Scythians had. And Concordia's human civilization was barely clinging to existence.

If humankind disappeared from the galaxy tomorrow, would the impact be significant? Wilder didn't think so. The Assembly had no particular reason to help them, yet it was. Wilder didn't fully know why. Perhaps Quinn was right when he said her human perspective made it hard for her to understand. Whatever the Assembly's reasoning behind their decision, what more could she ask of it than what it was already freely giving?

In the end, after some hesitation, Wilder had ended her message to Kes by saying, *I haven't decided what I'll ask for in return for the a-grav. Maybe I'll think of something on the journey. I wish I could ask for your advice. I bet you'd be able to suggest something else as well as saving all our asses. Anyway, I'm going now. Quinn wants us to set out right away. Stay safe. You better still be there when I get back.*

To help pass the time while she lay in the acceleration seat, Wilder had watched old Earth vids on the ship's data files, including that weird one where Aubriot had been advertising the *Nova Fortuna* Project. But she'd seen many of them before during the long months of her trip to the Assembly space station.

For a short while she searched for something new to watch before finally giving up. Next, she tried to sleep, closing her eyes and performing a complicated mental calculation as she usually did when she wanted to drop off. But, as usual while she was experiencing acceleration, she found it was impossible to fall asleep. She was simply too uncomfortable, and she was tense with worry about Piddle and Puddle, though they both seemed to be adjusting to the bouts of extreme force on their small bodies.

"Quinn," Wilder said.

It was a moment before the Fila answered. "Yes?"

"I was wondering if you had any suggestions on what to propose to the Assembly as recompense for the a-grav machine?"

"That is for you to decide as a representative of humanity."

"Huh? I'm seventeen years old. I'm the last person who should be making this decision. I wish I'd thought to talk to the Leader about it before we left."

"I understand your uncertainty and concern, but I don't believe it would be ethical or wise for me to voice my opinion and influence you."

"I'm not asking you to tell me what to say, I'm only asking for a little *advice*."

"Wilder, though we are good friends, you know the difficulties we have in understanding each other at times. Human lives are like blips in spacetime to me. I am already mourning your passing. The current needs of Concordia are plain to the least intelligent human, and you are certainly not among those ranks. The colony's immediate needs do not require stating. Beyond that...You are human, and I am not. There is no more to be said."

"But I would like to help the Fila too. You share the planet with us."

Long seconds passed before Wilder realized Quinn wasn't going to reply.

She heaved a sigh and shifted uncomfortably under the pressure forcing down on her.

CHAPTER TWENTY-FIVE

Tycho looked deep into Kes' eyes as he shook his hand.

"I want to make something clear before I go," the old man said. "I'm doing this of my own free will and I accept the consequences, whatever they may be."

A cold breeze was blowing across the parking lot outside the warehouse refuge. Kes gripped Tycho's hand tightly. "I understand what you're saying, and I appreciate why you're saying it."

Would Tycho's words make him feel less guilty if the vaccine was a dud and Wilder's friend went to his death? Kes doubted it. But perhaps, when the biocide arrived at the refuge and his own end came, he might be able to take comfort in the fact that he had done all he could, even to the extent of accepting an elderly man's offer to risk his life.

Kes watched Tycho walk calmly and steadily toward the heli that would transport him to a dead zone. Kes squinted in the bright sunshine. How long had it been since he'd seen natural daylight? More than a week. Seven days was the shortest time it would take for the human body to develop an immune response to the vaccine. Kes would have liked to have waited longer—three or four weeks would have been sufficient time to give them reliable data.

But they didn't have that long. At its current rate of approach, the biocide was expected to close in on the refuge in five days. No one knew how long it would take to breach the firebreak, but after it did, the colonists in the shelter would have only hours remaining to them. The scientists needed every moment they had left to mass produce the vaccine and send it out to all the known refuges. They had already begun production despite their ignorance about the vaccine's effectiveness. They had no choice.

The future of the colony was staked on a hypothesis.

Tycho reached the heli and climbed into it, clearly struggling to force his old, stiff body to make the maneuver. At the distance, he looked frailer than ever.

The heli door closed and the reflected sunlight on the transparent shell hid the interior. Tycho had disappeared from view. The rotors started up and within a few seconds the heli was rising into the sky.

As the days had passed and Tycho continued to show no ill effects from the biocide vaccine, other members of the refuge, upon hearing what Tycho had done, also stepped forward to be guinea pigs. The scientists had vaccinated four more individuals and were keeping them under close observation in the lab's meeting room.

Despite the apparently positive progress, Kes was filled with a sense of doom, though he'd been careful to mask his feelings around the others. He'd become convinced that the vaccine recipients had remained in good health because the vaccine was ineffective. His reasoning was sound. The literature he'd read indicated that mild fevers post immunization were common, but the experimental subjects remained entirely unaffected. The biocide worked so fast and was so devastating, a robust physical response to its vaccine would have been expected.

However, the morale of the refuge was a knife edge. Meredith's suicide hadn't helped matters. The spreading news of the vaccination experiment had renewed hope in the colonists' hearts. They had begun to believe they might survive this latest onslaught. Kes didn't want to put that hope in jeopardy by stating his doubts.

He tried to tell himself that unrelated feelings were triggering his disquiet. He missed Isobel and Miki. Comms between the warehouse refuge and the Chimera excavation site were slow and erratic and he hadn't been able to speak directly with Isobel since she'd arrived. His only source of information about his wife and daughter was the general report from the site organizer, stating their names on the list of occupants. Other than that, he had no idea if they had enough food and water, or somewhere safe and comfortable to sleep.

He realized he was staring at empty sky and the chill wind was penetrating his flimsy lab coat. Even the sound of the heli had faded away. He returned to the refuge, slipping through the gap in the large warehouse door and pulling it closed. The air inside was stale and not much warmer than outside. Kes guessed he only had a short time before the heli reached the test site.

A camera had been fixed to the outside and angled downward to record whatever went on below the vehicle. The pilot would be too focused on her controls to operate a recording device, maintaining a stable, steady hover at a fixed distance above the ground in the strong breeze. Kes had advised Tycho to take off his shoes and socks before the pilot lowered him to the ground, in order to facilitate immediate contact with the biocide in the dead zone.

Kes entered the lab. It was empty. Every scientist in the place was in the meeting room and watching the wall interface that was linked with the heli camera. The more optimistic among them had suggested broadcasting the test to the entire refuge or even across Concordia, but Kes had stated a firm refusal. The last thing anyone needed to see was an old man dying from the deadly effects of the biocide.

"He's nearly there, I think," said Tricia over her shoulder as she noticed Kes entering the meeting room.

The other test subjects were sitting up in their beds, hooked up to various monitors, watching the wall screen as avidly as the clustered scientists.

Kes saw the ground skimming beneath the heli. In those parts even the unpoisoned landscape was dry and bare, but occasionally green scrub or groundcover would flit past.

"Good idea to suggest the pilot drops him at an advancing border," Tricia continued when Kes reached her side. "I agree that the biocide may be less concentrated and weaker in the dead zones, where it'll eventually run out of living organisms to sustain it. It'll be the most potent along the lines where it's advancing. Though if you're right about the former, it gives me hope."

"Why's that?" asked Kes.

"Maybe the dead zones will eventually be safe for us to return to—if the biocide becomes inactive once it's consumed all available life."

"It's only a guess, and not one I'd like to stake my life on. I'd be happier if we can vaccinate the population, providing the vaccine works."

"It looks like we're about to find out," said Tricia.

The image on the interface had stopped moving. The heli was hovering over a patch of dry, brown soil strewn with small rocks. Thick leaves of a native plant Kes didn't recognize were clinging to life in the inhospitable conditions. They were green, but somewhere off-camera a line of death crept closer.

A heavy silence had fallen in the meeting room. The

camera beneath the heli only recorded video, not sound. Tycho and the pilot could speak to them over comm, but neither were choosing to voice their thoughts or fears. Only the soft hum and gentle beeps of the medical equipment broke the silence, somehow adding to the tension.

"Can I say something?" asked Drew. "We haven't discussed what we'll do if the vaccine is ineffective."

"We'll continue working on it," someone replied.

"No, I mean, what do we tell people?" Drew said. "Do we give out the details, or do we keep quiet about it?"

"I'd suggest that if the test is a failure," said Kes, "we keep that information within these four walls."

"We can't do that," Thom said. "People have a right to know."

"Usually, I'd agree with you," Kes replied, "but in this case—"

"There he is!" Tricia exclaimed.

Tycho had appeared, dangling from a harness, slowly spinning, his bare feet thrust out from pants gathered up by the straps. The camera focused on the top of his bald head, fringed with white hair.

The tension in the room screamed silently in Kes' mind. All he could see was the leisurely rotation of Tycho's head and his uncovered feet sticking incongruously below it.

If the biocide killed him, how long would it take? From what Kes had seen, the chemical's effect was pretty much instantaneous, but if the skin on Tycho's feet was thick and hard as it often was on older people, it might take a second or two for the virus to work its way up the microorganisms on his skin to reach tenderer, more vulnerable parts.

"He's down!" someone yelled.

Kes could hardly believe it. How had the old man reached the ground so quickly? But there he was. The line from the harness slackened as it no longer bore the old man's weight.

But he'd alighted on rocks, not on the soil. And the biocide hadn't yet reached the spot. Tycho was busy unfastening the harness and stepping out of it. What was he doing? There was no need for him to do that. Then Kes guessed Tycho's reasoning: the biocide could creep up the line to the heli and affect the pilot, whether Tycho was immune to it or not.

As soon as he was free from the harness, Tycho stepped out of shot.

"Where's he going?" asked Tricia. "He was supposed to stay there and wait for the biocide to reach him, wasn't he? Do you think he's changed his mind? I don't think he'll be able to outrun it."

"No," replied Kes. "I don't think he's changed his mind."

The scene on the interface expanded. The heli was rising, trailing the empty harness and line. Tycho came back into view, smaller due to the increased distance. His bald pate was shiny, reflecting the sunlight. He looked like a toy figure as he stomped rhythmically across the dusty earth. He seemed to want to break into a run if only his old body would let him.

He was advancing toward his death with all the speed he could muster.

Now that the pilot had risen higher, the line of death became clear. Where life survived, green hues colored the brown earth. The dead zone contained no green. The brown was deeper, peppered with the darker brown and black of destroyed vegetation.

The line that demarcated the two zones was moving, paradoxically as if it were alive. It sped toward Tycho's small figure at an alarming pace. In spite of his age, he finally mustered the energy to run. He headed directly toward the biocide, his arms and legs pumping, his feet no doubt being scratched and cut by sharp stones.

At the last moment, with the line of biocide only

meters from him, he halted. Putting his hands on his hips, he bowed slightly forward, as if catching his breath. Then he straightened up, facing the chemical's deadly approach square on.

A beat later it reached him.

In the meeting room, a collective breath was drawn. Kes felt his neck and back grow rigid. He wanted to turn away from the screen, unwilling to witness the death of this brave man, but he could not wrench away his gaze.

And so it was he saw Tycho fall. As the dead zone encroached on and passed the spot where he was standing, the old man fell to his knees. He plummeted forward and hit the ground belly first.

"Shit," muttered Drew.

"Oh god, I can't watch," Tricia said, shielding her eyes.

Kes bowed his head. His intuition had been correct. The vaccine was a dud. Either that, or they hadn't waited long enough for Tycho's body to develop an immune response. Or perhaps his entire idea that the biocide could be defeated by a vaccine had been wrong.

What would they do now? How much longer did they have before the biocide reached the refuge? If only they had more time, they might think up an alternative strategy, or perhaps the Assembly ships would reach them and they could evacuate the planet. But time was the one thing they didn't have.

Then someone shouted, "He's getting up!"

Disbelievingly, Kes raised his head to look at the screen. His eyes registered the small figure of an old man, surrounded by death, clambering to his feet, but his mind couldn't grasp what he was seeing. His mouth dropped open.

Tycho was standing. Tycho was *alive*. It was impossible, yet it was true. The old man walked in a small circle. Then he turned toward the camera on the heli and waved.

Dimly, Kes heard yells and hollers as the scientists erupted into celebrations. Hands slapped his back. Others grasped his right hand and shook it. Bright, grinning faces danced across his vision.

Someone was holding his shoulders and peering into his face. He recognized Tricia.

"Kes," she said, "are you feeling all right?"

"Huh?"

"Are you okay? You know you did it, right? You and Drew. You did it. You saved us. You've saved the colony."

"Huh?"

"I think you better sit down."

Kes felt pressure on his shoulders as Tricia forced him into a seat.

"We did it?" he asked her.

"We did it," said Tricia. "Nearly. We still have a lot of work ahead of us, but I think everyone's going to be okay."

CHAPTER TWENTY-SIX

Memories of her time at the Assembly space station were vivid in Wilder's mind as she traveled through the umbilicus that led to the aliens' ship. Quinn had told her the species she was about to meet performed the role of the organizers of the space station, and that Kes had named them Immani giganticus.

She didn't need reminding of the size of the alien 'organizers' she'd seen at the station—she recalled that one of the individuals she'd seen had measured about seven meters tall. They were quadrupeds and their legs made up half their immense height. Their upper half formed a dome, but due to the EVA suits they'd worn, Wilder hadn't been able to see their eyes or mouth(s) or any other part of their faces, assuming they had faces.

Wilder shivered slightly and pulled herself along the line the Immani had provided for her. It was hard to imagine that she was traveling at near light speed. Quinn had matched the speed of the *Opportunity* with that of the Immani ship, and now the two vessels were hurtling toward Concordia together.

The interior of the umbilicus was brightly lit, but she

couldn't see the source of the light. It seemed to come from the umbilicus material itself. The light at the end of the flexible tunnel was even brighter. In anticipation of entering the glare, Wilder increased the tint on her visor.

On the remainder of her trip to the Immani's ship, she had begun to work on a second problem. Now that she'd perfected her understanding of how to produce an a-grav force, it seemed obvious that without too much trouble she should be able to construct a device that would *create* gravity. The Guardians' ship, the *Mistral*, had carried just such a device. Though the ship had been destroyed, the majority of its plans had been transferred to the colony's data banks.

If she could offer a-grav *and* a gravity-generating device, that would be a hell of an advantage in negotiations with the Assembly. But she hadn't had time to work on the idea between the long bouts of acceleration and then deceleration, and she lacked tools and equipment. It wasn't only a matter of repurposing the a-grav machine's parts.

Still, she felt fairly confident she could commit to producing a gravity generator at some point in the future.

The closer she got to the end of the umbilicus, the larger the exit loomed. The effect was to make her feel even smaller and younger.

"Quinn?" she asked.

"Yes, Wilder?"

"I just wanted to check my comm would go through to you. You're sure we won't be cut off from each other while I'm aboard the ship?"

"I cannot think of any reason the Immani would prevent us from speaking to each other."

"Okay. Cool."

Wilder stopped hauling on the line. She'd reached the Immani's ship. She clung to the slim, metallic rope with one hand, floating free, and assessed the distance between her and the other side of the portal. The opening looked wide enough for the *Opportunity* to pass clean through it.

Inside, the glare made it hard for her to distinguish the ship's bulkheads. No one seemed to be awaiting her.

"Quinn, I reached the ship but I don't know where to go."

"If none of them are there to greet you they must have left something to indicate where you are to go."

"I can't see—oh." Wilder's eyes had adjusted to the extreme light—she imagined her pupils must be pinpricks—and she saw a disturbance in the beams. A line of even brighter light stood out along one bulkhead. "I think I know what I'm supposed to do."

After her many days of weightlessness aboard the *Opportunity* while in orbit above Concordia, Wilder was adept at moving in zero-g. She guessed she was supposed to follow the line of light. She set off accordingly, launching herself across the wide, bright space.

It seemed odd that the Immani had sent no one to greet her, but then there was no knowing what it meant. Perhaps they were being polite.

As she reached the far side of the entrance bay motion in her peripheral vision caught her eye. The door to the umbilicus was quickly closing.

"Quinn? Can you hear me?"

"I can hear you."

Wilder forced herself to relax. She was letting her nerves get the better of her. Her Fila friend was right: the Immani had no reason to wish her any harm.

Her visor displayed rising levels of gases, predominately carbon dioxide. The Immani were filling the entrance bay with the atmosphere they breathed. Wilder kept her helmet on. The gases that were essential to the Immani were poisonous to her.

The line of slightly brighter light led out of the bay along a wide corridor. Wilder had to take care to remain close to the sides. If she lost contact she could find herself floating helplessly, unable to push on anything to provide her with momentum. It might require several minutes of awkward and somewhat embarrassing maneuvering to work her way back to a solid surface.

Were the Immani watching her? Assuming they perceived their surroundings at least partially by sight it was likely they were, though she couldn't see anything resembling a camera. That was no surprise—she was having problems seeing anything at all in the brilliant light. Her eyes already ached despite turning up her visor to full tint.

Something flew across the junction at the end of the passageway. Wilder slammed her hand against the nearest surface, bringing herself to an abrupt stop.

"Quinn, did you see that?"

"I'm not receiving a visual from you."

"You aren't? Damn. I saw something. I don't know what it was."

"My guess would be that what you saw was an Immani, considering you are aboard their ship."

Though the translator's tone was emotionless, Wilder detected the Fila's sarcastic note. "Okay, okay. Don't forget I'm alone in a ship full of giant aliens. You've got to admit a little jitteriness is only to be expected."

"My advice is to attend the meeting with the Immani as soon as possible in order to overcome your nervousness."

"I'm working on it."

Wilder resumed her progress. She was finding it hard to maintain close contact with the walls. She was glad she'd decided to not bring the a-grav machine. Quinn was confident the Immani wouldn't simply take the machine from her and kick her out, but Wilder was not so trusting. She had dismantled the machine and deleted all recordings of its operation from the ship's data before leaving the *Opportunity*. But in any case, transporting the machine through the Immani ship would only have made things more difficult.

She pushed herself gently along, turning her head slightly as she did so. Something huge was rushing toward her from behind. Wilder gave a small shriek and sped away, fast.

In fact, she moved so fast she failed to notice the creature approaching her from in front. She collided with it, sinking into a soft, billowing surface. For a moment, she was lost in folds of white and she struggled, trying to find her way out. Then the spongey surface hardened and she was forced outward, ejected into the passageway.

An Immani floated on each side of her, blocking any possibility of escape. The creatures looked different from how Wilder remembered them. At the space station they'd been wearing EVA suits and their four limbs had been held to the floor by magnetism. Here on their ship she was looking at them from a different angle. She guessed what she was seeing was the top of their dome-like upper halves.

A circle of black dots wreathed each white head. Were the dots eyes? And where were their mouths? If they didn't have mouths, how did they breath? The creatures' four long legs were beyond Wilder's field of vision.

"Welcome aboard our ship, *does not translate*," said a voice.

"Thanks," Wilder replied, wondering what they had called her.

"Before we begin negotiations," said the voice, "I must warn you that Scythian vessels have been sighted approaching this sector. Our talk must be brief. We may not have time to come to a clear agreement before you must return to your ship and the life support system that can sustain you in the event of an attack."

"Holy crap," said Wilder.

"That term has no equivalent in any of our languages. Could you please rephrase?"

"We're going to be attacked by the Scythians?"

"That appears to be their preferred behavior."

"But what's drawn them here?"

"It's possible they tracked your ship departing your planet's star system, or they may have intercepted and deciphered the comms the Fila sent about your work with gravity devices. The technology is priceless. For obvious reasons, the Scythians would prefer only they possessed it."

"Wow, this is super bad." Wilder had never been the sole target of a Scythian attack. She didn't like the special attention.

"That's an accurate summation of the situation," said the voice. "Let us begin negotiations. What's your desired payment for the a-grav technology?"

"Well," said Wilder, "I just thought of something, or rather, some things."

CHAPTER TWENTY-SEVEN

Pain lanced into Cherry's knees and the heel of her hand, but she had no choice except to crawl on. She could already feel death edging toward her. She couldn't remember the last time she'd sweated, and she could only produce a few drops of dark amber urine. Blinding headaches and muscle cramps plagued her so badly she could barely sleep. When she did nap for a few minutes, she dreamed of wide pools of fresh, clean water, lying only meters from her. She would drag herself toward a pool, scoop a handful of the precious fluid, lift it to her lips—and wake up.

If she could produce tears, she would have cried. But crying would not fix her water condenser, which had broken one of the two times she'd fallen onto her backpack or when the Guardian had slammed her into a wall.

However, she was nearly at the boundary of the Scythian city. If she could make it there and push through, her comm might reach someone in Chimera.

How long had it taken her to navigate the maze-like drops that covered the ground from the buildings to the city boundary wall? Cherry could not remember. In her weakened state, it took her hours to traverse the long, roaming fissures that threaded the surface, and all the concentration she could muster to avoid falling into them. She recalled she'd spent at least one rest period lying on a lane, terrified she might move in her sleep and tumble to her death.

In spite of the ambient temperature of the underground city, Cherry shivered with cold whenever she stopped moving. She had long since abandoned her sleeping bag and all other equipment except her night goggles, her knife, and the bag that contained the Guardian's head.

When her dehydration had gotten so bad she could no longer walk and was forced to use her only hand to crawl, she had slung the string of the bag across her body. As she dragged herself along, the bag hung awkwardly beneath her, its contents catching on the ground and bumping her knees.

But now she was on that final, straight lane that led all the way to the boundary. If she could only make it that far, she might be okay. Doggedly, Cherry forced her hand to reach forward. Grimacing, she placed it on the ground. She had wrapped it in a sleeve she'd ripped from her top. The layer of cloth offered some protection but her skin had chafed away and her flesh was bruised, sore, and weeping. Her knees were in an even worse state. She hadn't looked at them in days, fearing that what she might see would dampen her resolve to make it back to Chimera.

It wasn't that she wanted to live so badly. Her motivation was spurred by her need to find out what secrets hid within the Guardian's electronic brain. It had gone to the city for a reason, a reason that could be vital to the colony's survival.

How much farther to go? In her current mental fog, she couldn't estimate the distance. Like the pools in her dreams, the wall seemed impossible to reach. But she'd come so far, she couldn't give up.

The journey back had been much more arduous than she'd imagined. The effort to climb out of the room where she'd deactivated the Guardian had nearly killed her. By the time she'd climbed up to the arched opening, her hand was a bloody mess, her teeth and jaw felt ready to detach from her head, and her leg and stomach muscles shook. She'd collapsed on the narrow ledge between two rooms, already perceiving an inkling of just how hard her return trip was going to be.

If she'd only had water she might not have suffered so much, but after each sleep she'd woken up thirstier, and as time went on the parched atmosphere had sucked her dry.

The rooms that she'd climbed into and out of quickly on her way through the city had turned into monumental trials of effort and willpower. She'd reached the end of her reserves of energy yet had been forced to continue onward, digging deeper to the utter limits of her strength.

She'd never liked spending time in the Scythian city, but during the course of her return journey she'd grown to hate it. She detested the stench of the air—though she could no longer smell it—she loathed the piles of fragmented decay that blanketed some of the rooms, and she despised the arched openings that provided the only method of moving through the metropolis.

Why didn't the Scythians use roads? Surely they needed roads? It made no sense. It was almost as if the aliens had created the habitation hundreds of thousands of years ago with the express purpose of making her journey as difficult as possible.

Cherry reached forward, but this time her hand didn't land on the smooth black surface of the floor. It touched a soft surface that gave a little under the pressure.

She'd made it! She was at the boundary wall.

Her eyes screwed up and a hoarse croak issued from her throat, but no tears came. She sat back on her haunches. The bag she was carrying rested in the hollow between her hip bones. Was the wall the right color? Her vision was blurry. She concentrated her gaze on the vertical surface in front of her. It was green, the softest of the materials the Scythians used in their constructions. Yet despite the fact that it was the easiest material to force herself through, Cherry wasn't sure she had the strength to do it.

There was nothing for her to do except to try. She leaned forward and pressed her head against the spongy surface. Her forehead sank into it, but the wall held under the meager pressure she exerted. Her shoulders sunk and she struggled to remain upright. Her knees were screaming in agony.

She had to get through the wall somehow, but she wasn't strong enough to do it unaided.

Then she remembered her knife. She had blunted the blade somewhat when she'd sawn through the silicon, metal, and plastic of the Guardian's neck, but the boundary wall didn't require a sharp edge to penetrate it.

Cherry took out her knife. Holding it like a dagger, she pierced the green surface with its tip and then drew the blade downward. A slit appeared. Before the material could rejoin, she slipped the knife into its sheath and forced her fingertips into the barely visible line. Pulling it to one side, she created a hole and caught a glimpse of the area beyond the city. She even thought she could see the far cliff face and the excavation vehicle that stood at its top.

She pushed the top of her head into the gap she'd created. The soft material closed around it, but Cherry moved forward quickly, easing her shoulders into the softened space. As her chest entered the wall, the bag around her torso caught and dragged. She forced herself onward, knowing this was going to be her last expense of effort for a long while, perhaps forever.

Finally, somehow, she was mostly through the wall. She collapsed, her calves and feet still embedded in the green matter.

She tried to comm, but her throat made only a choking noise. She coughed dryly and tried again. "Hello? Can anyone hear me?" she whispered.

***

Water, sweet water, was dribbling between her lips. At first, Cherry thought she was dreaming. She thought she'd finally reached the pool in her dream and that when she woke up she would be back in the dry Scythian city, in pain and alone, far from people who cared about her.

But this time when she opened her eyes a different sight greeted her. She saw a dark green cloth hanging near her face. She could also hear noises. The deafening silence of the Scythian city was gone. She could hear movement and indistinct voices.

The water was real. It was real. Cherry reached up and blindly grabbed at the space the water seemed to have come from. Her hand met flesh. Her grip folded around an arm, though her tender, injured palm protested at the touch.

"Whoa, take it easy." The arm removed itself from Cherry's grip. "I'm glad to see you're feeling better."

Cherry turned her head to see the owner of the voice. It was a young man she didn't recognize.

"I get it. You're thirsty," he said. "But I have to rehydrate you slowly. Your organs are on the brink of failing. If they receive too much water too fast it could overwhelm them and tip them over the edge. But a little more is okay." He held a sponge over Cherry's lips and gently squeezed it.

More exquisite moisture entered her mouth. She

swallowed. The taste wasn't exactly like water: it was a little sweet and salty.

"If I had a drip I could be more scientific about this," said the young man, "but none of the supplies I asked for have arrived from Lyonesse yet, and the Suddeners didn't bring any intravenous infusion equipment from Port City. Don't worry, though. I think you're going to be fine. Though if you'd spent another few hours longer in this state I might not be saying that."

"Who are you?" Cherry asked.

The young man smiled. "I'm sorry. I'm Dr. Zhang. I'm in charge of medical care at Chimera."

"You're from the warehouses?"

"That's right. I came over on a heli. There are a lot of vulnerable people here who require care."

"Wait," said Cherry. "Where's my head?"

Dr. Zhang's mouth rounded to an O. "Er, you need a little more rehydration. Here, have some more of this." He lifted the sponge.

"No," Cherry said, "I need to activate the head. I have to find out what the Guardian was doing in the city." She coughed weakly.

"Oh, you mean that thing you brought back with you? It's a head? Okay. That's kinda weird. I think it's around here somewhere."

Cherry tried to sit up. She saw the interior of a tent, then everything went black. When she came around, Zhang's face was close to hers, his features creased with concern.

"Please don't do that again. You must remain still and rest until you're better."

"I need the head," Cherry insisted.

"All right," Zhang replied. "If it's that important I'll ask someone to find it for you. But you must promise me you'll stop trying to get up."

"Just get me the head," Cherry said between her teeth.

***

In the end, it was two days before Cherry could get out of bed. When she walked, she hobbled like someone twice her age. Her knees and hand were covered in thick scabs under their medical gauze, and her pillow was covered with her hair, which had fallen out while she lay recuperating from her near-fatal bout of dehydration. What remained was thin and patches of baldness showed through it.

During her waking moments she'd gotten to know the inside of the medical tent better than she liked. There was nothing for her to do except look around it. She had no interface, and Doctor Zhang had taken out her ear comm, probably concerned about high stress levels impacting her recovery.

The place they'd put her only accommodated two beds. The other one was empty. In her minute examination of the tent, she'd noticed holes in the material stretched above her head, but they didn't matter in the depths of the Chimera site.

Her only other distraction had been the sounds that came through the thin material. The place was noisier than it had been when she left it. She guessed that the vulnerable colonists that Zhang had mentioned were arriving all the time from Lyonesse, swelling the numbers sheltering in the safest place in Concordia.

The second time she'd woken, Zhang had told her the Guardian's head had been found, but he refused to allow her to have it. The pleasant-mannered doctor had become almost belligerent.

What do you imagine you're going to do with it in your current state? he'd demanded. *Lie still. Get better. Then you can do whatever you want with your precious head.*

Now she *was* better. Maybe not a hundred percent, but she could move around without falling over, and that was good enough for her.

She had walked up and down the narrow space in the center of the tent three or four times without leaning on the bunks. She felt strong enough to go outside. This time, she wouldn't ask Zhang for the Guardian's head, she would demand it. As far as she knew, she remained the general of the colony. She could do whatever she wanted. No one had the authority to boss her around. Not unless a new Leader had been elected, and Cherry doubted anyone had time for that.

Cherry shuffled unsteadily over to the tent flap. She ran her hand down the join, breaking it open. But before she could go out, someone appeared on the other side. Cherry almost collided with the new arrival. Startled, she stepped backward and almost fell.

Isobel entered the tent, looking as surprised as Cherry felt. Or maybe her expression was more horrified than surprised. The woman's belly seemed larger than Cherry remembered it, impossibly large.

"*Cherry*?" Isobel exclaimed. Then she quickly added, "Here, let me help you back to bed." She reached for Cherry's arm.

"I'm okay," Cherry snapped, moving her arm out of Isobel's reach. "I need to leave."

"Why? Are you looking for this?" Isobel lifted up a full bag.

Cherry recognized it instantly. "Yes. You have the head?"

"I was bringing it to you. Please, sit down. I hate to say it, but you look awful. Sit on the bed and we can look at the head together. Zhang told me I'd better bring it to you soon or he wouldn't be answerable for what you might do. I've been working on it ever since you brought in."

"Working on it?" Cherry asked. "What do you mean? What have you done to it?"

Isobel had moved to Cherry's bunk and was sitting on it. The cast from her lower leg was gone. "Nothing risky. Come over here and I'll explain."

She waited until Cherry had sat down next to her before removing the head from the bag. Cherry hadn't looked at it since hacking it from the Guardian's body. Close up in the clear light of the tent's lamp, it looked hideous. The head's single eye was frozen half open. The area underlying the missing half of its face was a mess of blackened, melted plastic. Half the mouth was gone and the tongue and inner surface of the teeth on the remaining side were clearly visible. Frizzy remnants of fake hair clung to the mostly bald scalp.

Removing the head from the rest of the body hadn't been easy. Cherry's sawing and slicing had left a ragged shambles of a neck below the ravaged face and skull.

"I think I found out how to reactivate it," said Isobel, resting the head against her bulbous belly. "It's this nodule here, right?" She turned the head over and pointed to the small, colorless bump behind the ear.

"That's right," Cherry said. "How did you know?"

"My field is robotics engineering," Isobel replied. "I've worked in construction robotics for most of my career. Not exactly the kind of profession you might imagine for the spouse of the colony's chief xenobiologist, is it?"

"I hadn't really thought about it," Cherry replied. In truth, she'd found it hard to see past Isobel's extremely conspicuous pregnancy. She couldn't imagine anyone doing any kind of job while so physically encumbered.

"Anyway," Isobel said, "when I heard you'd been here and you'd gone into the Scythian city, I asked Alun what you were doing. I knew Kes would be worried about you and I thought I could give him an update. Alun explained the situation about the Guardian. Then I heard you were back and you'd brought something very strange with you. I was curious to know what it was, and it wasn't hard for me to get hold of it." She turned the head face downward in her lap. "No one else wanted anything to do with it. I've been taking a look at it while you were recovering. I'll show you what I've found."

Isobel inserted her fingers beneath a flap at the back of the scalp and slid if off, revealing a pale gray skull made from artificial material. Though the outer surface of the Guardian's head had been severely damaged in the heat generated by passing through Concordia's atmosphere, the interior seemed intact and unharmed.

Cherry recalled the android telling her that its memory had been damaged. Had it been lying?

"It was a little tricky to open it," said Isobel. "Whoever made this thing did *not* intend anyone else to mess with it. It's entirely intact. The CPU communicates with the rest of the body wirelessly. In fact, I only found the entry point because it had been forced previously. It was the marks left behind that showed me where to look."

"No kidding," said Cherry, leaning closer to the head. Even so, she could only just see the tiny scratch marks on the smooth artificial skull.

Isobel took a slim piece of metal from her pocket and pressed the edge into an invisible join. She gently worked the metal downward and then gave it a twist. The skull cracked open like a nut.

"It's an absolute marvel of engineering," Isobel said. "I would so love to meet the team that put this together. Unfortunately, it's been tampered with."

"Has it?" Cherry asked.

"Uhuh. Can you see here, and here? Those parts aren't the same as the others. And there are more additions and circumventions if you look closer."

To Cherry's untrained eyes, the sections Isobel pointed at didn't look any different from the rest of the contents of the Guardian's skull, but she was willing to take the woman's word for it.

"Have you tried to reactivate it yet?" she asked.

"No," Isobel replied. "I thought I would wait until you were feeling better and we could do it together. What do you think?"

In light of what Isobel had told her, Cherry was unsure what to do. "The thing is, what if the Scythians were the ones who tampered with the skull? There aren't any other likely candidates. They might have booby-trapped it."

Isobel drew back from the head, covering her bump with her hands. "What makes you think the Scythians have worked on this?"

Cherry briefly told her the story of how the Guardian had returned to Concordia. "But on the other hand," she continued, "if the head were booby-trapped, I'm pretty sure it would have gone off when you opened it."

Isobel had turned pale. "I had no idea. Why didn't Alun tell me? I would never have touched it."

"I didn't have time to explain everything to him, and it was only a guess anyway. But now you've told me someone's tinkered around inside the head, it adds up. I think the Scythians collected the remains of one of the Guardians after the *Mistral* exploded on impact with their ship, and they figured out how to alter its programming to..."

"To what?" Isobel asked.

"I still don't know exactly," Cherry replied.

The two women sat in silence, gazing at the exposed interior of the Guardian's head.

Finally, Cherry said, "I take it you didn't see anything that looked like a booby trap while you were poking around in there?"

"No, I didn't. Nothing at all." Isobel still looked scared. "You're going to activate it, aren't you?"

"I am. I have to. I have to try to find out what it was doing in the city."

"Okay," said Isobel. "Well, I'm going to leave you to it. I'm sorry, but I don't only have myself to think about."

"I understand," Cherry said. "But before you go, could you remove the parts that were added to the CPU?"

Isobel bit her lip. "I'll try. I can't remove all the non-original parts or it won't work, but I think I can take out most of them. Though I'll have to botch it." She reached into the pocket of her smock dress and took out a tiny screwdriver.

Cherry waited as Isobel worked. Thrity minutes later a small pile of hair-fine wires and tiny chips sat on Isobel's lap. The head's interior didn't look any different to Cherry.

CHAPTER TWENTY-EIGHT

Wilder lay down in her seat, glad to be going home. She only hoped she wasn't going back to a lifeless planet. If that was the case, her brief meeting with the Immani would have been for nothing. Not that they had agreed to her terms in the matter of the a-grav machine. As only one member of the Assembly they didn't have the authority. She would have to wait until the organization held a formal meeting before she would know if she'd secured the payment requested.

The *Opportunity* began its first round of deceleration. The load pressed down hard onto Wilder's body, squeezing her rib cage and squashing her pelvis into the soft padding. Her jaw was slowly being forced open. She clenched her teeth to hold it closed.

"Quinn," she said through barely open lips, "are the Scythian ships still approaching?"

"Yes," the Fila replied. "They appear to be intent on following us back to Concordia."

"How fast are they going? Will they catch us?"

"Unfortunately their ships are faster than the *Opportunity* and, according to the Immani, no other ship in the convoy can outpace them either. They will certainly arrive at Concordia at the same time as us if not before. But perhaps they aren't interested in the planet any longer, imagining that it's only a matter of time before the biocide does its work. They may only wish to attack the convoy."

"But surely they won't dare attack all these Assembly ships? They only attacked Concordia because they thought we were weak and defenseless. As soon as things got too tough for them they dropped their biocide and ran. And when I went to the Assembly space station they didn't assault the station itself, they only tried to kill us, the representatives of humanity. It seems to me they're cowards."

"Or smart and pragmatic," Quinn said. "I cannot read their minds, Wilder. All I know is that we must return as fast as we can and attempt to protect the remaining populations of Fila and humans."

"Maybe we should turn and fight them. Make a stand, you know?"

"That would delay the convoy's arrival at Concordia and the rescue attempt."

Wilder had no reply for Quinn and her jaw ached from trying to speak while under the deceleration load. She gave up talking with the Fila and tried to distract herself from her discomfort by mentally working on the problem of reversing the a-grav force in order to generate gravity.

After a few hours, just when Wilder was thinking she'd reached the limit of her endurance of the deceleration, Quinn mercifully slowed the ship. He set the speed to create an effect roughly equivalent to Concordia's gravity, so when Wilder climbed off her seat she could walk around the ship. Her leg muscles remained weak from her weeks in micro-g. She walked slowly through to the living quarters and immediately went to Piddle and Puddle's pouches.

When she opened the tops of the pouches, Piddle and then Puddle immediately climbed out, ran up her arms, and sat on her shoulders. Knowing what they expected next, Wilder walked to the cupboard that held her rations and gave each of the creatures a piece of Stephie's hard-baked cookies. After they'd eaten it would be grooming time. Wilder returned her pets to one pouch they could share for the activity.

Piddle and Puddle were in much better shape than her. After their period of adjustment, they seemed to be thriving aboard the starship. Their coats were shiny and soft, and they'd both put on weight, developing a roundness to their bellies that was irresistible. Wilder gave each of the tummies a rub and then closed the top of the pouch.

The same couldn't be said about her own stomach, which was concave with her two hip bones protruding on each side. Wilder took out one of the remaining meals Stephie had cooked for her and heated it up.

As she was eating, Quinn spoke.

"Wilder, I've been thinking about our conversation about the Scythian ships. I've had an idea, but it requires your agreement."

Wilder swallowed and put down her fork. "Shoot."

"As I said before, it's possible that the Scythians aren't interested in preventing the Assembly from helping Concordia. They may know about your a-grav device and want it for themselves."

"The Immani said that too. They said the Scythians may have deciphered your comms with them."

"If that's so," Quinn said, "then they're chasing us because they want the *Opportunity*, or, more specifically, the a-grav machine. Or, failing that, its inventor."

"Huh," said Wilder. "How flattering. So what's your idea?"

"The *Opportunity's* defenses are no match for the

combined weaponry of the Scythian ships, but what they perceive as our weakness could actually be our strength. We can use the *Opportunity* as bait."

"Bait? What's that?"

"You don't recognize the word? It's a term used when hunting animals."

"Oh. I don't think a lot of that goes on in Concordia."

"The bait is the food or prey animal used to attract the hunted animal in order to capture or kill it."

"Uhuh," Wilder said uncertainly. Now she understood what Quinn meant, she was getting a little worried about where he was going with his idea. "You want to use me as a prey animal?"

"We would need to work out the details with the Assembly, but essentially, yes. We may be able to use the *Opportunity* to draw the Scythian ships into a disadvantageous position and then attack them."

"Right," Wilder said. "Ummm. I'll need a few minutes to think about that."

"While you're thinking, I'll arrange a second rendezvous with the Immani ship. We cannot risk our comms being intercepted again."

CHAPTER TWENTY-NINE

The moment the news arrived from Lyonesse, it spread through Chimera like wildfire: the scientists had developed a medicine that protected against the biocide. They were creating it in bulk and sending it out to all the refuge sites as fast as they could. All the colonists had to do was sit tight and wait for their doses to arrive.

"Is what I heard right?" Cherry asked Zhang when he came to check up on her. "There's a treatment that protects people from the biocide?"

"Look up," said Zhang. He was holding a pencil light and he shone it in her eyes. He turned off the light and put it on the camping table. He pinched the skin on her arm, released it, and peered at the spot. "Your color and tone is better today." The doctor began to take out more equipment from a case. "Yes, you heard right. It's called a vaccine. It's a prophylactic treatment that stimulates an immune response. It's very interesting. Give me your hand."

Cherry held out her hand and Zhang clipped something to her finger.

"I haven't seen the schedule for rolling out the treatment program," Zhang continued, "but it would make sense if Chimera were to be the last refuge to receive it. It's the site most remote from the biocide."

"Yeah," said Cherry, "that does make sense." For what she had in mind, she wouldn't need the medicine for a long while. She would probably be the last to receive it after she returned.

As Dr. Zhang completed her checkup, she complied with his requests, opening her mouth and poking out her tongue, allowing him to carry out his various tests. She gave him the urine sample he'd asked for. While he ran it through a device that checked it for who knew what, she said, "I feel a lot better now. Pretty much back to normal."

"That's good," said Zhang, reading the results of her urine test on his interface. "You aren't quite there yet, though. You must get as much rest as you can over the next few weeks. After that I recommend monthly checkups for a year, followed by bi-annual checkups."

"But I feel fine," Cherry said.

"You nearly died of dehydration," the doctor replied. "That isn't something you recover from within a few days. The effects will be long lasting. They may last a lifetime."

Cherry frowned.

"It isn't so bad, is it?" Zhang asked. "Better than the alternative."

"I'll just have to take along several water condensers when I return to the Scythian city," Cherry said.

Zhang paused, carefully put down his interface on the table, and turned to face her. "Tell me you're kidding."

"I have to go back in there," Cherry said. "It's a lot to explain, but if I don't, the *Opportunity* is going to be shot to pieces and so will all the Assembly ships when they arrive." She wasn't even sure the *Opportunity* hadn't already been destroyed, but she guessed that if the Scythian defense system had fired she would have heard about it.

"You can't go back in there," Zhang said. "It's out of the question."

"I have to go. No one else here can do what needs to be done." What that was exactly, Cherry wasn't sure. Perhaps Faina would know. But the Scythian defense system had to be put out of action.

Zhang put away his equipment and snapped his case closed. "I'm sorry, but that isn't happening. You'll have to find someone else to do the work for you."

"I told you, there isn't anyone else," said Cherry. Who could she trust to listen to an android's wrecked head? She could barely stand to look at it herself. And traveling through the Scythian city was like enduring a waking nightmare. At least *she* knew what to expect. "Anyway, you can't stop me from going."

Zhang tilted his head. "Can't I?"

"No. I'm still the general of this colony."

"And I'm only a doctor. I get it. But you're forgetting I can declare you mentally incompetent." Zhang's pleasant manner had entirely disappeared. His gaze was frank and unblinking. "I can have you restrained— for your own safety."

Cherry opened her mouth to speak but then closed it again. She muttered, *"Shit."*

Zhang's expression softened. "Cherry, if you go back into that place in your current condition, you'll die. There's no doubt in my mind. Then who's going to do this thing that's so important for the safety of the Assembly ships?"

"I'm telling you, no one else can do it."

"Neither can you." Zhang picked up his bag. "The colony's problems are beyond my remit. I just fix people. If I could help you, I would, but you'll have to figure this one out by yourself." He left the tent.

Cherry lay down on her bed. She couldn't deny she still felt weak. Her comment to the doctor about feeling much better had been bravado. He was probably right that her body wouldn't cope with another feat of endurance. Yet who could go into the Scythian city in her place? People like Alun and other members of the Chimera site excavation team were fit and strong, but finding and deactivating the Scythian defense system would take more than fitness and strength.

The job required someone who understood at least a little about military defenses, and who wouldn't be freaked out by Faina's head. Kes fell into the latter camp but he already had his hands full producing the medication that protected against the biocide. Cherry racked her brains. Perhaps someone in the military could do it. If only Phy were still alive. She could always be relied upon to do a job right.

When the obvious answer popped into her head, Cherry sat up. She swung her legs off her bunk and stood up. She needed an external comm to Lyonesse, fast.

CHAPTER THIRTY

Kes watched the brown, dead landscape pass beneath the heli, trying to stay awake. Zapata, the pilot, had woken him to say they were only a few minutes from the refuge. Kes had dropped off as soon as the heli had taken to the air and slept for the entire hour's trip, yet he remained exhausted.

He hadn't seen his bed since Tycho had survived contact with the biocide. Every moment of his and the other scientists' time had been devoted to manufacturing the vaccine. The scientists were administering the vaccine, too, as there were more helis than doctors at the refuge. It was a monumental effort to complete the immunization of Concordia's population as fast as possible.

Kes' fatigue was making him airsick and the noise of the rotor was pounding into his head despite his ear mufflers. While he waited to reach the refuge and begin work, he mentally went over the progress of the vaccination program. After vaccinating everyone at the warehouses, they had flown out to the refuge nearest the Vimur. The green country surrounding Concordia's largest river was rapidly being laid waste by the biocide, and if the virus reached the water it would kill every Fila sheltering there. The team that had vaccinated the people at the river refuge had left equipment and instructions on how to create a similar firebreak to the one that had been built around the warehouse site. Sterile zones at the river's edge might not provide the Fila with permanent protection but it would buy time until the colonists figured out a better solution.

The military sheltering at the missile silos had also been vaccinated. The possibility of the Scythians' return when they realized their attempt at annihilation had failed was high. The idea of a second, and probably final, onslaught, filled Kes with despair. How could the colony continue to survive, faced by a technologically superior enemy who was determined to destroy it?

So many times, the colony had hauled itself back from the brink and gone on to enjoy periods of peace and plenty, yet it would never be free from the possibility of attack. But what else could all Concordians do except battle on, as they had always done? Kes closed his eyes. He suddenly felt old and jaded. All he wanted to do was see Isobel and Miki again.

"I can't see them," said Zapata.

Kes opened his eyes, confused momentarily, thinking the pilot was referring to his wife and child. "What?" He adjusted his mic, which had slipped under his chin.

"According to the most recent report of their location, they should be right down there," Zapata said. "I can't see them. Can you?"

Kes leaned to one side to get a clear view of the ground beneath the heli. It was as brown and dead as the rest of the landscape. If anyone was down there, they were dead. However, Kes couldn't see any signs of bodies or a habitation.

"They must have moved on when the biocide

approached," he said. "I guess they would have followed the highway."

Zapata nodded and took the heli higher before flying it in the direction of the long gray ribbon that dissected the dull landscape. In a few minutes they reached the creeping line of the biocide and flew over it. Kes glimpsed it moving beneath them, consuming all in its path.

Roughly fifteen minutes later they found the refuge. The assembled tents looked weatherbeaten. No people were visible on the ground. The place looked in a bad way.

Zapata set down the heli on a patch of level, green ground a considerable distance from the tents out of fear that the rotor's downdraft would blow them away. Kes jumped out and ran with his bag of vaccine doses over his shoulder to the refuge. Drawn, scared faces looked out from open tent flaps as he approached.

"Have you brought us water?" asked a teenage boy, climbing out of a tent.

"No," said Kes. "I've brought some medi—"

"We need water," the kid said. "We're nearly out. I sent in a request four days ago."

"I'm sorry," Kes replied. "I don't know anything about that. But I'm sure someone's on it. You're the coordinator here?"

"Yes. We need food too."

Kes looked the boy up and down. He couldn't be much older than fourteen. He checked out the faces peering from the other tents. They all seemed very old or very young. He stepped over to the coordinator and held out his hand. "What's your name?"

"Niall," the boy replied, shaking hands.

"Hi, Niall. I'm Kes. You're doing a great job, but I have to tell you, we flew over the biocide line only about forty miles from here. You need to pack up soon and move on."

"I know it isn't far away," said Niall, "but I heard there's another line approaching from the north. The only way we can go is south but the terrain there is hilly and difficult. We're getting squeezed in a trap. And we can't move fast. Some of us can only walk slowly."

"I hear you," said Kes. "I'll try to arrange some help. Maybe..." Kes wondered if the helis could come in and airlift everyone at the camp to the warehouses, where they would be safer. But the helis were all needed for distributing the vaccine. "I don't know exactly what we'll do yet, but at the very least we'll get water and food out to you as quickly as we can. Meanwhile, I'm here to give you some medication to protect you from the biocide."

The boy's face lit up. "Does it really work? Then we won't need to go anywhere."

"It does work," said Kes, "but it takes at least a week to become effective."

Niall's face fell. "The biocide will be here long before then."

"Yes, it will, so I'm afraid after I give you the vaccine you must move. And there's something else you need to know: the treatment probably won't be effective for everyone."

"You mean some of us could still die if the biocide arrives?"

"Not *if* the biocide arrives," Kes said. "When. There's nothing we can do to halt its progress. When it catches up to your group, it's possible one or two of you may not be protected by the medication."

"Is there any way to tell which of us that will be?" Niall asked.

"There is, but we simply don't have the time or the equipment to check, and even if we knew who wasn't protected there's nothing we could do to help them. It's just going to be a matter of luck."

Niall's face fell. "I'll try to keep them away from the

biocide as long as I can."

Kes pitied the boy, who was carrying far more responsibility than he should have to at his age. "I know you'll do your best. Could you gather everyone together? I'll administer the vaccine now."

CHAPTER THIRTY-ONE

Cherry waited for him outside Chimera, standing in the shade just inside the tunnel entrance. It was midday, and until her eyes adjusted the sunlight had been blinding. In spite of her protected position the heat hit her, radiating from the sand and the sun-warmed tunnel wall, and gusting in on the hot breeze.

Aside from the murmur of the wind, the desert was so quiet she heard the heli before she saw it. Then a black dot appeared in the sky. The heli was flying low and its form flickered and shifted in the shimmer of heated air. The aircraft landed in the same place Zapata had set down when Cherry had arrived, next to the road that led to the excavation site. The solid gate in the perimeter fence blocked her view, and as the heli lowered she lost sight of it.

The noise of its engine and rotors didn't cease. Within less than a minute the heli was airborne again and swooping around, heading back to Lyonesse. No doubt the machine and its pilot were needed to deliver the medication that protected against the biocide. None had arrived in Suddene yet.

The person guarding the gate seemed to be a woman, though the copious amounts of light, flowing fabric swathing the figure made its gender ambiguous. As far as Cherry knew, Laurie hadn't been assigned gate duty after the incident involving her. The guard prepared to open the gate. It had all been arranged with Alun's approval.

Cherry waited, sweat droplets crawling down her face, neck, and back. How long had it been since she'd seen Aubriot face to face? It had to be weeks, or months. It felt like years. Their long history traveled a path in her mind in the few minutes it took him to walk from the heli drop off to the gate. From its beginning in the ruins of the first settlement, through the tense months in Sidhe while the colony awaited the full wrath of the Scythians to descend, and on to the aftermath, the rebuilding *again*. Then had come the mission to the Assembly space station, when, after weeks of coldness, Aubriot had angrily confronted her about her true feelings for Ethan.

Had she wronged him? She didn't think so. Their arrangement had been platonic and mutually beneficial, she'd thought. She didn't think she owed him anything, and she hadn't expected any more from him than she'd gotten. But either there had been a misunderstanding or something had changed along the course of their relationship and she'd missed it.

After returning to a Concordia fifty Earth years on from the one they had left, Aubriot had withdrawn from her and gone a little crazy, neglecting his duties, drinking too much, and sleeping around. But lately he'd been better, calmer, and warmer toward her, trying to make her feel better about the terrible effects of the decisions she'd made. Now, she had no idea how things stood between them.

When she'd asked him to go into the Scythian city to find and disable the aliens' military defense system he'd quickly agreed. It had taken a day for a heli to collect him from Cerberus and bring him to Suddene.

The guard opened the gate, and then there he was, walking toward her. A rush of confused emotions swept over her: gratitude that he had come to do the work she could not, a sense of affinity that only the four who had experienced the leap into the future shared, and a pleasant warmth at the familiar sight of him. They had shared many good times even though things had gone bad later. And something else.

He stepped into the shadow of the tunnel entrance, already dusty and sweaty from his short walk.

"Hi." He dropped his bag onto the sandy tunnel floor and regarded Cherry impassively.

"Hi," Cherry replied, looking up at him. "Thanks for coming."

"What was I going to do? Say no?"

Ugh. She'd almost forgotten what an asshole he could be.

"Come on," she said. "We have to drive down to the excavation site."

Alun had loaned her one of the survey vehicles and she'd driven it up the tunnel herself, though with difficulty. She was used to cars that mostly drove themselves, and having only one arm hadn't made things any easier.

Aubriot threw his bag on the back seat and peered at the vehicle's controls. "Want me to drive?"

"Sure," said Cherry. She climbed into the passenger seat.

"It's been a while since I actually *drove* a car," Aubriot commented as he started up the engine. The headlights turned on and they set off down the tunnel.

"How long is it?" asked Cherry. "A couple hundred years?"

"Longer than that," Aubriot replied. "Over two hundred and fifty or thereabouts. I lost count. It doesn't matter. Time's a weird concept when you think about it. I mean, how old am I? If I hadn't left Earth I..." He didn't complete the sentence.

Cherry glanced at Aubriot's profile, puzzled about why he'd stopped speaking. They were beyond the reach of natural daylight. His features were outlined by the minimal lighting in the tunnel and the backwash of the car's headlights. His expression told her something was bothering him.

"What?" Cherry asked.

Aubriot scowled. "Before I go into the city, I need to talk to you."

"You can talk to me now."

"No. It might take a while." Aubriot threw her a quick look before returning his attention to the road. He seemed in a bad mood. Surely he wasn't still sore at her? After all this time?

"Okay," Cherry replied.

After a couple of minutes' driving in silence, Aubriot said, "I want to take a team with me into the city. I hoped to bring a few good soldiers from Cerberus, but transportation is a problem."

"You might find some volunteers among the excavation crew. I warn you, it's a hellish place to navigate. You'll have to take plenty of water."

"I know," Aubriot said. "You already told me. And I'll have to take the head."

"Yeah, the head too."

"You know, when I told you to cut the Guardian's head off," said Aubriot, "I wasn't expecting you to actually do it."

Cherry gave a grim, tight smile. "Neither was I."

***

Alun had begun the preparations for the expedition into the Scythian city before Aubriot's arrival, so it only took a couple of hours to gather additional supplies to support the two men and one woman who volunteered to accompany Aubriot. Alun was one of the volunteers, and the one Cherry was least concerned about. The site supervisor was already somewhat familiar with the strange, stinking place beneath Suddene's desert. She hoped the other two—the man was named Simon and the woman was called Abby—had strong stomachs and minds.

When all was ready, Aubriot told the team to check all the equipment one more time and then to relax and wait for him. He asked Cherry if there was somewhere they could talk privately.

She took him to the medical tent where she had recuperated. She'd since moved out of there and was sharing a place with Isobel and Miki, but she knew the medical tent was currently unused.

Cherry closed the tent flaps after she and Aubriot went inside. The enclosed place smelled faintly of antiseptic ointment. She climbed onto her former bed, her muscles tensing up with apprehension, though she didn't know what Aubriot wanted to talk about. It was out of character for him to want to have a serious discussion about *anything*. He was the champion of flippant remarks and emotional distance.

Aubriot sat on the other bunk. Cherry's shorter legs swung from her bed, but his feet were planted flat on the ground, his knees akimbo. He leaned forward and rested his elbows on his knees. His brow furrowed into deep creases as he mentally wrestled with whatever was troubling him.

"Sorry," he said.

Cherry lifted her eyebrows. She couldn't remember ever hearing Aubriot apologize. The effect was unnerving.

"It's hard to know where to start," Aubriot continued. He glanced at the tent wall. "Are you sure we can't be overheard?"

"As sure as I can be," Cherry replied. "We can walk

to the other side of the site if you want. No one will hear us over there."

"No, no. It's fine." Aubriot sighed and straightened up. He rubbed the side of his nose.

"You know," said Cherry, "if this is about us...what you accused me of while we were aboard the *Opportunity*..." It was the only thing she could think of that might explain why he wanted to have a serious discussion with her. She recalled his fury vividly.

Aubriot waved dismissively at her. "Water under the bridge." He frowned. "All right. Here goes. The thing is, well, something you should know is, I can't have kids." He studied her, watching her expression to see how she felt about this news.

"Oh, uh, I'm sorry." Cherry was even more puzzled. Was this revelation really *that* important? Then a realization struck her. "Hey! I always made sure we used birth control and we didn't have to! Why didn't you tell me this before?"

Aubriot shrugged. "I don't go around telling everyone. It's private."

"What we were *doing* was private!" Cherry heard her voice had become loud with indignation. She lowered her tone lest their discussion attract unwanted attention. "What we were doing was private, and I wasn't just *anyone*. Or at least I hope not. We were lovers and I *thought* we were friends, for a long time. Why didn't you tell me?"

"I don't know. It didn't seem important. Not at first, anyway."

"Right," Cherry said. "Well, if that's all you wanted to talk about, like I said, I'm sorry. But I don't understand why you're telling me this now. Alun and the others will be waiting, so maybe you should—"

Aubriot reached across the narrow space between the bunks and grabbed her forearm. His large hand encircled it. "That isn't all I have to tell you." He stared into Cherry's eyes and didn't release his grip. "The reason I can't have kids is due to a decision my parents made when I was just a fertilized egg in a petri dish. They selected a range of genetic modifications for me, including the one that made me infertile. They didn't tell me about it until I was fifteen, when they suggested I undergo fertility testing. Sterility was a risk the doctors warned them about with this particular modification, but they took the risk anyway, on my behalf. I had no say in it."

"You're hurting me," said Cherry.

Aubriot let go of her arm. "I'm sorry." He got up and then sat down next to her. Reaching around her shoulders, he pulled her close. "You're the first person I've ever told about this. I want to ask you to never tell anyone else, though I suppose it's bound to come out eventually."

"About your sterility?" Cherry was becoming alarmed by Aubriot's behavior. Infertility was extremely rare among Concordians, but she had heard of one or two cases. It wasn't shameful, however, and she didn't understand why he would want to keep it a secret.

"No. That's only a side effect I wanted you to know about." Several moments passed, and then Aubriot let out a long exhale. "Cherry, the genetic engineering my parents requested that ended up making me sterile was an experimental and illegal procedure. It was designed to confer extreme longevity."

"Right, so you're going to live for a long time. That doesn't seem too bad. Do you know how long?"

"I don't know for sure. Before I left Earth I had myself tested for the last time. By then I was forty-five and my cells displayed no signs of aging. I might live an extra two or three hundred years, or a thousand, or maybe I'll never die from old age. I just don't know."

Cherry rested her head on Aubriot's chest, digesting this new information. Suddenly, she sat upright. "When it became obvious that you weren't growing any older, wouldn't your parents have been arrested? Is that why you created the *Nova Fortuna* Project? Because you wanted to leave Earth?"

"Both my parents had died before I began the project," said Aubriot. "It turned out that all the money in the world couldn't save them from drug addiction. I assume they died happy. But, you're right, I was worried what might happen to me as time went on. When your face is one of the most well known in the world it's hard to hide the fact that you never grow older. I could have faked my death, had surgery, and done the same again and again, but I would have spent my life always worrying about being found out. The Earth I left wasn't kind to people who altered their 'natural' state. I hadn't chosen to be what I was, but that wouldn't have made any difference to them. I might have faced imprisonment and maybe even execution."

"So you thought if you came to a new planet, where the culture and the rules were different..."

"My problem was only one of the reasons I started up the project, but, yes, I thought if I lived somewhere things were different, somewhere maybe *I* made the rules, then I could live without looking over my shoulder."

Cherry's gaze roved Aubriot's flawless features, his smooth skin, and his hair, which was entirely free of the gray that had already begun to pepper her own. She imagined the years marching on and Aubriot never changing, like a statue or a painting, while all Concordia and everyone in it aged and died, and new life appeared and grew and then also died. It was hard to imagine what it must be like to know your life might never end.

"It's a lot to take in," Aubriot said. "I know. You don't have to say anything. I don't need your pity."

"Pity?! Why would I pity you? Who wouldn't want to

live forever?"

"Think about it. I certainly have. It isn't so great if you're the only one. What's it going to be like for everyone I know and love to grow old and die while I carry on living?"

Cherry didn't reply. She'd never heard Aubriot talk of loving anyone. She wasn't even sure he was capable of it. But though she didn't comment, her face must have given away her thoughts. Aubriot's features stiffened in anger.

"I'm not a monster," he spat.

She threw him an irritated glance and hopped down from the bunk. "The others are waiting for you."

He grabbed her arm again. "Wait. Please. I haven't finished. Maybe I *am* immortal, but I'm not indestructible. I have to get this off my chest in case I never see you again."

For some reason she didn't fully understand Cherry's eyes filled with tears. "What is it you want to tell me?"

Aubriot swallowed. "I've had a lot of time to think over the last few weeks. After we cleared up the silo and fixed everything that was fixable, there was fuck all to do at Cerberus except wait for the biocide to get us. I've been thinking about my time here, right from when I came out of cryo until you comm'd me after the battle to find out how I was doing. It hasn't been easy. Living this new life has been a lot harder than I thought it would be.

"I know how I come across, Cherry, and for a long time I didn't give a shit. However I behaved, it didn't matter. I always got what I wanted no matter what it was. *Women* wanted me. But not you. You could take me or leave me. To you, I was a convenience, a substitute for the person you wanted but couldn't have. That was quite a blow to my ego, let me tell you.

"I tried to get over myself. After all, you weren't doing anything worse than I'd done myself. Why should

I care? But I couldn't get over it, because it hurt. There I was, the man with the cast iron ego, and my *feelings* were hurt." Aubriot held out his hand. "Come here."

Cherry took a step toward him. He took her hand and broke eye contact, dropping his gaze to the floor. "Before I go down into that place, I want to tell you how much I care about you. If I were to live on after you died of old age, I'd find that hard to bear. I'd wish my parents hadn't laid this curse on me. I know I'm not the easiest person to get along with, or the most likable, and maybe I'll never be this frank about my feelings for you ever again. But I want you to remember what I said. It's true and it's never going to change."

Aubriot raised his head and looked Cherry in the eye. She had never seen an expression on his face like the one she was now seeing. It was like she could see inside him. She took another step forward until they were almost touching and wrapped her arm around his neck. "You mean a lot to me too," she said awkwardly. It wasn't the most romantic conversation but she guessed it was probably the most romantic the two of them were ever going to get.

Aubriot hugged her. As they held each other in silence, Cherry realized how alike they were. Aubriot might be an asshole but in the right circumstances she could be a real bitch. They were pretty well suited.

"I have to go," said Aubriot.

"I know," Cherry replied, but neither released their hold on the other.

Finally, Aubriot was the one to end it. He kissed her briefly on the lips and then stood up. "I'll be back in a few days, barring any disasters."

"Don't forget the head," Cherry said.

Aubriot smiled and bent down to kiss her again. Then he was gone.

CHAPTER THIRTY-TWO

Wilder watched the screen anxiously as the Scythian ships approached. No one knew why they were there or what they planned on doing, and they certainly weren't going to tell. As well as the Immani's guess that they knew about the a-grav machine and wanted it for themselves—or wanted to prevent anyone else from having it—Wilder wondered if they only wanted to destroy the *Opportunity*.

The Scythians knew the ship. They had tracked its journey to the Assembly space station and tried to kill its human occupants after slipping through the station's defenses. At their most recent 'visit' to Concordia, they must have wondered where the ship had gone, but they'd failed to find it where Quinn had hidden it behind the second planet out from the sun. Maybe the Scythians had since seen the *Opportunity* depart the system and they were determined to prevent any human or Fila from escaping.

Or maybe it was all a coincidence. The Scythians could simply be on their way to Concordia to check their biocide had done its work and the planet and everything on it was dead.

Whatever their motivation, Wilder hoped the hostile aliens would fall into the trap the Assembly had set and their fleet would be destroyed. She also hoped the *Opportunity* would survive unscathed. But it would be a close-run thing.

The Scythians had supplemented the fleet that had fought the previous battle, replacing the ships that had been destroyed and returning the number of their fleet to ten, including two of the massive, four-coned vessels with their central pulse-emitting spikes. Some of the ships' forward-facing cones bore the ravages of the conflict, however, and one of the larger ship's splayed fans to the rear was half wrecked. Wilder wondered if these sections of the larger ships were some form of heat-dispersal device. She couldn't guess what other function they could serve.

Against the background of far-distant stars the Scythian ships appeared frozen in space, but Wilder knew they were traveling at tremendous speed.

"What's happening, Quinn?" she asked. "I can't tell *anything* from looking at this interface."

"The Assembly ships are slowing and spreading out. The Scythians will catch up to them more quickly now, but unless their fleet breaks formation they won't be able to engage with all our ships effectively. The distances will be too great. Some of the ships—the Parvus' vessel in particular—are going to pretend to leave, as if in fear."

"Yes," Wilder said. "The Scythians might believe that, considering it was the Parvus who turned the battle against them last time." Despite the dangerous situation, she was feeling excited at the thought of the forthcoming fight. When the Scythians had last attacked she'd felt guilty that she'd never been in any danger like her friends on Concordia. It was good to finally have an active role to play.

"They might," Quinn replied. "Especially because they cannot possibly reach a star to operate their starpower harnessing weapon before the Scythians catch up to them. Without that capability they are quite weak. And it would be reasonable to assume the Scythians would target their ship in vengeance."

"What happens if the Scythians do break formation and go after individual Assembly ships?" asked Wilder.

"I'm not certain," replied Quinn. "I would need to ask the Immani about that."

"After all," Wilder continued, "it would probably only take one or two of the Scythian's smaller ships to destroy the *Opportunity*."

"Perhaps, but she can mount an impressive defense for a vessel her size. And it's unlike the Scythians to take risks."

Quinn was right. The Scythians had consistently shown an element of caution—or even cowardice—in their military engagements. The scout ship that had attacked the first settlement had left when the *Mistral* had shown her bite, and the fleet had fled after the Parvus had redirected the power of Concordia's star at their ships. Wilder hoped the Scythians would take the bait and home in on the *Opportunity*. An entire fleet ganging up on one little ship would be just their style, and also their downfall.

"Can I see the other ships?" Wilder asked. Staring at the Scythian ships was becoming unbearable.

"You can only see them separately," replied Quinn. "They are already too far apart to appear within one screen."

The scene shifted to a silvery, cylindrical ship with rounded ends. Lines of lights ran along the sides, and at what Wilder assumed was the rear, two squared shoulders protruded. A long, wide slit ran across the back. Did the shoulders house the ship's engines? It seemed a reasonable guess, but Wilder knew she could just as easily be wrong. The slit could also be for heat dispersal.

A galaxy of technological development lay beyond Concordia, which was primitive in comparison. Wilder hoped she would live to see and learn about all of it, even if it took a whole lifetime.

"Ah," said Quinn. "The Scythians have broken formation."

The scene switched back to the enemy's vessels. Three were peeling away from the main bunch. They were all the smaller, single-crescent ships.

"Do you know where they're heading?" Wilder asked.

"Extrapolating from their current headings, I would guess they are following the Parvus' starship."

"Oh no," said Wilder. "That wasn't supposed to happen."

"Perhaps they found the prospect of exacting their revenge too hard to resist."

"What will the Parvus do?"

"Fly," Quinn replied. "Their ship is fast."

"But not as fast as the Scythians."

"I don't think so."

"Isn't there something we can do?"

"Others are coming to their aid, circling back."

"This is going to mess up the entire plan," Wilder said.

The screen continued to show the original Scythian fleet, now missing three of its number. Wilder clenched her fists. It was incredibly frustrating to not be able to see what was going on.

"Is anyone firing?" she asked. "What's happening?"

"Nothing, yet," Quinn replied, "but there's no doubt the breakaway Scythian vessels intend to attack the Parvus' ship. They're heading straight for it."

Meanwhile, the remaining seven Scythian ships were drawing ever closer to the *Opportunity*. They seemed to be taking the bait. Nevertheless, it would take a strong attack to defeat them. Would the Assembly force be too weakened by the loss of the ships that had gone to defend the Parvus?

"We are within Concordia's star system," said Quinn.

"We're nearly home!" Wilder exclaimed. "I hope everyone's still okay. Is there any way you can find out?"

"Not at the moment. The remaining Assembly and Scythian ships will draw together somewhere above the planet's surface. Assuming we survive, we will find out what's happened on Concordia after the battle."

CHAPTER THIRTY-THREE

"Ooooooh!"

Cherry jerked awake. She'd been dreaming she was still in the Scythian city and trapped under soft fragments of debris. A nightmare. When she woke she was relieved to realize she was breathing fresh, clean air and that she was in Chimera, in Isobel's tent at night. The light from the lamps at the center of the excavated cavern—lowered due to the lateness of the hour—gently glowed through the tent walls.

A quiet gasp came from the other side of the tent, and Cherry remembered a similar sound had awakened her.

"Isobel?" she whispered. "Are you okay?"

"Uhuh," came the reply.

Cherry let out a mental sigh of relief. The last thing she wanted was for Isobel to give birth right then. The conditions were far from ideal, and though Zhang was there for that kind of thing, Cherry dreaded the prospect of being asked to help out. That had been her first thought when Isobel had offered her a place to sleep, sharing the tent with her and Miki. Cherry would have refused if she hadn't felt a responsibility to look after Kes' wife. She hadn't needed to ask him if he would like her to do it.

Miki was cute, and she hadn't minded playing with her to give Isobel a break, but babies and even the *thought* of childbirth made her anxious and uncomfortable. She hoped Isobel wouldn't pop until she was safely back with Kes on Lyonesse. It seemed like the baby had only kicked her or something like that. Cherry really didn't know or want to know the ins and outs of all the various aches and pains pregnant women suffered.

"I'm okay," Isobel said softly. "It's just...I think the baby is coming."

"What, now?!"

"No, but soon." Isobel gave another quiet gasp. A pause followed, then, "I've been having contractions for a while but I didn't want to wake you."

"You didn't..." Cherry sat up, pushing down her sleeping bag. Isobel was shadowy in the darkness. A shadow with a large bump. Miki lay still beside her, sound asleep. "I'll go and get Dr. Zhang."

"If you wouldn't mind, that would be great. And then could you take Miki to the tent next to ours? The woman there, Carol, offered to look after her when the time came. She has a little boy the same age as Miki."

"Of course I don't mind," Cherry said. She was already pulling on her pants. She pushed her feet into her boots and then went to the tent entrance. "I'll be back with Zhang as quick as I can." Opening the tent flap, she slipped out into the half-light of the Chimera site at night.

The place was never entirely silent but night time was peaceful. Snoring and the cries of fractious babies were the only sounds she heard. The tents threw long shadows on the cavern's walls, which were scored with marks left by the excavators.

Cherry ran quietly to the group of medical tents, where she hoped to find Zhang already working. The first two tents were empty. The next two held a patient each, and the final one held a nurse too, but none of them knew where Zhang was. The nurse thought he was probably sleeping and she told Cherry where to find his tent.

Cherry found it without any problems but Zhang was not inside. Another man was in there, who told her that Zhang had left to attend a birth.

Cherry was momentarily confused. How had Zhang known that Isobel had gone into labor? "When did he leave?" she asked.

"About an hour and a half ago," the man replied.

"Damn," Cherry said. Zhang was attending another laboring woman. "Do you know where he went?"

"No, but…Do you need him for an emergency?"

"Yes, my friend's about to give birth too."

"Whoa," said the man. "Bad timing. You know you can comm him, right?"

"Stars, I didn't think of that! Thanks." Cherry backed out of the tent. How had she managed to forget she could comm the doctor? She was panicking. After a lifetime of facing danger and death, she was panicking over a woman in labor. She took a deep breath and sent the comm.

Zhang's answer was terse. "Yes?"

She explained the situation with Isobel.

"How far apart are her contractions?"

"I don't know. Does it matter?"

"Not at all," Zhang replied acerbically. "I was just making conversation. Look, I'm attending another birth right now and I may be some time. This is Isobel's second labor so it should be straightforward. I'll see if the nurse is available to come over soon, but while you're waiting, time the period between the beginning of one contraction and the beginning of the next. If they get to two minutes apart, let me know. Stay with her and look after her until I can get there." He closed the comm.

Look after her? What did that even mean? But Isobel had been alone for several minutes now. Cherry ran back to her tent. As soon as she poked her head inside, Isobel said:

"Is the doctor here?"

Miki was awake and playing with her teddy.

"He's coming soon," Cherry replied as she climbed into the tent. "Miki, it's time to go and see your friend. Mommy's going to be busy for a little while."

"Yes," Isobel said, "and when you come back you can meet your little sister."

"Oh!" Miki grinned and squeezed her teddy. "I want to meet Nina now!"

"Not yet," said Isobel. "Soon."

Miki stood up and walked to Cherry, who was holding out her hand. Cherry took her to the next tent and quietly woke the sleeping woman inside.

"Tell Isobel good luck," the woman said as Cherry left. "I hope everything goes okay."

"I will," Cherry replied.

When she returned to Isobel's tent she halted outside for a moment. She closed her eyes. *You can do this.* Then she scolded herself. It was Isobel who was about to give birth, not her. Putting on a cheery, confident smile, she went into the tent.

Isobel gasped. "What's wrong?"

"Huh? Nothing's wrong."

"You never smile," said Isobel. "Something's wrong. What is it?"

"I was just trying to put you at ease," said Cherry.

"Don't ever smile at me like that again," Isobel said. "Oooooh!" She put her hands on her belly and sucked in a long breath. She continued to breath slowly and steadily for several moments, then she relaxed.

"Was that a contraction?" Cherry asked. "Zhang told me to time them. What time is it? Where's my interface?" She scrabbled vigorously in her bag, trying to feel for the smooth screen in the dark.

"Cherry, calm down," Isobel said. "I've done this before. It's going to be all right. Ahhhh!" She clutched her belly again.

"That's way sooner than two minutes!" Cherry exclaimed. "Shit! Where's Zhang?" She bolted outside the tent and comm'd the doctor.

"What?" Zhang asked.

"Isobel's contractions are really close. Much closer than two minutes apart."

"Are you absolutely sure? Did you actually time them?"

"I didn't need to," said Cherry. "I know the difference between two minutes and thirty seconds."

"Damn," Zhang said. "I'm not going to make it there. This baby is coming now too and it's breech. I'll talk you through it."

"What? No way! There has to be someone else who can help. What about that nurse you were talking about?"

"There's no time. You'll have to do it. Can you see the head yet?"

A loud groan came from Isobel's tent.

Cherry darted inside.

Isobel was on all fours. "Is the doctor here?" she gasped.

"He'll be here any minute," Cherry said. "I'll help you until then."

But Isobel was beyond hearing what Cherry was saying.

***

Cherry held little Nina in the crook of her arm. Zhang had explained how to swaddle the infant and now she'd gone to sleep, apparently not remotely interested in this new world she'd entered. Cherry didn't know who she was more in awe of: Isobel, who had just given birth without any anesthetic and hardly making a fuss, or Zhang, who had directed Cherry through everything while at the same time attending a woman enduring a long and complicated labor. With great timing, the nurse had arrived after the exciting part was over.

Isobel was resting. She'd asked Cherry to wait until morning before going next door to tell Miki it was time to meet her new sister. Cherry thought that was a great idea. She didn't want to deal with an excited toddler *and* a newborn, even a peacefully sleeping one. The entire night had been a nerve-wracking ordeal. She marveled at Isobel's ability to take it all in her stride. Cherry would rather return to the Scythian city than undergo the same experience.

"You can put her down if you want," Isobel said. "I made a little bed for her a few days ago. Over there."

"I see it," Cherry replied. Isobel had lined the lid of a packing case with cut down blankets. She gently laid the sleeping infant in it.

"Not the nicest crib, is it?" Isobel asked.

"I really don't think she minds," replied Cherry. "I'll get you an external comm as soon as the coordinator wakes up so you can talk to Kes. He'll be ecstatic. How are you doing?"

"Good." Isobel smiled.

"You look good too," said Cherry. It was true. Even in the half-light Isobel was radiant. "It's hard to believe, considering what you just went through."

"It's the post-birth hormones," Isobel said. "It's quite a rush. Maybe you'll find out one day."

Cherry held up her hand in mock horror. "Nu-uh. Not happening. But I'm happy for you."

Isobel winced and touched her stomach.

"You don't have another one in there, do you?" Cherry asked.

Isobel laughed. "Stars, I hope not." She winced again. "It's only post-birth contractions. They aren't as fun as the hormones."

"Is there anything I can do? I can't believe Zhang still isn't here. I'll comm him again."

"Ahhh!" Isobel sat up and half doubled over. Her jaw dropped as she peered downward. She pulled back the cover. A wide, wet patch spread over the bottom half of her torso and across her thighs. The bedding beneath her glistened faintly. In the dim light the liquid looked black but Cherry knew what it was: blood.

Isobel's gaze rose to meet Cherry's, and for a beat they stared at each other in horror.

"Zhang!" Cherry yelled the doctor's name even before he answered the comm. "Isobel's bleeding badly. You have to get here now!"

"Some blood is normal—"

"This isn't normal! Get over here."

"Cherry," Isobel said, her tone high and soft, "help me." Her eyes were wide and dark.

Cherry grabbed towels to help soak up the blood. She pressed the material to the dark patch. But she didn't know what else to do. What could she do? If Isobel had been wounded Cherry would have known how to suppress the bleeding, but the blood was coming from inside her.

"It'll be okay," Cherry said. "Zhang will be here in a minute. He'll figure something out."

Isobel lay down on her side and covered her face with her hand.

Cherry touched her arm. "Don't worry. You're going to be all right." But as she spoke, she saw fresh blood surge out through Isobel's nightgown and onto the bed linen.

There was a rustle at the tent door. It opened and Zhang came in. His first reaction at seeing Isobel struck fear into Cherry. The doctor looked shocked. But he closed his mouth like a trap and resumed his professional attitude.

"Okay, Isobel," he said, "I'm going to try a few things. Cherry, you might want to leave."

"No, please stay with me," Isobel said.

"I'll stay," said Cherry, sitting on the floor near Isobel's head and taking her hand.

Numbly, she watched Zhang work. All her discomfort and squeamishness about childbirth was gone. All that she could feel was a growing sense of dread. It didn't matter what Zhang did, he couldn't stop the bleeding. Cherry had not imagined a single person could hold so much blood.

Isobel lay quietly, in fear at first, but then as time went on her eyelids began to droop and she drifted in and out of consciousness. Zhang told Cherry to try to keep her awake, so she asked Isobel about Miki and what she would need the following day. Isobel's replies became gradually less intelligible until Cherry was simply talking to her without expecting an answer.

An inestimable period of time later, Zhang stopped what he was doing. He sat back on his heels. His shirt was stained and so were his forearms up to the elbows. He looked exhausted. "Cherry, can I speak to you outside?"

She turned to Isobel to ask if it was okay to leave her alone, but her eyes were closed.

Cherry followed Zhang out of the tent. The camp was beginning to wake up. People were moving between the tents. Cherry regarded the doctor, knowing what he was about to say but not wanting to hear it.

"I've tried everything I can," Zhang said, "but nothing's working. She doesn't have long."

"What about a blood transfusion?" Cherry asked. "If we're the same type I'd happily donate some and so would others, I'm sure."

"Even if I had the equipment for a transfusion it

wouldn't help. The only thing that will save her is a hysterectomy. I don't have the facilities to perform a major operation like that and if I tried to do it any other way the shock would kill her. To be honest, she's too far gone anyway. There isn't anything else I can do." Zhang put a hand on Cherry's shoulder. "You're her friend. I'm sure she would appreciate some company in her final moments."

"I'm not..." Cherry swallowed. "Okay. I'll do it."

She returned to the tent. Baby Nina was stirring in her crib, making quiet chirruping noises. Cherry carefully picked her up and placed her next to Isobel's face. The movement caused Isobel to open her eyes. The corners of her lips curled up.

Did she know what was happening? Cherry didn't know if it was cruel or kind to tell her.

Isobel's gaze left her infant and roved a little before she found Cherry. "Tell Kes I love him," she whispered. Her eyes moved again until they alighted on her daughter once more, and then she left the world.

CHAPTER THIRTY-FOUR

"The *Opportunity* is back!" Tricia exclaimed.

Kes looked up from the vaccine pods he was loading into a case.

Tricia was the lab's main contact with the refuge's coordinator. She was holding her ear comm as she listened to the rest of the message. "Apparently the satellite picked up its signal a while ago, but now it's entered the system and it's on its way to Concordia."

Kes stopped what he was doing. Tension he hadn't known he was carrying drained from his body. Wilder was going to be okay. The girl was like a sister to him. He couldn't bear the thought of anything happening to her.

"Oh." Tricia's happy expression faded. "Scythian ships are on its tail."

A collective gasp sounded around the lab.

"They're back so soon?" asked Thom.

"We're screwed," Drew said. "And after all we've done. We'll never fight them off again."

The despair in the room was almost palpable. Kes stared at the pods in his hands, the products of countless hours of exhausting work. Tycho and the other volunteers had risked their lives. The colony had lived in fear for weeks, only for it all to come to nothing.

"I don't honestly know what we were expecting," Thom said bitterly. "They're never going to leave us alone. I wonder if they let some of us live on purpose, just so they could return and torture us more."

"How many ships?" Kes asked Tricia.

"The satellite's picked up seven."

"That's three less than last time," said Drew.

"We destroyed some of the fleet last time," Tricia said. Her hand rose to her comm again. "Uh, the vid from the satellite is going to be broadcast all over Concordia. We can watch it in the meeting room."

The scientists dropped what they were doing and moved toward the meeting room en masse. Kes hesitated. They still hadn't vaccinated the entire population. No one at Suddene had been immunized against the biocide and there were a few small refuges they hadn't reached yet. On the other hand, if the Scythians were returning, was there any point to what they were doing?

The Parvus had left, and the *Opportunity* couldn't defend the planet on its own. Perhaps Cerberus and other silos that weren't too badly damaged could be resurrected...

Kes' shoulders slumped. He was tired of living under a constant threat of annihilation, forever rebuilding the colony after each successive attack. And now a young woman whom he loved like family might be about to die. He understood Thom and Drew's attitude. It was almost too much to bear.

As his co-workers departed for the meeting room and the lab emptied around him, Kes continued to stoically fill a case with vaccine pods. In less than a minute he stood alone, the rustle of the soft plastic pods loud in the newly quiet room. No sounds came from the meeting room as all inside were undoubtedly focused on the drama overhead unfolding on the interface screen.

Kes' resolve to not watch the battle broke. He didn't want to see the *Opportunity* felled from the sky, but he had to see whatever was about to happen.

He strode from the lab into the meeting room. The scientists nearest the screen were sitting down. The ones behind them stood, their arms folded or their hands resting on table tops as they leaned forward, their gazes fixed on the screen.

As it had always been, the satellite's single vantage point was inadequate. The Scythian ships it had picked up were not yet visible. Only the *Opportunity* could be seen, a small speck growing steadily larger. Its dark gray hull made it difficult to distinguish against the backdrop of stars set in the black velvet of space.

"Is that it?" a voice asked uncertainly. "That thing in the middle? It looks like a smooth asteroid."

"Yes," Kes replied. "That's it." He thought about comming Wilder, but the messages would take too long to travel the distance separating them. By the time Kes heard her reply it might all be over and he would be listening to her as he watched the *Opportunity* be obliterated.

She had gone to the approaching Assembly ships to negotiate a deal with them regarding the a-grav device. What had happened to their vessels? They had to be faster than the *Opportunity*. Why had Wilder returned ahead of them? Had Concordia's allies abandoned them?

"I think I can see one of the Scythians ships," Tricia said.

Kes studied the screen, then he saw it too: four bright spots making up the four corners of a square and a single dot right in the middle. It was one of the largest Scythian ships. The lone central dot was the vessel's deadly pulse weapon. One direct hit from it would spell the end of the *Opportunity*.

The Fila ship fired! The sound of a simultaneously drawn breath broke the silence in the meeting room. The distance between the *Opportunity* and its hunters was too great for the pulse to cause any damage, however. The speeding needle of light dissipated into space.

"What are they doing?" Thom asked. "They should be trying to escape, not drawing fire!"

"Our ship will never outpace the Scythians," said Drew. "And once they've destroyed the *Opportunity* they'll turn their attention to us."

Kes wanted to shake the man and tell him to shut up. Except he was right.

A second pulse erupted from the *Opportunity's* rear pulse emitter.

"What the hell is Quinn doing?" Kes blurted.

"It's like he's trying to bait them," said Tricia.

A heavy weight settled on Kes' chest. It was like the *Opportunity* was acting as bait to draw the Scythians into the system. It was the only explanation that made any sense.

"More ships are approaching the edge of the system!" Tricia exclaimed, relaying another message from the refuge coordinator.

"More Scythian vessels?" asked Thom.

"No. Their engine signatures are different, and different from each other too."

"It's the Assembly ships," Drew said. "They've arrived at last. That changes things a little. The *Opportunity* might make it."

"I hope so," said Tricia, "but she's cut off from the other ships by the Scythians."

Silence fell as every gaze in the room strained to see what was happening. The *Opportunity* was now clearly visible, and Kes could also distinguish the outline of a Scythian ship. Moving points of light in its general area had to be the rest of the fleet. He could see nothing of the Assembly ships whatsoever but he didn't doubt the report relayed from the refuge's coordinator, who was reading the satellite's data.

"She's never going to make it," said Tricia softly, though her words were easy to hear in the hushed room. She turned to Kes, her expression full of fear. "How can she make it?"

Kes had no answer.

"What's that?" asked Thom. "Is there something there?" He pointed at the top right of the screen.

Kes couldn't see what he meant at first, then he realized it wasn't a ship that Thom was pointing at, but a moving absence of light. A dark shape was moving across the starry background, blocking out the tiny points of light.

"I see it," Drew said. "Whatever it is, it's massive."

Light exploded from the dark mass and shot across space faster than any ship was traveling. Nevertheless, the pulse faded by the time it reached the Scythian ship. It hit but Kes doubted it did much damage.

The trajectory of the Scythian ships began to alter. The largest ship returned fire. The pulse from the spike found its target at the massive Assembly ship and was absorbed into the darkness.

"More Assembly ships are approaching," Tricia said, "but I can't see anything."

"It's hard to tell what's going on," Drew said.

Aside from the small, dark gray shape of the *Opportunity*, all that could be seen of the other ships was visual suggestions of their forms and the brilliant but tiny sparks of light that traveled between them. In silence, hundreds of thousands of kilometers above their heads, a pitched battle was being fought.

Kes thought he guessed what was happening. The Scythians must have been spotted returning to Concordia—perhaps by Quinn and Wilder aboard the *Opportunity*—and a plan had been hatched to use the

Fila ship to draw the enemy vessels forward and then attack them from all sides except their front, which faced toward their origin planet.

The Scythians had an escape route: all they had to do was fly onward, away from the Assembly ships. But for the time being they were not choosing to do so. Perhaps they wanted to prove their might against the Assembly, especially while in their home planet's system.

Kes was somewhat relieved that the *Opportunity* seemed to have been forgotten. The ship continued to move closer to Concordia. He wished Quinn would fly it around to the other side of the planet or to some other place where he and Wilder would be safe.

The room's tense silence burst into exclamations and hollers. A flash of light had lit the screen. One of the Scythian ships had exploded.

"That'll show 'em!" someone shouted.

"They're not going to like that," said Thom.

The fighting intensified and drew closer to Concordia as the Scythian and Assembly ships continued along their trajectories. Some Assembly ships remained invisible, only the pulses that arrived from space giving away their position. The remaining six Scythian ships could now clearly be seen. They were firing in all directions. A second of their largest ships was concentrating its fire on the black pit that showed the location of the massive Assembly ship. Now, it was no longer simply absorbing the fire. Each pulse briefly lit its surface, spilling across it like water splashing on a stone.

Somewhere in distant space a light flickered and was gone.

"We just lost an Assembly ship," Tricia said.

Then another Scythian ship turned into a ball of quickly snuffed fire.

The Assembly seemed to have the edge. Would the Scythians turn tail and run? For the moment, they were choosing to tough it out. Concordia's planetary system had become the battleground where the simmering tensions between the Assembly and their hostile neighbor was to be played out.

Glancing at the *Opportunity*, Kes decided to comm Wilder. He wanted to tell her to advise Quinn to fly the ship out of immediate danger. He sent the message, not knowing when he might receive a reply.

"That's another one!" Drew yelled. A third Scythian ship had fallen.

The enemy's flagship continued to pound out pulses at the dark, gigantic block of a starship. Kes could make out some of its form now. He thought he could see tall towers like a medieval castle's. The dark ship looked like a massive citadel, flying through space.

Could the large ship continue to withstand the onslaught from the Scythians? Kes hoped so because its return fire was having a devastating effect on the Scythian fleet.

"Three down, four to go," Drew said gleefully. "I knew the Assembly would save us!"

Kes thought Drew's jubilation was premature. Even if the Assembly did defeat the Scythians this time around, there was nothing to stop them from returning to take out their anger on Concordia when the Assembly ships were no longer around. Concordia was too weak to put up an adequate defense and it would remain so for a long time.

Light flared from the citadel ship, but it was not the light of pulse fire. Part of the ship had broken away. The stars blocked by its presence grew fewer as the dissected tower tumbled off into space. The ship instantly responded. A blaze of light hurtled across space. The spike of the Scythian ship was its target and it hit it full on. This caused a chain reaction that spread down the ship. The joined crescents ruptured and disintegrated, dissolving in light.

"That's it," said Drew. "That has to be it."

As if they had heard his words, the remaining Scythian ships began to speed up. They were going to take the only remaining escape route: to fly past Concordia and out the other side of the system. Kes expected the Assembly ships would give chase and attempt to inflict more damage while they were in range.

The Scythian ships sped closer. Kes' concern for the *Opportunity's* passenger grew stronger. Would the Scythians attack the small ship out of malice and spite? The ship continued to slowly move closer to Concordia.

"The Assembly ships are coming in too," Tricia said. "We should be able to see them better soon."

The crescents with their strangely scrawled patterning were now easily visible. Kes guessed that anyone standing outside would see them moving in the night sky.

One of the ships fired. As Kes had feared, the shot was aimed at the *Opportunity*. The pulse briefly lit up the Fila vessel on impact, but it didn't seem to cause any serious damage.

The Scythian ships flew on. The Assembly ships didn't seem able to match their speed.

Then the *Opportunity* exploded.

"NO!" Kes shouted. He gaped at the screen, watching the fragments of the Fila ship scatter into nothingness. *No. Wilder! No.* He collapsed into a seat.

"Damn," said Drew. "Who was aboard? Does anyone know? Why did the Scythians have to do that? She wasn't even firing on them any longer."

"I don't think a Scythian ship did that," Thom said. "Did anyone else see another pulse from the Scythians?"

"Perhaps it was a delayed effect," said Drew.

"It doesn't work like that," Thom said.

Tricia frowned. "I thought I saw something coming

from our direction."

"From Concordia?" asked Drew. "Great. It must have been one of the silos. Those idiots shot at our own ship."

Kes' head was in his hands, his mind reeling. Wilder was gone. That bright, happy young woman had hardly lived, and now she was gone.

"Kes," Tricia said, "are you okay?"

He was not okay. A sweet girl had died, and he didn't think he would ever get over losing her.

CHAPTER THIRTY-FIVE

Cherry spent the time following Isobel's death feeling like she was walking through a fog. When people spoke to her their voices sounded distant and muffled. She had to strain to hear what they were saying. Everything she saw appeared as if she were looking at it through a veil. Nothing seemed real except for the fact that Isobel had died.

Cherry had hardly known her. She'd mostly thought of her as Kes' wife, and then as someone smart enough to figure out how to work on the Guardian's head. Isobel had also been a loving, kind mother to Miki and, in the short time Cherry had spent with her, she'd come to believe that despite their different personalities, they could also have been good friends.

Life in Chimera continued on, the ripple caused by the death of a woman in childbirth seeming to have barely any impact. Miki remained with the neighbor who had cared for her while Isobel was in labor. The woman Zhang had been attending while Isobel gave birth offered to feed Nina as well as her own baby until other arrangements could be made.

Cherry remained in the tent where Isobel had died. Places to sleep were hard to find, and she'd recovered from her time in the Scythian city so she couldn't stay in a medical tent. She removed all the blood-stained linen and spent hours simply sitting in there, reliving the final hours of Isobel's life and recalling all the terrible things that had happened on Concordia over the years of colonization.

When she left the tent she vaguely heard comments about the Scythians returning and the Assembly ships defeating them. She also heard the program to medicate the population to protect them against the biocide was showing success. A group that had received the treatment and was subsequently overrun by the biocide had nearly all survived.

But these pieces of information that made it through the fog seemed insignificant. More vivid to Cherry were the rotting bodies of thousands of Fila, floating on the ocean waves, or the sight of Garwin being cut to pieces by Scythian spiders. She had seen too much death, and she felt unbearably tired. Not fatigued or sleepy, but deep-down tired. Tired of life.

Perhaps two nights had passed—Cherry wasn't sure —when Aubriot poked his head into the tent. Cherry was so deep in the fog she almost didn't recognize him.

"I heard what happened," he said, coming in. "Must have been awful."

He sat on the floor next to Cherry's sleeping bag. She was lying down, curled up, on top of it.

"I had the easy part," she replied.

"I don't think so," said Aubriot. "It can't be easy watching someone die."

Cherry didn't disagree. She'd watched Ethan die, too, and that had torn her apart. She didn't have the energy or willpower to argue with Aubriot and there was no point. Suffering wasn't a competition.

"We found the Scythian defense system control

room," Aubriot said, "with plenty of help from Faina's head. I was thinking it was weird how easy it was for us to circumvent the security inhibitor they wired into the Guardian's CPU. They stopped it from verbalizing the intel but didn't prevent it from tapping it out on a keyboard. I was wondering if the Scythians don't have an equivalent to fingers. It's kind of like when we built Sidhe and we thought we'd hidden all evidence of our presence on the surface, but the spiders found us by scent, not sight. We'd made the mistake of assuming the Scythians perceived the world the same way we did. Maybe they made a similar mistake when they added their security to Faina's CPU. What do you think?"

"Maybe," Cherry replied. "I don't know." She didn't move. She hoped Aubriot would go away because she guessed where the conversation would end up and she didn't want to go there.

"Yeah, maybe. I suppose we'll never know. I don't think they'll be coming back in a hurry, not after what the Assembly ships did to them. It's just a bloody shame we didn't manage to put the Scythian defenses out of action until after they had fired on the *Opportunity*."

This piece of information pierced Cherry's dulled senses sharply. "What?" She sat up.

"The Scythian defenses took out the *Opportunity*. Didn't you hear? We didn't manage to disable them in time. It only took us another hour or so." He looked downward and shook his head. "We were so close."

"But Wilder was aboard the *Opportunity*," said Cherry. "And so was Quinn. Are you telling me they're both dead?"

"I'm sorry," Aubriot replied.

"Oh, stars," said Cherry, her hand rising to clamp over her mouth and nose. "Who else? Who else has to die? Poor Wilder. I never got the chance to apologize to her and now I never will." Cherry fell onto her side. So much death. So much pain. She couldn't bear it.

Aubriot remained with her in the tent, his legs crossed and his head bowed, as new grief overwhelmed Cherry. How long he sat there she didn't know. By the time she was done the lamps had been turned down in the cavern and the tent was nearly dark.

"I heard someone's arriving with the vaccine tomorrow," Aubriot said. "When we've built up immunity to the biocide we can go back to Lyonesse. Start sorting things out and rebuilding."

Apprehension clutched at Cherry. "Do you know who's bringing the medication?"

"No, but maybe it'll be Kes. He'll probably want to see his kid and new baby." Aubriot studied Cherry's face. "What's wrong?" When she didn't answer, he repeated his question.

"I can't face him," Cherry said, choking on her words. "I can't tell him."

"Tell him about his wife?" Aubriot asked. "You mean he doesn't know?"

"I don't think so."

"I thought she died a couple of days ago. Why haven't you told him yet?"

Cherry had no answer.

"You have to tell him," said Aubriot. "Maybe it is better he doesn't hear it as a comm, but it's best he hears it from you."

Cherry knew it was true but she couldn't bear the thought of breaking the terrible news to her friend. "I feel like this is all my fault somehow. Everything I touch turns to shit. Everyone I come in contact with dies. Even Wilder. She's gone now too."

"You're seriously blaming yourself for the death of Kes' wife? How on Earth could her dying be your fault? That doesn't make any sense. It was an accident. Childbirth is always a bit risky, especially in conditions like these." Aubriot put a hand on Cherry's shoulder. "You need to get over yourself. If anything, that woman's death should teach you that bad things happen and sometimes there's fuck all you can do about it."

***

It was Kes who brought the medication to Chimera.

The colonists sheltering there were the last people to receive it. By then, the biocide had ravaged most of Lyonesse and turned it into a barren wasteland. No Concordian life forms remained alive. As far as anyone could tell, not a single microorganism lived in the soil or the ocean. The trees of every forest were dried skeletons of dead wood. The rest of the plant life had turned to brown husks. The animals lay dead upon the ground, unable even to rot and decay because not even the bacteria remained alive.

Only the humans and some of the Fila had survived. Not all of the humans had been protected by the vaccine. Out of every hundred that waited in dread as the biocide finally reached them, one or two would fall, killed instantly. There was no telling who it would be, and each family and friend said their goodbyes, not knowing if they would be the ones to die.

Chimera was the only refuge that had remained safe. The biocide had traveled slowly through the desert and other unoccupied regions of the dry continent. Yet everyone knew it would reach Chimera eventually, and those sheltering there would have to leave some day and travel to places where the Scythian's poison might still linger. It was essential they all receive the vaccine.

Cherry waited for Kes at the bottom of the tunnel that led from the surface. Nina hung from her front, suspended in a cloth wrapped around her torso, and she held Miki's hand. While she'd been waiting for a chance to speak to Kes in person, she'd tried to formulate the right words to tell him about Isobel. But she'd come up with nothing. If the right words existed, she did not know them.

Miki was excited to see her daddy. She jiggled and

swung on Cherry's hand. "Is Daddy coming soon?" She tried to pull her hand out of Cherry's, probably because she wanted to run into the tunnel to meet him.

Cherry gripped the little girl's hand tightly. "Daddy will be here in a minute."

The moment Cherry was dreading arrived. The lights from the vehicle that was bringing Kes from the surface lit up the dark interior of the tunnel, and she heard the approaching engine's noise. The car emerged from the darkness. Alun was driving. Cherry had asked him not to say anything—that she would tell him herself. Kes was easily distinguishable by his red hair in the front passenger seat.

A great heaviness pulled at Cherry's heart. What she had to do would be the hardest thing she'd ever done and she would live with the moment for the rest of her life.

The car stopped. Kes had already spotted Cherry and his children. His door opened and he climbed out. His expression was happy but a little uncertain. Clearly, he was wondering where Isobel was. As he walked over, Miki managed to rip her hand from Cherry's and run to her father.

"Daddy! Daddy! Daddy!"

Grinning, he squatted down as Miki reached him and he lifted her into his arms. He walked the remaining distance to Cherry carrying Miki, who was holding his neck tightly and planting kiss after kiss on his cheek.

Kes held Cherry's gaze all the way. She didn't need to tell him anything. Her face said it all. With each step that he took, realization pierced his happy but bemused state. His features fell. His eyes questioned hers, pleading with her for it not to be true. By the time he reached her he knew, and he broke.

"Mommy's gone away, Daddy," Miki said. "Far, far away. Can we go and see her?"

"When?" Kes asked Cherry, his voice husky.

"Three days ago. I'm so sorry. I didn't know how to tell you."

He nodded.

Cherry untied the knot at her shoulder and began to unwrap Nina. Kes helped her, and then gently lifted out his new daughter. The baby was sleeping, as she had done for most of the time since she'd been born, according to the mom who was feeding her.

"I can take the children if you'd rather be alone for a while," Cherry said.

Kes gave a slight shake of his head. He cradled little Nina expertly in one arm while the other supported Miki. He walked away without another word. Cherry watched as he stopped in an area of shadow near the tunnel entrance and sat down on the ground with his daughters.

Cherry turned away to give the man some privacy and nearly bumped into Dr. Zhang, who was standing right behind her. She hadn't heard him approach.

"Poor guy," Zhang said.

"Yes."

"I'll talk to him later about exactly what happened. He'll need some time to take in the news first."

"Yes." *A lifetime.*

"He must have left the medication doses in the car," Zhang said. "I'll see to them. Don't forget you need a dose too. I know you've been through a lot lately. I don't want you wandering off and forgetting."

"I won't forget." Cherry left the doctor and walked back to the main group of tents. Aubriot was waiting for her in Isobel's old tent.

"How did it go?" he asked.

"I didn't need to tell him. He guessed." Cherry sat down on her sleeping bag. Now that her task of conveying the sad news about Isobel to Kes was over, she felt no better. She didn't think she would ever feel better.

Though the colony had survived yet another brush with disaster, the future held no prospect of improvement of its situation. Concordia was now barren. They had food and seeds in storage, and so if the biocide burnt itself out they wouldn't starve, but now they were living on a world where the ocean and lands were dead. The only seeds they had were for food crops, not trees or shrubs or ground cover plants. Until life evolved again on Concordia, the place would be an empty, bleak wilderness, nothing growing or moving as far as the eye could see.

And the threat of the Scythians' return remained. The Assembly might have defeated them this time around but the Assembly ships could not stick around forever. They had their own planets to protect and journeys to undertake.

"Everything's shit, right?" Aubriot asked.

"That's a good way of putting it," Cherry replied.

"Yeah, well, we've got each other. That's something."

Cherry frowned. This new, affectionate side of Aubriot was going to take some getting used to.

"Right?" Aubriot asked.

"Right," Cherry replied. "I guess."

Sounds of a disturbance started up outside the tent. Voices rose louder, chattering in excitement. Cherry and Aubriot's gazes met as they noted the new noise.

"Is that good or bad, do you think?" asked Aubriot.

"Only one way to find out." Cherry got up and went to peer out of the tent entrance, wondering what she was about to see. She didn't think she could take another disaster, but she'd felt that way about the previous several events and her feelings hadn't prevented them from happening.

All she saw was a knot of people near the tunnel.

"What is it?" asked Aubriot, pushing in beside her.

"I don't know. I wish they wouldn't congregate there near Kes, though. He deserves some peace and quiet."

"I'm going to take a look," said Aubriot, going out.

Cherry decided to join him. She hated being in the tent alone, after what had happened in there. She walked with Aubriot across the open, rocky ground. Other colonists were also wandering over, attracted by the gathering crowd.

Cherry was glad of Aubriot's large frame and bossy attitude as he pushed through to the center of the throng. She followed in his wake. It wasn't until she reached the middle that she saw what the fuss was about.

Kes was standing facing away from her, his arms wrapped around someone. Miki was holding onto his leg and a woman in the crowd was holding Nina. Kes' back obscured the face of the person he was holding, but Cherry could see a woman's arms around Kes' back and her skinny legs in pants.

She stood on her tiptoes to peer over Kes' shoulder.

"Wilder!"

Wilder raised a hand and waved. "Hey, Cherry!"

Cherry was frozen in surprise for a moment before she broke free and ran to her two friends.

"I thought you were on the *Opportunity* when it was destroyed," Cherry said.

"No, no," Wilder replied, still in Kes' embrace. "I wasn't aboard. I stayed on the Immani ship. We used the *Opportunity* as bait, that's all. I knew you guys would be worried about me after the ship blew up but I couldn't comm from the Immani vessel. Only the Fila stations can receive their comms and they've all been abandoned. Quinn said Immani sensors showed the biocide hadn't reached this refuge yet, so I thought it would be safe to come down in a shuttle we'd brought over from the *Opportunity.* It was the only way I could let you all know I was okay."

Wilder had spoken so fast she was breathless. She also seemed to be gasping because Kes was hugging her so tightly. Cherry went to hug her too. Wilder's survival was just the kind of miracle she needed right then.

"Careful!" Wilder exclaimed. "You'll squash Piddle and Puddle."

"Huh?" Cherry took a step back and Kes finally released Wilder too.

Wilder reached into two deep pockets in her pants and pulled out a small furry creature in each hand.

"The famous Piddle and Puddle," Kes said, his voice hoarse. His eyes were red and his face wet. "Can I?" he asked, holding out his hands.

"Of course," Wilder replied, handing over the animals.

The crowd around them began to dissipate, now that they'd witnessed the surprise arrival.

"I'm glad you made it," said Aubriot. He reached down to give Wilder a hug.

She accepted graciously but over his shoulder she raised her eyebrows at Cherry.

Cherry shrugged and stifled a smile.

Aubriot released her and said, "So how did you survive on the other ship? Do these Immani breathe oxygen like us?"

"No," Wilder replied. "They're the organizers of the space station. Do you remember?" She lifted her hand high to indicate a great height.

"Hard to forget them," said Aubriot.

"They're used to generating environments for all kinds of species, and their ship is *huge*! When Quinn hatched the plan to use me and the a-grav as bait, the Immani said the Scythians might think that I and the a-grav machine were aboard the *Opportunity*, but there was no reason we *had* to be. They created environments for me and Quinn along with the rest of the Fila crew. Quinn flew the ship remotely."

Aubriot went to speak but Wilder flapped her hands

excitedly to quieten him. "There's more! The Immani think they can save the remaining Fila. They're going to collect them from the Vimur and any freshwater lakes that the biocide didn't reach and fly them up to their ship. Isn't that great?"

"That *is* great," Cherry said. She couldn't help but give Wilder another hug, rejoicing that this young woman whom she'd wronged so badly was alive and seemed to have forgiven her.

"I don't know what's going to happen after that, though," Wilder said. "This place is a disaster zone. I could see in the vids aboard the Immani ship. My forest is *dead*."

"My guess is the biocide virus will die out when it's run out of organisms to infest," said Kes, "but I doubt anything will survive it, except us." He paused and held up one of Wilder's creatures for closer inspection. "Though it's possible a small percentage of each species may have natural immunity. If so, over time, those populations would grow. We may see some dramatic imbalances as things sort themselves out."

"And meanwhile the Scythians will send another fleet to wipe us out," Cherry said, coming down from her high with a bump.

"If they do, we'll be ready," said Wilder.

"You mean we should rebuild the silos?" Cherry asked. "I suppose we'll have to."

"We can rebuild the silos, and more," Wilder said. "I made a bargain with the Assembly. They *really* wanted the a-grav machine and any other gravity technology I could develop, and they asked what we wanted in return." She grinned like a child.

"Are you going to tell us what you asked for?" asked Cherry.

"At first, I thought the best thing I could ask for was the protection of Concordia in perpetuity. I mean, we could always use defenses, right? Considering we kind of stole someone else's planet. But then I thought, no. It's time we stop relying on other people and stand on our own two feet. So instead, I asked for…" Wilder smiled, enjoying everyone's anticipation. "A gift of the latest and most useful technology from each of the Assembly member species. We get to choose. It could be starship engines, robotics, mining equipment, weapons, who knows? Just imagine. All those new machines!"

"Smart," Aubriot said. "Very smart. I wouldn't have liked to go up against you in a business deal."

"Fantastic," Cherry said. "If we can get our act together we won't have to ask for anyone's help in defeating the Scythians. In fact, if they hear about our capabilities, they might even leave us alone."

"Maybe," said Aubriot. "Or maybe they'll go somewhere else instead."

"Sounds good to me," Cherry said.

"Don't speak too soon," said Aubriot. "I haven't told you what happened to Faina. After we'd disabled the Scythian defense system controls, she asked me to deactivate her and leave her down there."

That unfamiliar pang of pity for the Guardian hit Cherry again. "And did you?"

"Yeah. She could have been useful, but it seemed the right thing to do. But before I shut her down, she told me that she had the impression the Scythians had extracted Earth's coordinates from her. She didn't suggest a reason why they did that but it's obvious, isn't it? They would only want the coordinates of our home planet if they planned on going there."

Wilder said, "We took their origin planet, so…"

"They're going to take ours," Cherry finished.

"With all this new technology we're going to have," said Aubriot, "it doesn't seem fair that we keep it to ourselves while the Scythians destroy Earth. I don't know about the rest of you, but I think it's time for me to go home."

The story of Space Colony One continues

in:

Space Colony One, Part Three

Sign up to my reader group for a free ecopy of *Night of Flames*, the prequel to *Space Colony One*, more free books, discounts on new releases, Review Crew invitations and other interesting stuff:

https://jjgreenauthor.com/free-books/

ALSO BY J.J. GREEN

STAR MAGE SAGA

SHADOWS OF THE VOID SERIES

CARRIE HATCHETT, SPACE ADVENTURER SERIES

THERE COMES A TIME
A SCIENCE FICTION COLLECTION
LOST TO TOMORROW

DAWN FALCON
A FANTASY COLLECTION